He'd never let her leave without him

The thought caused Merissa to hurry. *Just get your things, and walk quietly to the boat.*

She almost felt guilty sneaking away from Cagan in the dark, especially since she'd be leaving him stranded in such wild surroundings. But if she didn't, he'd only catch up to her again, take her back to Baton Rouge where the authorities were waiting to arrest her for a murder she didn't commit.

Besides, she was only playing by his rules. And she was certain he had his own agenda.

She looked at Cagan one last time and her heart constricted. Asleep, as awake, he exuded rugged power. Someday she'd have to finish a kiss with him.

Finish it to the very end.

Dear Reader,

They're rugged, they're strong and they're *wanted!* Whether sheriff, undercover cop or officer of the court, these men are trained to keep the peace, to uphold the law. But what happens when they meet the one woman who gets to know the man *behind* the badge?

Twelve of these men are on the loose...and only Harlequin Intrigue brings them to you—one per month in the LAWMAN series. This month meet Cagan Hall, the sexy bounty hunter.

Author Joanna Wayne takes us into the steamy bayou, which this Louisianan knows well. And the trip reads like something right out of the sexy thriller movie *No Mercy*—with Cagan playing Richard Gere! Joanna's descriptions are so vivid you can actually feel the heat!

Be sure you don't miss Cagan's exciting story—or any of the LAWMAN books coming to you in the months ahead...because there's nothing sexier than the strong arms of the law!

Regards,

Debra Matteucci
Senior Editor & Editorial Coordinator
Harlequin Books
300 East 42nd Street
New York, NY 10017

Extreme Heat
Joanna Wayne

Harlequin Books

TORONTO • NEW YORK • LONDON
AMSTERDAM • PARIS • SYDNEY • HAMBURG
STOCKHOLM • ATHENS • TOKYO • MILAN
MADRID • WARSAW • BUDAPEST • AUCKLAND

In memory of Dean and Mary Gibbs and my wonderful parents whose romance spanned seven decades. And to my husband, Wayne, who never stops encouraging me.

ISBN 0-373-22389-7

EXTREME HEAT

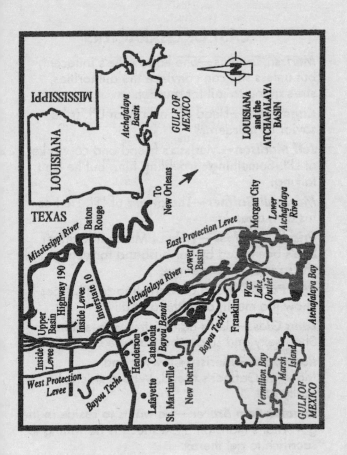

LOUISIANA and the ATCHAFALAYA BASIN

CAST OF CHARACTERS

Merissa Thomas—She knows she's innocent, but unless she can convince the authorities, she's going to jail for murder.

Cagan Hall—Head of Security at LPI. Is he savior or murderer?

Jeff Madison—Merissa's friend and co-worker at LPI. Something's troubling him, but he isn't talking.

Marshall Gaffner—The owner of LPI. He has his own agenda.

Priscilla Gaffner—Wife of Marshall Gaffner. She's been used by her husband for years, and she's ready for a change.

Rick Porter—Head of Marketing at LPI. Does he know too much, or nothing at all?

Lana Glass—Jeff's administrative assistant. She's sexy and smart, but can she be trusted?

Rod Lopen—Merissa's lawyer and Marshall Gaffner's friend. Whose side is he really on?

Senator Sam Bracer—He wants to reside in the governor's mansion. How much is he willing to sacrifice to get there?

Chapter One

Cagan Hall stopped in the shade of a towering pine tree to wipe the perspiration from his brow. Louisiana in June. Who in his right mind would want to go off on a fishing trip in weather like this?

The kind of people he got mixed up with, obviously. He kicked a rock with the toe of his mud-splotched sneaker and sent it flying up and over the patchy undergrowth that bordered the dirt path.

A week at the lake with two new friends. Well, not friends, actually. More like tools of his trade. New friends were as dangerous as that water moccasin he had almost stepped on yesterday.

Nonetheless, here he was spending the week with a guy who was suspect at best. Jeff Madison claimed to know a lot, though he hadn't shared his information with Cagan. And what he had shared with other people was speculation without any real facts to back him up.

It might just be sour grapes talking. Jeff had been busted from being one of the top dogs at Louisiana Prosthetics, Inc., to a whimpering puppy. That meant anything he said was suspect. Everything at LPI could be strictly on the up-and-up.

Cagan's instincts told him differently. His instincts and the information he'd gotten from his cohorts, Tommy and Luke. Everything pointed to a lot of extra money floating around for the right man to pocket, if he was smart enough.

So the way things stood right now, Cagan had plenty of doubts about Jeff. Ditto for his other fishing companion. Merissa Thomas, tall, blond and naively sensual. In fact, the only thing he was sure of about her was that she was a woman. *All* woman. The kind you dreamed about on lonely nights. He should know. He'd had almost a week of it.

A curse rumbled under his breath. Merissa was just the type of woman he needed to stay way the hell away from at a time like this. Previous events had hammered that lesson into every crevice of his brain. The problem was when she was around, his brain had difficulty overruling the rest of his body.

For the past six days and nights, he'd talked, laughed, even cooked with Merissa, and he'd found not one thing about her he didn't like. That was the problem. Who could trust a woman like that?

Cagan picked up his pace. He was almost to the lake's edge and eager for a dip in the cooling water. Just thinking about Merissa made chilling out seem more of a necessity than the pleasure he'd originally intended.

A mosquito buzzed around his ear, and Cagan swatted at it—at least he started to. He stopped in midswat and swallowed the low whistle that rose in his throat. He closed his eyes, but the breathtaking mirage did not go away. It was as if an image of Merissa had materialized from his thoughts. Except the woman standing at the water's edge was all too real.

He watched silently as she kicked her leather sandals from her feet, her painted toenails gleaming in the fading glow of the setting sun. A welcoming breeze stirred, tousling her hair, and she gathered the silky blond strands into a ball and knotted them atop her head.

Cagan groaned inwardly. He had been avoiding this type of agony all week. He'd battled the urge to look at her too closely, strangled the need inside him that had hardened into painful knots every time she'd stood too near.

And, as she'd been all week, she was oblivious to the mesmerizing power she held over him. She slipped her hands inside the front waistband of her white shorts, undoing the button that held them up. Anticipation surged inside him, awakening every nerve in his body. He should say something, call out her name to let her know he was here.

He opened his mouth but nothing came out. Lost in an awe-inspired trance, he watched as the white shorts skimmed her long, tanned legs and dropped in a snowy heap at her feet.

He let his gaze travel back up her long legs to the bikini bottom that hugged her flesh, a shimmering peach satin over tight little buttocks. He forced himself to look away. He hadn't been with a woman in weeks. No, make that months.

That's the way it had to be for now. Too much was riding on his temporary stint with LPI. Up until this week, he had been able to handle the celibacy just fine. Now, all of a sudden, he was worse than a panting schoolboy.

If he had a brain in his head, he'd turn around and beat a hasty retreat. But unlike the rest of him, his brain had grown soft. Instead of running for his life, he continued to stand as stiff and silent as a sentinel, watching while Merissa lifted one tempting foot and then the other, stepping out of her shorts.

He took a deep breath and counted to ten, determined to maintain some semblance of control as she tucked her hands under the smooth cotton of her tank top and peeled it from her body, dropping it beside the discarded shorts. The bikini top clung to her flesh.

She was a work of art, he acknowledged, as perfectly sculptured as a priceless statue. And from the scraps of gossip he'd heard at work, just as untouchable. Cool and calculating, and always in control. That's what Rick Porter had said about her. Funny, Cagan hadn't noticed those qualities at the lake this week.

Merissa paused at the edge of the lake, dipping the toes of her right foot into the water, testing the temperature. Her bronzed body was poised like a heron, her neck high and regal, her legs shapely and sure.

He ignored all the warnings his mind screamed and followed his instincts, stepping into the clearing and walking down to the lake.

"So this is where you sneak off to every afternoon," he said, failing to hide the gravelly tone that desire had added to his voice.

Startled, she jerked around. For a brief second, Cagan could have sworn he saw real fear in her wide eyes. But in an instant it was gone, replaced by a shy smile that lit her eyes and softened her features.

"I don't sneak. I just enjoy the privacy."

"Too bad. I was just thinking how nice your company would be." He watched as her cheeks became tinged in red. "But I'd never impose on a beautiful lady."

"No. I mean, that's okay."

"Okay you want me to leave?"

"No. Okay, I'd like for you to stay." She lowered her gaze and backed away as she spoke, stepping into deeper water, letting the caressing liquid rise above her waist. "It's just that this bathing suit is a little snug. Too much good Southern food since I've been in Baton Rouge, I guess."

"It looks fine to me." Hell, it looked dynamite, but he didn't elaborate. He was too busy telling himself he should back off and run, not walk, in the opposite direction. Physical attraction he could handle, but Merissa had all the makings of a woman who could burrow under a man's skin, mess up his thinking, cause him to make costly mistakes.

He wouldn't let that happen. Never again. This would be an afternoon dip in the lake. That's all. And a good chance to find out just how much Merissa knew about what was really going on at LPI. He loosened the catch on his shorts and stripped to his bathing suit.

He plunged into the water, not slowly like Merissa had done, but quickly and totally, depending on the cooling water to accomplish what his mind had failed at—make him see Merissa as a possible link to obtaining the information he wanted and nothing more.

She started to swim away from him, her strokes strong and rhythmic. Cagan swam after her, pushing hard to catch up. Finally, she turned and swam back toward the shore, stopping when she could rest her feet on the muddy-bottomed lake.

Cagan stopped a few feet away from her. He could see her body clearly, see the soft swirl of her breasts just above the water's surface, the sparkling drops of liquid sliding into her cleavage. He took a deep breath.

"You're a good swimmer," he said, trying to keep the moment light.

"Thank you." She shook her head and then pushed a few stray hairs back from her face. "I love the water. I guess that's the reason I badgered Jeff into bringing me along when his other friends backed out."

"Oh, you mean we're second choice?" He hesitated just a second before pressing the matter. Subtle. That was the best way to ask questions. "Who backed out?"

"Friends from LPI. Rick Porter and Lana Glass. He's head of marketing and Lana works in personnel with Jeff. Do you know them?"

Cagan nodded his head. "We've talked."

"Rick had a change of plans at the last minute," she continued. "Said he had to go out of town on family business. Something like that. And Lana had unexpected company coming in."

"Are Rick and Jeff good friends?" Cagan made his tone nonchalant, pretending to sound only mildly interested.

"I didn't think so, until Jeff invited him on this trip. It's strange but..." She stopped and a troubled expression pulled her lips into a frown. She didn't let it linger. Flashing Cagan a smile that would melt the polar ice cap, she stepped closer. "Here I go, reverting to shoptalk, and I promised myself I wouldn't do that this week. We still have one more night of vacation, and I plan to enjoy every second of it."

Before Cagan could duck, she slid her hand across the surface of the water, creating a wave and propelling it in his direction.

"So you want to play rough, do you?" he challenged, wiping the spray from his eyes. Before she could answer, he'd dived beneath the water and grabbed one of her legs, pulling her down. The water swirled around them and she struggled, pushing against him. They were a mass of legs, arms and slippery bodies, and Cagan felt his temperature climb to dangerous levels.

Finally, they bobbed to the surface, her hands wrapped around his neck. She knotted her fingers in his hair, pushing down as if to plunge him beneath the swirling water.

But she was no match for his strength. He tightened his hold on her tiny waist and pulled her closer.

"I give up," she said, her breath catching in a soft laugh.

But Cagan didn't let go of her. He couldn't. Not with her staring at him, her wide eyes moist, sparkling with half-hidden desire. It was wrong, all wrong. He knew it as well as he knew his own name, whatever it happened to be at the time. But he was just as certain that he was going to kiss her.

Her lips parted, pink and lush, unmistakably inviting. He lowered his mouth to hers, and she didn't back away. Instead, she pressed closer, the fullness of her lips opening. His breath pushed against his lungs as her tongue touched and tangled with his, her hot breath mingling with his own.

He wasn't sure how long it lasted, how much time he was lost completely in the feel and the taste of her. He wasn't even sure who came up for air first.

"We need to get back," he heard himself whisper hoarsely, almost surprised that he was finally obeying his own mental dictates.

"I know." She turned away and threw herself into the water, swimming hard and fast to shore.

He stood, watching her go, his body still aching from the passion that had been awakened but not nearly appeased. And it wouldn't be. At least not any time soon. The situation they were in was far too dangerous. He knew it even if she didn't. He'd been here before.

But this time it would be different, he vowed silently. He'd do what he had to do and get what he came for. But he'd walk away from Merissa no matter how badly he wanted her. He had to. One woman was dead because of him. The memory would burn inside him forever. And the only certainty in his life was that he would never let that happen again.

MERISSA STRETCHED her feet toward the dying campfire. The day had been incredibly hot and muggy, but a thunderstorm was brewing now, and the breeze blowing across Lake

Maurepas made the night air almost chilly. She listened to the easy flow of conversation between Jeff and Cagan. Before tonight, she would have joined in, been just another one of the boys. But after one heart-stopping kiss, everything seemed different.

Setting the nearly empty coffee mug on the ground beside her, she traced her lips with the fingers of her right hand. The taste of Cagan was still there, teasing her, taunting her temporary weakness. The last thing she had planned to do was let some macho ex-cop turned security guard get close to her.

This week was supposed to be the opportunity she needed to get her thoughts in order. She had so many decisions to make. A year ago, she had come home to Baton Rouge with high hopes that she could rediscover the foundation of her life. It hadn't worked.

If anything, she was more lost than ever, and far more disillusioned. The dream job Jeff had enticed her with was providing more complications than solutions. And then there was Jeff. At first, he'd wanted a lot more than friendship. She'd put a quick end to those expectations. But lately, something else was going on with him.

That was the real reason she'd wanted to come with him on this vacation. He needed a friend, someone to listen while he worked through whatever it was that was making him irritable and depressed. But she had gotten nowhere with him.

A deep sigh escaped her lips. Now she had Cagan to deal with, as well. She could feel her insides stirring again, as images of their afternoon encounter swept through her mind. Involvement was the last thing she needed at this point in her life. Especially with someone who'd left New York because his problems there had gotten out of hand.

Still, there was no use wasting energy blaming herself or him for what had happened this afternoon. It had been inevitable. The attraction between Cagan and herself had been brewing from the first day of the camping trip. From the moment she'd first stared at close range into his eyes, dark and intense. From her first encounter with his boyish smile and rugged good looks.

Oh, she'd seen him at the plant before, but only from a distance. From a distance, his devastating charms were manageable. Now that she'd been as close as a kiss, she'd have to be on her toes every second.

"So what is it with you tonight, Merissa?" Jeff asked, breaking into her silent thoughts. "Is our having to leave tomorrow getting you down?"

"That must be it." She forced a lightness into her voice. "It's been a perfect week." Until this afternoon, she added silently. "But I think I'll turn in now since we plan to get started back early tomorrow. And next week will be busy. I have a lot of work left to do on that new design I promised Gaffner."

"Work." Jeff shrugged his shoulders. "I knew sooner or later someone would bring up that repugnant four-letter word. And as for Gaffner, you know what I think about him."

Merissa cringed at the unmasked disgust in Jeff's voice. He shouldn't be talking this way, especially not in front of Cagan. A few idle words and everything could get blown out of proportion and then delivered to Gaffner. It could prove disastrous for Jeff, especially after all the grumbling and complaining he'd done of late.

"That's not the way you talked a year ago, Jeff," she reminded him, "when you talked me into leaving my position in Dallas to come to work with you here. All I heard then were praises of LPI and Marshall Gaffner. The best boss in the world, according to you.''

"A year ago. Seems more like a lifetime ago.''

"Sounds like you have a few gripes.'' Cagan stopped talking to swat at a mosquito. "Feel free to unleash on me if you want. After all, I'm the new kid on the block and just in security. I've got no clout at LPI.''

"Who does anymore? But why spoil the last night of a perfect week talking about LPI?'' Jeff grunted. "Besides, if anyone is complaining, it should be you. Safeguarding a bunch of plastic limbs after what you were used to.''

"Yeah, well, believe me, what I was used to wasn't so great. Everything's work once you've done it for a while.''

Merissa watched Cagan's face. It revealed nothing. She'd noticed that before. If the conversation took on a serious note, his face and eyes adopted a hardness that blocked any access to his real feelings.

But it hadn't been that way earlier in the afternoon. His eyes had burned with emotion, and his lips, though hard and demanding, had been anything but cold. Merissa stared at the ground as the sudden memory rocked her brain.

"You say that,'' Jeff continued, apparently unaware of the crimson hue that must surely be coloring her cheeks, "but working for the New York City police force had to be pretty exciting.''

"It had its moments. Good and bad, like everything else.''

Merissa watched as Cagan walked over to the coffeepot that rested on a bed of hot coals. She curled her legs under her, giving him room to pass. She needn't have. He went the long way around, making sure he didn't come near her. Apparently, he shared her certainty that, inevitable or not, this afternoon had been a mistake that shouldn't be repeated.

"Is the Big Apple police chief begging you to come back yet, Cagan?" Jeff asked. "Or is he still on his kowtowing-to-the-press kick? Trying to make it look like you were in the wrong?"

"It doesn't matter. Like I told you when you hired me as head of security for LPI. I did my job. If the yellow-bellied chief doesn't like my methods, well, that's just too bad. He'd have to beg before I'd go back. And that's not his style."

Irritation colored his words and flamed new fire into his dark eyes. He had made it clear all week that he didn't like talking about his past. The only information Merissa possessed about Cagan Hall had come from Jeff, except for the gossip around the plant. The talk there was that he asked a lot of questions. According to Jeff, he was a godsend, just what LPI needed. Cagan had shown up about four months ago looking for work. Jeff had been impressed with his credentials, particularly his ten years on the New York City police force. It was the rest of his reputation that disturbed Merissa. He'd been the force bad boy, the one who hadn't played by the rules.

"Guess we're in the same boat, Jeff," Cagan commented. He took a long sip from his mug and then leaned back against the trunk of a tree. "From what I understand, you got dumped on, too."

"I don't know what you mean."

"Word around the plant is that Rick Porter was moved into your spot as marketing supervisor and you got bounced down to personnel."

"I'd hardly call that being dumped on," Merissa protested, coming to Jeff's defense. "It was a lateral move, not a bounce. Marshall Gaffner knows how valuable Jeff is to the company. He wants him to learn the workings of every department."

"Oh. I guess I didn't think of it that way. Is that how you see it, Jeff?"

"No way."

Merissa could feel the anger rising inside her. She'd heard that Cagan was always snooping around the plant trying to cause trouble, asking questions that were none of his business, meddling in everybody's affairs. Tonight's behavior was proving it. Once a cop, always a cop.

She shot Jeff a heated glance, warning him to keep quiet.

Jeff ignored her. "I don't claim to know what Gaffner's thinking, but I do know one thing. Prosthetics are not the first priority at LPI anymore. Even Lana Glass says that." Anger punctuated his words, firing them through the night air like bullets.

"It sounds to me like Gaffner made a big mistake," Cagan said.

"Well, it's not his first. Merissa can tell you about that." Jeff shrugged his shoulders disgustedly. "But she probably won't. Gaffner's got her fooled like he does everyone else. But that won't last much longer."

"Why not? Do you know something we don't?"

"Yeah. I know plenty. But I'm not talking. Not yet anyway. But the last laugh may be on Gaffner."

"What about you, Merissa?" Cagan turned and stared at her, obviously eager to dig deeper into company dirt.

She glared back at him. "There's nothing to tell. Gaffner canceled one of my design projects because he didn't feel the expenses justified the possible results. Besides, I'm sure you have more important things to worry about than the petty little happenings at the plant." She faked a yawn. "Now if you two will excuse me, I'm going to bed. It's been a long day."

Cagan stepped away from the fire, this time moving in her direction and stopping to stand over her, much too close.

"Not nearly long enough," he whispered, extending his hand to pull her to her feet.

Merissa's heart made a deceptive lurch. Only a minute ago, she was ready to kill him. So why was she suddenly trembling inside? In spite of herself, she raised her head and was captured by the desire in his eyes.

"Long enough for me," she responded huskily through the lump that clogged her throat. She ignored his outstretched hand and pushed herself to a standing position. "The week has been nice, restful. But I'm ready to get back to town and something a little more exciting."

"Is that a fact?" Cagan said, his eyes and voice hinting of amusement. "I found it extremely exciting. Especially this afternoon."

Merissa refused to make eye contact. "To each his own," she quipped, turning on her heels and heading in the direction of her tent. Hopefully, getting away from Cagan would give her a reprieve from his relentless virility. If not, sleep would be a long time in coming.

MERISSA TOSSED RESTLESSLY, the sleeping bag imprisoning her legs. Half asleep, half awake, she rubbed her eyes. Something had startled her. Some unfamiliar noise, some movement. Pushing away the dregs of sleep, she tried to concentrate.

She pushed herself to a sitting position and stared through the narrow screened opening of her tent. Blown recklessly by the wind, dark shadows danced across the window, and a brilliant flash of light zigzagged across the sky before crashing into a growling clap of thunder.

Nothing but a summer storm. She let herself fall back to the top of the sleeping bag. Now that she knew what had wakened her, she just wanted to go back to sleep.

"You're a damn fool if..."

The loud voice startled her, beginning like a booming drum and then fading into the wind. Raking her fingers across the ground at the side of her sleeping bag, she fumbled for a flashlight and her watch.

"... stupid cop idea..."

She was getting only bits and pieces of the angry words, but it was enough to tell her that Cagan and Jeff were arguing. Switching on the low beam of light, she directed it to the face of her watch. Half past midnight. She climbed from her bed and walked to the door, peering out into the darkness.

"Rick in... with him... and Gaffner's... money..."

Jeff's voice was raised and slightly slurred. Probably he was drinking again. It was a side of him she'd never known until a few months ago when the problems at LPI had begun to unfurl. But at least it was the first time this week.

Pulling a white kimono across her shoulders, Merissa stepped outside. A light mist had begun to fall, and her bare feet sank into the slippery dampness. She waited, her eyes adjusting slowly to the stormy blackness that encompassed her.

"... none... damn business..."

Jeff was ranting like a child having a tantrum. She reached inside the tent and grabbed her sandals. Cautiously, she made her way through the moss-draped trees toward the tent the two men shared. The rain grew harder, pricking her face and shocking her back to her senses.

She wasn't Jeff's keeper. He was a friend, but even she knew there was no reasoning with him when he went off on one of his tirades.

Let ex-cop Cagan Hall deal with Jeff's temper, Merissa decided, turning back to her tent. As for her, she'd had enough of them both for this week. In fact, she'd had enough of Cagan for a lifetime.

She slipped out of her damp robe and sandals and slid back into bed, this time nestling her naked body between the warm layers of her sleeping bag. An icy chill slithered down her spine, and she was suddenly filled with an almost desperate urge for morning to come and the camping trip to be over.

It had started out so well to end like this. Bringing Cagan along had been the fatal mistake. Not only did he egg Jeff on, but he held a strange, unexplainable fascination for her. Still, she had to face facts, not intuitive urges. He was not her type, and even if he had been, she wasn't about to get involved with him.

No matter what he said, she was sure he was only in Baton Rouge until things in New York cooled down. Danger and excitement were in his blood. He reeked of it, the same way he did of masculinity. And she didn't intend to be the temporary plaything of any man.

She turned onto her side and restlessly combed her fingers through her tangled hair, pushing the wispy strands away from her face.

"Merissa."

Her heart flew to her throat as the startling voice sliced through the darkness. She jerked her head around and stared at the tall, broad-shouldered figure that had ducked inside her tent.

"I thought I saw a beam from your flashlight. I just wanted to make sure you were all right."

Cagan's voice wrapped around her like a blanket. There was no slurring there. Apparently, he hadn't shared in Jeff's drinking. Still, she didn't want to feel his warmth. Not here. Not now.

"I'm fine, Cagan. The wind and rain woke me and I got up to check the time."

"That's all you heard? Just the wind and rain?" He inched closer.

"That's all," she lied. She didn't want to hear him explain why he and Jeff were arguing, and she certainly wasn't going to encourage him to stay. He turned to go, and the scent of him, musky and masculine, wafted on the still air inside the tiny tent. She all but cursed the unexpected desire that suffused her body. "And all I want to do now is go back to sleep," she whispered, praying he would hear only her words and not the deceptive pounding of her heart. She turned her back to him as if to prove the truth of what she'd said.

"Of course," he answered.

When she turned around again, he had gone.

Merissa lay awake for a long time. The wrathful sounds of the wind and driving rain continued, but the ballistic voices that had wakened her subsided. Still, she couldn't put them from her mind.

Not them and not the feelings Cagan had stirred inside her. There was something about him, some undefinable quality that intrigued yet frightened her. Or was it only her past, the broken engagement with Bruce, that had left her gun shy around any man she found attractive?

No matter. Either one was reason enough for her to stay far away from Cagan Hall.

Chapter Two

Morning brought sunshine, dazzling rays that sparkled like diamonds on the wet grass. Merissa moved with a spring to her step. The smell of moist earth and the wake-up chorus of a dozen species of native birds pushed last night's problems to the back of her mind.

She breathed deeply. The smells, the sounds, the feel of the sun on her skin were as potent as a youth serum. They conjured up delightful memories of running barefoot through the slippery mud, of lazy afternoons fishing with her grandfather on the banks of the Atchafalaya River and the various bayous that fed it.

The bayou country, the Atchafalaya Basin. Raw. Wild. Beautiful. She shook her head, willing the distant past to recede as it should. It had all been so long ago. She wondered if she'd ever look back at this point in her life with the kind of longing she felt for her youth.

Probably not, if the past year and a half were any indication. The broken engagement, the move to Baton Rouge, and now the growing problems at LPI. And the hits just keep on coming, she reminded herself, thinking about her ridiculous attraction to Cagan Hall.

She glanced toward the men's tent, but there was no sign of movement. No surprise there. Their arguing late into the night would have kept them from getting much sleep. Still, it was the first time this week she had risen before them. The first time they hadn't wakened her with loud teasing and calls about the fish they were always about to catch.

Fighting off the first pangs of hunger, Merissa lifted the lid of the camp stove and lit it. She wasn't going to bother with a campfire this morning, but she would surprise them with breakfast and coffee. In truth, she had probably been a little tough on both of them.

Jeff had every reason to be upset about the way he had been treated by Gaffner. She had even talked to Gaffner about it herself, but to no avail. She hadn't mentioned that to Jeff. He'd be horrified that she had tried to run interference for him.

Jeff Madison and Cagan Hall. The most unlikely of friends. Jeff was the head of personnel for one of the fastest growing companies in the state. Cagan was an ex-cop and the newly hired head of security. Jeff, usually mild and easygoing, had always tried to get ahead by playing the game according to Hoyle. Cagan, intense and ruggedly handsome, was a man who apparently tossed aside rules like old underwear.

There was no explaining the attraction she felt for Cagan. He wasn't her type. Not to mention that she'd been immune to anything with even the possibility of romantic complications since her breakup with Bruce Travis over a year ago.

But Cagan Hall was definitely getting to her. Adjusting the flame of the butane burner, she placed an iron skillet on top of it. Still, it wasn't entirely his fault, she admitted.

After all, could he help the way he looked? Dark and muscular, with shoulders as broad as a giant's. Could he be blamed that his eyes were dark and fiery or that the air be-

tween them crackled every time they were anywhere near
each other?

But even that didn't explain her reaction to him. She was
around handsome men at the plant all the time, and none of
them made her tremble in anticipation with just a look. She
sighed, resigned to her own weakness.

It was the aura of excitement about him that had her
weak-kneed and even weaker-brained. Life on the wild side,
a hint of danger. It always raised her level of interest. Blame
that on her grandfather, too, she thought, groaning, pulling the last package of bacon from the cooler.

Pa Pa' had been the one who'd lured her outside while the
women had cooked the steaming pots of gumbo and fried
the freshly caught fish. He'd had her slipping through the
still bayou waters, moving in and around half-hidden alligators, avoiding assorted slimy creatures and soggy mud
holes that sucked you inside them. Life with him had been
anything but dull.

Alligators, snakes, bayou quicksand. They were play-
things compared to dealing with men, Merissa reminded
herself as she pulled the thick, honey-cured strips of bacon
apart and placed them side by side in the hot skillet. She'd
already learned that lesson far too well.

The meat sizzled, splattering a drop of grease onto her
arm. The pain was a welcome release from her thoughts.
Breakfast and packing her gear to go home—those were all
she needed to think about now.

CAGAN STRETCHED HIS LEGS as much as he could in the too-
short sleeping bag he'd borrowed from Jeff. He drew in a
breath, and the smell of bacon awakened his nostrils.
Groaning, he lifted himself up on his elbows. His joints
ached as if he'd been beaten with a club. A week of sleep-

Extreme Heat

ing on the ground was not his idea of fun. Not that he'd gotten a whole lot of sleep last night.

He'd wanted Jeff to talk. Instead, he'd drunk a few beers and started ranting like a kid who'd had his candy stolen. This was not the man Cagan had met four months ago. Something big-time was going on with him. And one way or another, Cagan planned to find out exactly what that something was.

Squeezing his eyes shut, he shoved himself into the sleeping bag again and dropped his head back to the lumpy pillow.

"Are you guys ready for a cup of coffee?"

Managing to open one eye, Cagan stared at the stream of sunlight that poured into his previously dark tent. Merissa stood in the center of the stream, her blond hair reflecting the rays of sunshine like glass.

"Where's Jeff?" she asked, her gaze wandering from him to the empty sleeping bag on the other side of the tent.

"Beats me. I smelled breakfast, so I thought he was out there cooking."

"No. I gave up on you two and decided to do the honors today."

Cagan pulled himself up to rest on his elbows again, crossing his bare legs under the mound of insulated fabric. He stared at Merissa. Big mistake. Her white shorts and T-shirt all but gleamed against her deeply tanned body. And her blond hair fell halfway down her back, loose and inviting.

One more day, he told himself, shaking away the last of his grogginess. That's all the time he had to resist the forbidden Louisiana goddess. Merissa walked nearer and stood over him, holding out a mug of steaming brew.

"This must be my lucky day," he said, smiling up at her. "Not only bedside service, but I won't have to suffer through Jeff's bitter coffee."

"You might want to hold off on the praise. Mine is even stronger than Jeff's."

She returned his smile and leaned down, placing the cup in his hand. Her hair fell forward, brushing his fingers, and Cagan felt a rush of testosterone that punched below the belt.

"We don't think of it as bitter," she continued, her voice still early-morning husky. "The chicory just gives it an extra bite. If you stay in Louisiana long enough, you'll learn to love it."

"Sounds intriguing."

"Strong coffee?"

"No, staying around awhile."

She averted her gaze to the ground. Steam from the mug of coffee she held in her right hand swirled about her face, painting her soft, pouty lips shades of misty pink. Cagan ached, the desire to hold her translating into a painful knot that settled in his gut. She was so damned enticing.

But not for him, he reminded himself. This was not the place or the time for courting disaster.

Silence grew thick between them, but still Merissa made no move to leave. Instead, she hooked her foot around the leg of the camp chair and dragged it to the side of his sleeping bag. "What did you and Jeff argue about last night?" she asked, easing down to the chair.

"We didn't." He kept his face poker-hand cold. The less she knew about their argument last night, the better off they'd both be. "He had a couple of beers and got a little loud. That's all."

Merissa took a long sip from the mug of coffee she had originally brought for Jeff. "It sounded like arguing to me."

"No, just a spirited discussion. Sorry if we woke you." He studied her face. Doubt shadowed her eyes. God, he hated lying to her. But he had no choice. He never did.

"So, where do you think Jeff is now?"

"I have no idea. Like I told you, I just woke up to the smell of bacon." He set his cup on the ground beside him and leaned over on his elbow, staring up at her. "And a beautiful woman bearing coffee."

"And now the bacon's getting cold," she commented, rising to her feet. "I vote we eat without him."

"I agree." He didn't really. He wanted to stay right here, just the two of them, holding back the day and the return to Baton Rouge and reality.

He watched as she turned to leave. Her foot caught on the edge of his sleeping bag, throwing her off balance. Instinctively, Cagan reached out to catch her, but she righted herself, her graceful body almost catlike in its agility.

His coffee didn't fare so well. The movement of the bag had toppled his half-empty mug. Merissa bent down and picked up the cup, staring at the dark stain that spread over the blue flannel lining of his bag.

"I'm sorry," she said softly, dropping to her knees to get a closer look at the stain.

The clean, flowery smell of her washed over him, making him forget, or at least ignore, his resolve to stay away from her. "Leave it," he murmured, grabbing her wrist and pulling her so close that her shimmering hair cascaded over his chest.

Every nerve in his body reacted. What the hell was he thinking? He'd never be able to stop with a harmless kiss this time. Willing his mind to rule, he let go of her wrist.

But she didn't back away. His gaze captured hers and she drew closer, so near her warm breath fell on his face. Her lips were parted, just slightly, moist and all but begging to be kissed. Damn. She had to know what she was doing to him.

He reached out with the fingers of his right hand and traced the fullness of her lips. She opened them more, sucking his fingertips one by one, like a child with an ice-cream cone.

And he was only human, though even that had been debated before. Curling the fingers of his left hand into the silky strands of her long blond hair, he pulled her against him and pressed his mouth against hers, knowing he was too rough, too demanding.

He kissed her lips until his lungs strained for air. She should be damned thankful for his control. Otherwise he'd give in to the urge that rumbled inside him. He'd tear the clothes from her body and take her, wildly, instinctively, like the beast he probably was.

A low cry gurgled from her throat, followed by murmured words too soft for him to make out. It didn't matter. He didn't trust words. They always promised but never delivered. Instinct and action, those were the things he understood. Hungrily, he pulled her down beside him.

"No, Cagan. No." Her hands pushed against his chest. "I shouldn't have come in here. I'm sorry." Her voice was laced with desire, but her body had stiffened in restraint.

"You don't have to be afraid of me, Merissa. I won't hurt you."

He wouldn't hurt her. The words grew bitter in his mouth even as he said them. The truth was he could hurt her. Maybe not this minute, but before it was all over. Fatally. It had happened before.

His arms fell to his sides as reality jolted him back to his senses.

"It's Jeff," she whispered, answering a question he'd never asked. "I don't want him to find us like this. It would hurt him."

Jealousy flared inside Cagan. Not that he had any right to feel it. "What's between you two?" he asked through clenched teeth.

"Friendship. Nothing more." Merissa rose to a sitting position and straightened her T-shirt. "Jeff settles for that, but it's not his first choice. Sometimes, when he looks at me, I know he wants more."

"I'm sure." Cagan tucked a finger under her chin and tilted it upward so that he could look into her eyes. "I can't imagine there's a man alive who wouldn't want you, Merissa."

"I don't mean it to be that way."

The words weren't conceited, merely honest and straightforward. And strangely enough, Cagan believed her. Everything about her made him aware he was a man, but her sensuality was touched with naiveté, a fragility that made her all the more irresistible.

And it was all the more difficult for him to let her go now. His body still ached for her. But it was more than a physical need that drew him to her, though he wasn't sure exactly what it was he felt. He only knew that he had to let her go. Now and forever.

Silence encompassed them, thick and choking. "I'll go finish breakfast," Merissa offered, moving toward the door.

Cagan nodded agreement, knowing full well that mere food would never satisfy the craving that raged inside him.

THE COOLNESS OF MORNING evaporated quickly. By the time breakfast was ready, the sun had already started its sweltering assault. Merissa sat at the table long after Cagan had finished eating and excused himself to start packing for the trip home. She picked at a clump of cold eggs.

"As soon as I dismantle your tent, everything will be loaded and ready to go," Cagan called, walking back from the pickup truck. "Now all we need is for Jeff to get back."

"This isn't like him," she answered. She was still nursing the anger she'd felt all morning at his disappearance, but even with nurturing, the anger was slipping away fast. Now it was more of a gnawing fear that tiptoed around the edges of her mind. "Did you hear him leave the tent this morning?" she asked.

"No. The truth is I don't remember his even coming to bed last night. When I got back from your tent, I crashed. The next thing I knew, you were standing there with coffee, and Jeff's sleeping bag was empty."

"I'm worried about him, Cagan." There. She'd finally said the words out loud. "If he were all right, he'd be here."

Cagan walked over and caressed her with his eyes. She knew without his saying it that he didn't dare offer the reassurance of his touch. The tension of the morning still hovered over them like hungry birds of prey.

"He probably just got up early and wanted to get in one last chance at the fish," Cagan said. "He'll come walking up the path any minute."

"You don't know that. You don't know if he even came back to the tent last night. He might have wandered off in the dark and fallen or..."

"You're jumping to conclusions." Cagan sounded confident, but he paced the path between her and the truck as he spoke. "Besides, the boat's gone. He has to be fishing."

"I hope you're right." She struggled to accept this perfectly reasonable explanation, but her apprehension didn't go away.

"He'll be here any minute. I'm sure he just hit a spot where the fish are jumping in the boat with him and he's having trouble pulling himself away," Cagan continued. "You know how he likes to fish."

"I do now." But she wasn't convinced Cagan was right. It wasn't like Jeff to run off like this when he knew their plans were to leave early. "I think I'll go down to the lake and have a look around."

"Do you want me to go with you?"

"No, you stay here and finish loading the gear. I won't be long."

Grabbing her straw sun hat, Merissa started down the dirt path that led to the shoreline. Jeff and Cagan had put the fishing boat in the water about a quarter of a mile down the road at the public launch, but they had kept it here during the week, tied to the trunk of a towering cypress tree when they hadn't been in it.

Using a tissue to wipe the perspiration from her forehead, Merissa struggled to make sense of Jeff's disappearance. It was useless. The only reasonable explanation she could come up with was that the argument between the two men last night had been more serious than Cagan was admitting. At least it must have been in Jeff's eyes.

He might have still been angry this morning and gone fishing to cool off. But angry or not, he shouldn't have left them here waiting on him. He knew she had an appointment scheduled for this afternoon, and Cagan had to work tonight.

Waves from a passing boat crashed against the muddy shore as Merissa stepped into the clearing by the lake. She shaded her eyes with her hands and peered across the water. A man and two children waved at her from the speeding craft, and her heart sank. For a minute, she'd been sure it would be Jeff, but there was no sign of him or his fishing boat.

Disgruntled and perspiring, she turned to trudge back to the campsite. A red squirrel darted in front of her, then scurried into the bushes. She watched, catching a glimpse of him again when he jumped onto the trunk of a tree and scampered to the first branch. Pausing on his hind feet, he chattered at her mockingly.

She stepped off the path to get a better look at his antics. But the squirrel wasn't about to let her get too close. As if taunting her, he sprang to the next tree, disappearing into a cover of branches and pine needles.

A smidgen of color caught Merissa's eye. Red plaid, vibrant-hued, familiar. Like the shirt Jeff had worn last night.

"Jeff!" She called out his name, but the only response was the hammering of a woodpecker somewhere in the distance. "Jeff! If you're out there, answer me." She moved quickly, pushing aside vines and underbrush that wrapped around her arms and legs.

A rabbit bolted beneath her feet and she jumped, all but tripping over an outstretched root. She was getting closer, and the snatch of fabric was growing, taking shape and form. It was Jeff. She was sure of it now. No wonder he hadn't come back. He must have fallen and hurt himself just as she had suspected.

Her leg caught on a sticker vine that wouldn't let go, and a warm rivulet of blood trickled down her leg. She yanked the vine away, ignoring the pain. She had to get to Jeff. He wasn't moving, and for all she knew, he was unconscious or maybe worse.

Her breath stabbed at her chest as she forced her legs to run through a tangled mass of vegetation that tore at her shorts and legs. A shudder racked her body as she reached his side. He lay on his stomach, deathly still, his head resting on the hard, smooth root of a tree. One arm was stretched up the trunk, caught on a jutting twig. It was the blessed trace of color she'd seen from the path.

"Jeff," she gasped urgently, "what happened?"

She grabbed the edge of his shirt and rolled him over.

"Oh, God, no!" Her heart lunged, striking against her chest with such force she had to struggle to remain upright. The front of his shirt was coated with a sticky mass of deep crimson, the glinting handle of a knife protruding through the blood. His eyes...

She backed away. It was a bad dream. Not real. Turning, she stumbled away. Her legs and feet moved without her consciously telling them to. Forcing air into her lungs, she ran past low-hanging limbs that swatted at her face and arms. She had to get help. Fast!

Chapter Three

Cagan shaded his eyes and searched the woods for some sign of Merissa. Fifteen minutes ago, she'd gone in search of Jeff. Now she'd disappeared as well, and he was getting more than a little tired of the whole business. And nervous as hell. Tugging his fishing hat lower, he propped his foot on a half-decayed tree stump. A white egret flew low over the lake's surface and then swooped to the water's edge, landing a few yards from where he stood. It lifted one foot and stood quietly, waiting for the movement in the water that would signal breakfast had arrived. Seconds later, it dipped its beak below the surface and then took flight again, disappearing into the line of trees that bordered the lake.

Appear from nowhere, take care of business, then cut out. The choice modus operandi. The egret knew it from instinct. Cagan had learned it the hard way.

Something rustled the grass behind him, and Cagan spun on his heels. He heard a cry. Low, frightened. Female.

"Cagan!"

He jerked around. "Merissa." Her name fell from his tongue as she stepped from the bushes. Her eyes were wide and frightened, her lips trembling. He darted forward, reaching her just as her legs folded under her, her slender frame collapsing against him. Hugging her to his chest, he held her limp body upright. "What happened? Are you hurt?" His voice was strained, tripping over unspoken fears.

"No. It's Jeff."

"Where is he?"

"I...think..." Her breathing was ragged, punctuating her words with sharp jabs. "He's...in the woods." Her voice dropped to a shaking whisper. "He's hurt. He needs a doctor. Right away."

Cagan gripped her arms and held her in front of him. Her face was ghostly white, and the eyes that had looked at him earlier this morning with flickering desire were dark pits of horror and confusion.

"Take me to him," he told her, one arm circling her waist.

"He's over there. Behind a tree. In the grass." Her voice quivered and she held out a hand to point in the direction she had come from a minute before. Her hand was smeared with a sticky substance that looked like crimson syrup.

She started walking, and he matched her steps, one arm still around her trembling body.

"No, not this way." She turned and staggered back toward the path.

She was leading him in circles. Cagan ran his hand over his concealed weapon and cursed his skeptical nature. He had to be prepared for any possibility.

Merissa stopped, then turned in another direction, her gaze sweeping over the area. "I'm not sure, Cagan. I thought he was right here, but now..."

"Think, Merissa. Which way did you walk after you left him?"

"I can't remember." She shook her head and then turned from side to side. "That way, I think. I remember that bush," she said, pointing at a nearby shrub with a whitish flower.

Cagan dropped his hand from Merissa's waist and took her hand. He moved in front of her, pulling her along, picking up the pace to a near jog.

"Are we nearly there?" he asked as she directed him deeper into the woods, farther off the path she would have traveled to the lake.

"Yes, almost. Straight ahead." Merissa blurted out the words and then stopped dead in her tracks. She couldn't go on. Breathing was painful, and she had exhausted all her reserves of energy.

"What is it?" Cagan asked.

Dizziness washed over her in waves. "I can't go back again," she whispered. She had faced the gruesome sight of Jeff's body once. She couldn't do it again.

"It's okay, Merissa. I'm with you now."

"Please, Cagan. You go ahead without me."

"I can't leave you here alone."

Alone. No. She didn't want that. She let herself be led. A few steps through the trees, that's all it took, and then Cagan was bending over Jeff's still body, the same way she had done a few minutes ago. At least she thought it had been a few minutes ago. She wasn't sure now. Time was as lost to her as her sense of direction, her power to reason.

"Is he . . . ?" Dead. The word hammered inside her, but she couldn't bring herself to say it. Tears pushed at her eyes, and she tried desperately to hold them back. She watched as Cagan felt for a pulse, then cringed as the pain of seeing Jeff's body for himself carved new lines into his face. "We have to do something, Cagan. Call somebody. Take Jeff somewhere."

"There's no rush, Merissa." His voice was stony, and he stayed in his crouched position, examining the wound. "He's dead."

The ice in Cagan's voice penetrated her shock and jolted her back to reality. "But how...?"

"He was murdered."

"That's impossible. Who would've murdered him? It had to be an accident. He fell on his knife, that's all. He must have tripped while running. Or fell from the tree."

The words were tumbling from her mouth, but she hardly knew what she was saying. She only knew that Cagan couldn't be right. No one would have a reason to stick a knife into Jeff's heart.

A fillet knife. Jeff's. The one she had washed and dried last night when they'd cleaned the dishes. If someone had killed him, that someone had been in their camp. The murderer had been there with her and Cagan. Or else...

"Come on, Merissa. Let's get out of here."

Cagan draped his arm over her shoulder. The loud voices from the night before clamored and clanged inside her—the drunken slur to Jeff's words, the angry edge to Cagan's. But what was it they had said? She couldn't remember, not in the blur of confusion that clouded her mind.

Trembling, she wiped her hands on her shorts. The blood wouldn't come off. New panic gripped her. She had to get to the lake and wash the blood away.

Shoving with her elbows, she broke away from Cagan. She started to run, right through the thickest of the bushes and grasping vines. They clutched and tore at her, but she forced her legs even faster. She had to get away.

Cagan grabbed her arm and yanked her to a stop. "Where do you think you're going?"

"To...to the lake." She lifted her hands and stared at them, nausea attacking with renewed fervor. "I have to wash."

"The lake is the other way."

She shuddered, and tried to pull away.

Cagan muttered a curse under his breath. Merissa's eyes cried out to him, frightened innocence shimmering through the moisture. Regret played havoc with his will. All he wanted to do was hold her, protect her, but he didn't dare trust his emotions.

A warning shouted in his brain, one that had been programmed into existence. *Always consider the person finding the body a suspect.* He pushed it aside. It was only a rule of thumb, not carved in stone.

"I need to wash my hands, Cagan. And then we have to call the police."

"I know. I'll go with you." He walked beside her, near enough to touch, ready to reach out and grab her if she started to run again. God, how he hoped she wouldn't. Everything about her tantalized him—her walk, the tilt of her head, the bronzed body beneath the golden hair. Even in her state of semishock, this power she had to fill him with some male protective urge was overwhelming.

But was it shock at all? Or was she just an expert at illusion? He couldn't let her seductive powers blind him to the facts. He'd known beautiful women who'd murdered for a lot less than was at stake in the LPI scenario.

Merissa picked up her pace and he matched her stride for stride. He longed to trust her, but suspicion dogged his every move.

It was the way he lived, the way he stayed alive.

MERISSA SHIFTED in the uncomfortable wooden chair. She had been escorted directly from the lake to this dingy, cluttered room. For over an hour, she had been here, listening to one meaningless question after another. Stupidly, she had assumed that Baton Rouge police would show up to investigate Jeff's death. But, of course, they hadn't. Local lawmen answered 911 calls, and these particular locals were all but salivating over the prospects of a juicy murder case.

Eyes narrowed, she stared at her paunchy interrogator. His face was ruddy, and one cheek swelled with a brown lump of chewing tobacco that made an appearance every time he opened his mouth to ask a question.

"So how long did you say you knew the victim?"

The victim. Her throat constricted again, but she forced her mouth to answer. "I've already told you. He dated my best friend in college. Five years ago. When they broke up, Jeff and I remained friends. We were both in engineering and we had a lot in common." She stretched her back, giving only minor relief to the weary muscles. "None of which has anything to do with his being murdered," she added, her mind and body far beyond their normal level of endurance.

A door behind her squeaked open. Cagan walked back into the room, followed by the sheriff. He was a lean, mean guy who needed a shave and a bath, and a crash course in manners.

"Y'all 'bout done in here?" the sheriff drawled.

Merissa's Officer Friendly picked up an empty tin can and spit a stream of brown gunk into it. "Close," he answered, setting the can back on the floor. "Miss Thomas was just telling me about her relationship with the victim."

Cagan glared at the sheriff and shot Merissa a look that would have intimidated a gorilla. It didn't work on her, and from the look on the sheriff's face, it hadn't fazed him, either.

"We found the body and we called 911," Cagan growled at the tobacco-cheeked man. "We gave you the details about that. Anything else you want to ask the lady, you'll do it in the presence of her lawyer."

Merissa met his gaze with a scalding look of her own. "I don't need a lawyer, Cagan. I told you, I'm not afraid of their questions. I just want the killer found. And I'm tired of everybody treating me as if I have something to hide.''

She was tired of cops, too, ex-cops included, and their sneaky way of walking ten feet around every issue instead of going at it head-on.

''What the officer wants to know is whether or not I was sleeping with Jeff,'' she added tartly. ''He wants to know if the three of us were involved in some tabloid-type triangle where the odd man out got murdered.''

''Keep quiet, Merissa.''

''No, Cagan. I'm not keeping quiet. And I'm not going to sit here and listen to any more of their ridiculous innuendos.''

Patience stretched past breaking, she wagged a finger in the sheriff's direction and glared at Cagan, daring either one of them to stop her.

''I went on a fishing trip with a long-time friend whom I'd trust with my life. *And* my chastity. I wasn't sleeping with Jeff or with Cagan Hall, and I never have. So you can take your dirty little minds and point them in another direction.'' Her insides were trembling, but somehow her voice stayed fairly stable. ''And I didn't kill him,'' she continued when, surprisingly, no one interrupted her. ''So you'd be a lot better off finding out who did, instead of wasting your time giving me the third degree.''

''Oh, we're gonna find out who did it. You don't hafta worry your pretty little head about that.'' The sheriff tugged on the waistband of his baggy pants as he talked, hiking them up while giving her a quick once-over with his eyes. ''Or maybe you should.''

Standing up, she stepped in front of the sheriff. ''The only thing I'm worried about is your competence. Now, if there's nothing else, I'm getting out of here. You have my address and phone number. I'm sure you'll call if you need me." She spun on her heel and headed toward the door.

"Not so fast, Miss Thomas." The sheriff stepped in front of the door. "You'll leave when *I* say."

Cagan moved over to stand beside her. "Like Miss Thomas said, she's ready to leave *now,* and unless you have a warrant for her arrest or for mine, I suggest you move away from the door."

"Yeah, you talk mighty big, don't you? But you don't call the shots here. We're running this investigation."

"Oh, is that what you're doing?" Cagan snapped.

"And what would you call it?"

"A couple of clowns on parade."

The sheriff's face grew bright red, and he scowled so tightly it had to hurt.

"After the way you botched up the examination of the crime scene," Cagan continued, his voice low but hard, "I seriously doubt you'd be able to convict the murderer if he walked in here and kissed you on the—" he glanced at Merissa "—on the cheek."

"Don't worry about us." The sheriff rubbed his thumb over the hammer of his gun. "In case you haven't noticed, Hall, we don't play by big-city rules down here."

"You don't appear to be following any rules."

The sheriff strutted around the room. "You don't seem too good at following rules yourself. Not known for being a peace-lovin' sort, either, are you, Officer Hall?" A chuckle bared his yellowed teeth. "Excuse me, I meant *ex*-Officer Hall."

"So you did your homework," Cagan answered. "Do you expect me to be impressed?"

The sheriff stopped strutting and stood in front of Cagan, one hand on his hip. "Yeah, I know *all* about you. Not just that little spiel you gave us about being head of security for Louisiana Prosthetics. It only took a couple of phone calls to get the real scoop.''

"It sounds like you have me pegged about right. I'm rotten to the core. Now either arrest me or get out of my way.''

The paunchy guy spit again. "I say we arrest both of them. We got cause. They were at the scene. Nobody else was. As far as I can tell, they're prime suspects, at least Hall is. He's reluctant to give us pertinent information. Besides, what man wouldn't kill for something like that?''

His gaze wandered all over Merissa from head to toe, stopping a lot longer on some spots than on others. Her skin crawled under his slimy assessment.

But Cagan's skin was not crawling. It was pulled taut over muscles that were wound like ribbons of steel. She grimaced, knowing that the hands he had knotted into hard fists were dying to zero in on the officer's leering face.

"Nah. Let 'em go," the sheriff drawled. He wrapped his hand around the battered doorknob and twisted it, pulling the door open. "Like Miss Thomas said, we know where to find them. And if they try to hightail it out of the state... bang, we got 'em." He stuck out his finger, pointing it like the barrel of a gun. "Just a figure of speech," he added, his mouth twisted into a distorted grin.

Merissa followed Cagan to the pickup, all but running to keep up. He didn't wait for her or even bother to open her door. Climbing into the driver's seat, he slammed the door behind him.

"Slimeballs!" he muttered, punching the key into the ignition and revving the engine. Merissa braced herself, but not in time to avoid being thrown back against the seat as the tires spit gravel at the rapidly disappearing building.

The next few miles passed in silence, leaving Merissa to her own troubled thoughts. The splitting headache she'd developed while waiting for the police to arrive at the campsite had settled into a dull throb, but her confused emotions still tumbled about like new-fallen autumn leaves.

Leaning back and closing her eyes, she tried to sort out her feelings. She had been mesmerized by Cagan all week. A look, a touch, a kiss. That's all it had taken for him to throw her totally off center.

But things were different now, heartbreakingly different. One of her best friends was dead. Staring out the window, Merissa searched her brain for the scraps of argument she had heard last night. It was useless. All she could remember was that the voices had quieted shortly after Cagan had left her tent. But later, he'd denied that he and Jeff had argued at all. A spirited discussion, that's how he'd described it. And no one had seen Jeff alive since then.

Emotional confusion clouded her mind and dulled her senses. She'd like nothing better than to trust Cagan, but she didn't dare. Not until she knew the truth about what had really happened to Jeff.

"What kind of questions did 'Mr. Manners' ask you when I was out of the room?" Cagan finally asked, breaking into thoughts she was glad to have interrupted.

"Mostly stuff about Jeff and me, and about you."

"All of which was unnecessary at that point. With what you had just gone through, they could have shown a little consideration."

"They did at first," Merissa reminded him. "They were ready to take our statement and release us until you started telling them how to do their job."

"When did I do that?"

"About two minutes after they arrived at the lake."

"Yeah, well, incompetence bugs the hell out of me. Anyway, I'm sorry they were so rough on you back there. I probably deserved it, but you didn't."

Merissa turned to stare at Cagan. His hands clutched the steering wheel as if it might jerk from his grasp at any moment. His face was as hard as nails, his chin jutting out defiantly, his lips drawn into tight lines.

"What do you know about Rick Porter?" He glanced her way when he spoke, his eyes burning with a glint of steel.

"I don't know him well. Not many people at the plant do. He has a reputation for being difficult to get along with. But Gaffner obviously thinks he's capable. And Lana's dated him for a few months now."

"Ah, yes. Lana Glass. The dazzling darling of personnel. The redhead who has herself melted and poured into those tight little skirts."

"You noticed."

"I'm a red-blooded male."

Merissa was all too aware of that fact, but she wasn't about to touch it now. Instead, she worked on keeping her tone even and her own suspicions under control until she knew a lot more than she knew now. "All the men went gaga when Lana first came to work for LPI, but she didn't seem to notice any—"

"Except for Rick Porter," Cagan broke in, "the guy nobody else could get along with. She noticed him. She dated Jeff for a while, too, didn't she?"

"Briefly. Is there a point to this, Cagan?"

"No, I guess not." He accelerated, pushing the speed over the posted limit. "But there are a few points I need to make and you need to listen and listen good."

"No, Cagan. I don't need to listen. Not now." And especially not to you, she added silently before continuing her tirade. "I've been through all I can handle for one day. The only thing I need is to go home. I want to take a bath, a hot one, so hot I'll believe it's burning away the stench of what happened today. And then I want to sleep. For hours.

Maybe days." Her voice caught and trembled. "And I want time to grieve in some semblance of peace."

Cagan dropped his right hand to the seat and wrapped it around hers. A shiver, icy, bone chilling, skittered through her. A far cry from the heated tremors he'd inspired this morning. She pulled her hand away.

A man had been murdered. She and Cagan were prime suspects, maybe the only ones. And she knew *she* hadn't done it.

She shuddered. A few hours ago, there was nothing she wanted more than to be with Cagan, just the two of them and the burning desires he kindled inside her.

Now grief for a lost friend wrung her insides and wrapped clutching fingers around her heart. And to top it off, doubt and suspicion raced rampant through her mind, coloring her feelings for Cagan in shades of blue and nasty black.

What a difference a day made. And a murder.

MARSHALL GAFFNER STOOD at the window of his fourth-floor office and stared out his plate-glass window, the perfect spot from which to view his latest extravagance. Mardi Gras Lights. The winner's choice, the place to play and win, or so said his advertisements. Neon lights, glimmering paint, cheap glass jewels, all guarded over by a plastic masked queen. Gaudy, but it suited him. A lot more than running the stuffy prosthetics company dear old Dad had left him.

So did having the controlling interest in a riverboat casino. At least it had in the beginning, when he'd been convinced the money would pour into his bank account as rapidly as it slid through the slot machines. It had for a while, but only until the novelty wore off. Until competition moved in, always glitzier, luring away the gamblers he'd depended on to make Mardi Gras Lights pay.

Still staring, he poked a finger under his tie and loosened it, pulling it away from his sweaty neck. The damn thing was strangling him, just as everything and everybody else was doing these days. His creditors, his wife Priscilla, his girlfriend. Go for the jugular. That was the battle cry for all of them.

Especially Priscilla. Threatening divorce when she knew good and well he'd never split up their assets. He'd see her dead first. Sweat balled on his brow, and he yanked a linen handkerchief from his pocket and wiped it away. They were all after a piece of the rock.

And Sen. James Bracer was worst of all. The senator's constituents loved him, but then, they didn't know him as Gaffner did. They had no idea of the extremes he'd go to to make sure nothing got in the way of his lining his pockets.

Gaffner knew it now, just as he knew that the stakes in the game they were playing had changed, had grown to killer proportions. That meant the rules of the game would have to change, too.

In fact, they already had. They had changed a week ago when the doctored shipment disappeared, on the day one million dollars had slipped through his and Bracer's fingers. Someone had taken it. That meant someone knew way too much. This was not the way Bracer had promised him things would be.

All Marshall Gaffner wanted was enough money to enjoy life on his own terms. He wasn't cut out to be a criminal, didn't have the stomach for it. He was a far cry from the Southern gentleman his father had been, but he had his limits. At least, he'd thought he did. Now the need for survival was forcing him to stray outside the boundaries he'd set for himself, making him do things he found downright disgusting.

But he had no choice. He was playing with fire, and the heat was growing more intense. That was the problem with playing with fire. The hotter it got, the harder it was to contain. And the more casualties it claimed.

Gaffner rubbed his temple with the fingers of his right hand in a futile attempt at easing the dull ache. He left the window to pace the room, his hand-sewn Italian loafers sinking into the plush beige carpet.

Stopping at his desk, he reached into the top drawer for one of the Cuban cigars he had managed to acquire especially for his private stock. He liked the finer things, and there were no fine things behind the bars of a federal penitentiary.

That's why he'd take care of things himself now. And Merissa Thomas was at the top of his list. Smart, sweet, and a real looker. Regret tugged at his resolve. He hated to do this to her. But it all came down to survival.

Chapter Four

Merissa folded the newspaper and slammed it onto her desk. For the past week, evidence had piled up against her like Mississippi mud after a flood.

Her fingerprints were on the knife. Hers and no one else's. Jeff's blood had been smeared all over the front of her shirt, and her arms and legs had been covered in scratches as if she'd been in a skirmish. And she and Jeff had been *more* than friends. Those were the facts, according to the daily news reports.

She was innocent and she had no cause for alarm. Those were the facts, according to the high-powered, fast-talking attorney Gaffner had recommended. He and Gaffner apparently believed her story. She wasn't sure about anyone else, especially her co-workers.

Curious stares had followed her around the plant like cheap private eyes. She shouldn't really be surprised by that. The sheriff and his tobacco-spitting deputy had been to her office three times this week, flashing their badges and making sure everyone she worked with knew she was under investigation for Jeff's death.

A shiver rode her spine. In spite of her lawyer's reassurance, she was worried. Innocent people *did* go to jail. It happened all the time, and it could happen to her. On the whim of this incompetent sheriff, she could be arrested and locked away in a dingy cell, surrounded by every kind of criminal. And Jeff's real killer would walk the streets a free man.

Her hands began to tremble, and her stomach churned sickeningly. No matter how hard she tried to stay objective about this whole mess, she couldn't escape the fears that hounded her day and night. Struggling for a calming breath, she pushed her chair back from her desk. With slow, deliberate movements, she laced her fingers behind her neck, letting her head drop back as far as the stiff muscles would allow.

The tension eased slightly, and she stretched her neck from side to side, her gaze sweeping across her roomy office. The late-afternoon sun filtered through the tinted glass windows, casting a golden hue on the dark furnishings and brighter accents.

She let her gaze linger on each item, as if she were seeing them for the first time. As if they could pull her back from the nightmare that had started at the lake and grown more real every day. She cradled the crystal paperweight her parents had sent her from England. For the first time since they had left the States, she wished they were nearer, or even that she could call them and talk about the trouble she was in.

She wouldn't, not yet anyway. Her father had taken a year's sabbatical from the university where he taught in the science department to recuperate from his heart attack. First her grandparents' deaths, then her father's illness. Her mother had more than enough to deal with without Merissa adding to her problems.

With a heavy heart, she slid her fingers across the top of her desk. The wood was polished mahogany with a leather inset across the top that protected the expensive wood. Pleasant surroundings encourage employee productivity,

Gaffner had told her on that first fateful interview. Now the surroundings were more terrifying than pleasant. Of course, she still had Cagan Hall, head of security, around to make sure she was safe. Which to her way of thinking was worth exactly nothing.

She'd been as unpleasant to Cagan as she could. It hadn't fazed him. He was like a stalker, materializing at every turn. He had called her a half-dozen times a day, appeared from nowhere every time she stepped into the coffee room or out for a drink of water. Never threatening, at least not openly, but always there.

He had to stop following her. If he didn't, her rattled nerves would push her over the edge. Attraction, sensual anticipation and infatuation had run their titillating threads through every encounter at the lake. But suspicion colored their every meeting now, undermining every word and look that passed between them. She wanted him out of her life.

Merissa flicked off her computer. Work was impossible. Her inability to concentrate made designing tasks or even routine office activities seem like monumental feats. A week ago, her work as a prosthetics engineer had been everything. Now her office was little more than a prison.

She shuddered at the thought and the foreboding chill returned to haunt her. She'd go to Gaffner and tell him to keep Cagan away from her. The rest of the office and even the cops might be taken in by him, but as far as she was concerned, Cagan was number one on the suspect list.

"May I come in?"

The unexpected voice startled Merissa, and she twirled her chair to face the door. Lana Glass stood just outside the doorway, her mouth curved in a half smile.

"I didn't mean to frighten you."

"It doesn't take much these days." Merissa breathed a sigh of relief. At least it was Lana this time and not Cagan.

"How are you?" Lana asked, stepping inside the door.

"I've been a lot better."

"I bet. I just saw today's paper."

"Yeah, me, too. From the looks of the article, I'm all but convicted."

"Try not to let them upset you." Lana walked closer, her tight skirt making short steps a necessity. "It's a slow week, and they need a story."

"Then let's hope something exciting happens soon, before the newspeople have me frying in the electric chair. Anyway, that's enough of my problems," Merissa said, changing to her business tone. "What can I do for you?"

"Nothing. I just wanted you to know how sorry I am about what happened. It was bad enough without the cops trying to implicate you in the crime. But now it's completely ludicrous. No one who knows you would ever believe such a thing."

"Thanks for that vote of confidence. I guess it's too bad I don't know more reporters. Or cops. Believing I'm guilty doesn't seem to be a problem for them."

Merissa forced a smile to her lips and worked on relaxing. Evidently, not everyone had lined up against her. Lana had been to Merissa's office before, but always on business. It said a lot that she had dropped by just to offer a little sympathy.

"You do know one cop, Merissa. At least you know an ex-cop."

"Cagan?"

"Exactly."

A familiar throbbing began in the back of Merissa's head, and the muscles in her neck grew stiff. "Did Cagan send you to talk to me?"

"No. Why should he?"

"I don't know. Look, Lana, I don't need to talk to Cagan. I have a lawyer."

"But Cagan was right there with you at the lake," Lana insisted. "Maybe he could do something to keep you from all this police harassment? They don't seem to be bothering him."

"Of course not. You know the police and their macho fraternity code of ethics. Protect your own and damn the rest." Anger raised her voice.

"I don't think Cagan's like that, Merissa. Besides, if anyone around here knows anything, it should be him. He's always asking questions, and he and Jeff talked a lot before that trip to the lake. Several times..."

Lana paused, then ran her fingers through her hair as if deciding just how much she should say. Apparently, she opted for more.

"A couple of times," she continued, "I had to come back to the office at night, and I'd see them here, talking and laughing like the best of friends." Lana leaned against the desk, her gaze penetrating.

"They were friends, Lana," Merissa responded, "but I was Jeff's friend, too. I'll do whatever I can to help find the killer, but I don't need Cagan's help."

"I think you do." Lana's tone was almost pleading. "And I wouldn't trust any lawyer Mr. Gaffner recommended."

"What is that supposed to mean? Gaffner has no possible reason to sabotage my defense."

"Don't be so sure. Not in this case."

Picking up a pencil, Merissa drummed a restless rhythm with the eraser. Rumor had it that Lana and Gaffner were as thick as cream. Boss's pet, and she made the most of it, kissing up to him every chance she got.

Evidently, something had happened to curdle the cream. Filing her thoughts for later consideration, Merissa made an effort to get Lana to drop the subject.

"I appreciate your concern, Lana, but you really don't need to worry. I have one of the city's most respected lawyers and I'm cooperating with the police in every way I can. I'm sure they don't actually consider me a suspect. If they did, I'd be in jail."

Merissa stood, hoping Lana would take the hint and leave. Much more of her kind of encouragement and Merissa would be reduced to a shaking mass of tears. So much for sympathy.

She didn't get her wish. Instead, Lana reached out and squeezed her hand. "That's the other thing." Lana paused, her long eyelashes lowered as if she dreaded sharing what she was about to say. "Be very careful, Merissa. The deputy was here a few minutes ago. I overheard him talking to Gaffner and—"

"Just say it, Lana. Believe me, it can't be any worse than the things I've heard already from one source or another."

"Okay. He said your arrest is imminent."

Merissa's breath caught in her lungs as an unexpected wave of panic swept over her.

"I'm sorry. But I thought you should know, and I didn't think Gaffner would tell you."

"No. It looks like I'm pretty much on my own." The pencil slipped from her fingers, bouncing on and then off the edge of the desk. Lana's words echoed in her mind, setting off a thousand alarms. Cagan, Jeff, Gaffner. What kind of weird triangle had formed between them, locking her in the middle with no way out?

"If you need anything, even just a friendly face, call me." Lana opened the door and waited.

"Thanks. I will." The words came out in a shaky whisper. Merissa watched in silence as Lana gave a little wave and walked out the door. Still standing, she closed her eyes, willing her heart to calm and her brain to work in a halfway rational manner. She had to think, had to find some way to clear her name. And she had to do it fast, before the wheels of justice ran over her and left her buried in their dust.

There was only one place to start. Hands trembling, she picked up the receiver and dialed Gaffner's private office number, the one that didn't go through his nosy secretary. He answered on the third ring.

AN HOUR LATER, Merissa stepped out of the elevator and headed toward Gaffner's office. She'd wanted to see him at once, but he'd put her off, telling her he'd be busy for the next hour. He probably hoped her temper would have cooled by then. He'd be disappointed. If anything, she was hotter than ever. She'd always been honest and aboveboard with him. She expected the same kind of treatment.

Her pace slowed as a loud female voice cut through the air and echoed down the long hallway. Obviously, Merissa wasn't the only one who was unhappy with the state of events around LPI. She came to a full stop as the high-pitched voice sounded again.

"I don't care who hears me. I've told you for the last time. I'm tired of—"

The angry outcry was cut short as Gaffner's door slammed shut. A tempest was obviously brewing in his office, and he didn't want it to seep into the hall. Not that there was anyone around to hear except Merissa. The building had pretty much emptied of workers, most of them heading out a half hour ago when the clock had struck five.

She hung back, not wanting to eavesdrop. Unless the argument concerned her, it was none of her business. She didn't have to wait long. The door was flung open and Priscilla Gaffner stamped into the hall, sporting a scowl that a bulldog would have envied.

"Good afternoon, Mrs. Gaffner." Merissa offered a smile as Priscilla passed her in the hall. Priscilla's scowl remained.

"Oh, hello, Miss Thomas."

Her tone was cool, and she barely paused in her rush to the elevator. Merissa studied her back as the door closed. She'd met Gaffner's wife on several occasions, and she'd never been overly friendly. But at least before she'd made an attempt at polite interest. Something was obviously eating at the woman this afternoon.

Merissa turned and walked to Gaffner's door. Whatever the Gaffners' personal problems were right now, she was willing to bet they couldn't match hers.

Merissa's knock was answered by the boss himself, all smiles as if his wife had just bidden him a pleasant adieu instead of storming away in a fit of anger.

"Come on in, Merissa. I'm glad you called to see me. I was just about to ring you myself."

Good. Maybe she'd misjudged him, and he really was planning to tell her about the sheriff's visit. She followed him through the deserted outer office. Evidently, his secretary was one of the five o'clock disappearing crew.

"Have a seat," he said, motioning her to an overstuffed chair opposite his desk. He moved behind the desk and stood behind his chair, leaning his stocky frame against it. "I've been worried about you."

"Thanks. I'm getting worried myself."

"I know. I talked to Rod Lopen. He still says you have nothing to worry about. This matter will just take time."

"He's told me the same thing. That's one of the reasons I wanted to talk to you. I know you said he was a brilliant attorney and a good friend of yours, but I can't see how he's doing anything to help me."

"I'm sure he's doing all he can, Merissa. He's one of the best. He's handled a few things for me, and he handles all of Senator Bracer's law business." Gaffner cocked his head and delivered a stare one might give an impudent child. "Like he says, these things can't be rushed."

She glared back, not about to buy into his games. "I'm not sure I have a lot of time, Mr. Gaffner. What did the sheriff tell you when he visited you this afternoon."

"What makes you think I've talked to the sheriff?"

"Word gets around."

"You're right. It does." Gaffner pulled out his chair and dropped into it. "That's the other reason I wanted to see you, Merissa. I feel the constant talk around here about your involvement in Jeff's death is interfering with your job performance."

"My performance?"

"Yes. And to be frank, I have a proposition for you."

Merissa felt the blood rise to her cheeks as Gaffner presented his so-called proposition. She'd thought he was her friend. Before she left his office, she knew she'd been wrong.

CAGAN POURED A CUP of thick black coffee and downed a huge sip of the chicory-laden brew. Merissa was right. The stuff *was* growing on him.

Merissa Thomas. He rolled her name over in his mind the same way he had done so many times over the past few days. He had let her get to him in a way he hadn't let any woman for a long time. Not since the morning he had found Beth's mangled body stretched across her bed.

Old bitterness rose up inside him, so real he could taste it. He shook his head. This was not the time to deal with

ghosts. There were too many problems in the good old here
and now that demanded attention, and they were all hur-
tling ahead at breakneck speed.

Jeff's death couldn't have come at a worse time. Not that
any time would have been good for Jeff, but as far as Cagan was concerned, the last thing he needed right now was
to wind up on a murder-suspect list. Currently, he was running a distant second to the beautiful and mysterious Merissa Thomas, but since the two stooges were running the
show, his second-place ranking was subject to change at any
moment.

The bony sheriff with the terminal case of body odor was
itching to make a quick arrest. He wanted action while the
press was still supplying him with huge helpings of gratu-
itous publicity.

The number-one contender for arrest of the month was
Merissa. She was the sheriff's prime target, and bumbling
as he appeared to be, it was beginning to look like he might
have hit the bull's-eye this time.

Cagan's muscles hardened and his hands knotted into
fists. The very thought of Merissa locked up in some flea-
bag of a jail gnawed at his mind like a rat at a hunk of moldy
cheese. He'd never wanted to believe more in someone's innocence, but how could he when every new scrap of information he uncovered pointed to her guilt? Still, he'd done
his homework, and what he knew of her past didn't add up
to a murderess.

He drained the last dregs of the strong coffee and hammered the empty mug against the table, the thud echoing off
the LPI cafeteria walls. He was feeling tired and frustrated.
Last night, he'd met Rick Porter after work for a few beers,
hoping to find some new angle.

A few drinks and Rick's sardonic tongue had wagged a
mile a minute. Interesting tidbits about Lana, gossip about

Gaffner's wife, even stories about the after-hours parties in Gaffner's private suite at his riverboat casino.

Wild parties that both Rick and Lana had attended, apparently on a regular basis. No one else from LPI. Just Rick and Lana. That at least partially fit the rumors that ran rampant around the company. Gaffner had the hots for Lana. That would explain why Lana was invited, but not Rick. Unless Lana was actually on the up-and-up and had insisted she get to bring her boyfriend along.

No matter, Cagan still hadn't found the information he was after. So tonight would be another work detail. When the plant was his alone, he had some serious snooping to do, files to examine and records to sort through.

The digital beeper at his side vibrated, and he picked it up to check the number of the caller. He recognized it at once. Gaffner's, followed by 911, the big man's signal that he wanted to talk to Cagan on the double.

Grabbing the cellular phone from the loop on his belt, Cagan dialed the private number to Gaffner's office. The busy signal beeped annoyingly and he broke the connection with an irritated hit of the button. Cagan started for the hall.

Gaffner was the boss, and he liked immediate attention paid to all his orders. It irritated Cagan to no end, but he'd comply. This job was manna from heaven, and he wasn't about to let it slip through his fingers. At least he was here on the inside.

Cagan didn't bother with the elevator. There were only four floors to the building, and the stairs suited him just fine. This time he ran them, taking two at a time. Not that he thought Gaffner really had an emergency. He just liked the exercise. It wasn't as good as going to the gym, but it was the best he could do working both days and nights.

Breathing heavily, he pushed through the stairwell door and rounded the corner to Gaffner's office. Damn. Now what? Merissa was running down the hall as if she'd been shot from a cannon.

Head down and hair flying loosely behind her, she didn't even see him, not until she came crashing into his arms. Instinctively, he wrapped them around her, holding her close.

"Cagan." She whispered his name as if she couldn't believe it was him, and for the shortest of moments, she clung. "I'm sorry. I didn't see you," she murmured, regaining her composure and trying to pull away.

Cagan gripped her upper arms and held her tightly. She lifted her chin and her moist lips trembled.

"What's the matter, Merissa?"

"Nothing. Just let me go."

He couldn't. There it was again, like a virus that infected his mind and body. The urge to hold her to him, to feel the warmth of her skin on his, to protect her.

"Let go. You're hurting me."

He loosened his grip, but not enough for her to slip away. "Then tell me what has you so upset."

"It's nothing, really. Just a confrontation with Gaffner about a design I'm working on. I can handle it without your help."

"I'm sure." He released her arms and she backed away. "Is that why you didn't bother to return my phone calls?"

She tilted her head, and her gaze captured his. Her eyes were dark with the glint of fire and shimmered with fear. "I've been busy, Cagan. But you needn't worry about me."

"So I've heard. According to Rick Porter, you have the best defense attorney in town."

"Had. Rod Lopen is Gaffner's man. As of now, I plan to get my own."

"Is that what you and Gaffner were arguing about?"

"No. I told you. We weren't arguing. Just like you and Jeff *weren't* arguing the night before he was killed."

So that's what was eating at her. She knew he had lied. She started to walk away, but he grabbed her arm again.

"I think this is called harassment," she snapped.

"No, Merissa. It's called concern. I have to see Gaffner now, but after that, I want to talk to you. You're in trouble, and this game of hide-and-seek you're playing is not helping. When I finish with Gaffner, I'm coming to your office."

"I no longer have an office."

"Now what are you talking about?"

"Ask your friend Gaffner. He's the one who fired me." Yanking her arm from his grasp, she stomped down the hall and toward the elevator, her head high.

Cagan took a deep breath and forced himself to let her walk away. Denying the power of the undefinable force that tore at his resolve, he headed for Gaffner's door.

Once inside, he settled into the seat Gaffner offered. The office looked and smelled of the man who inhabited it. Everything was overdone, including the stale cigar smoke that hung in the air, strong and annoying.

"I'm glad you came on up, Cagan," Gaffner said, leveling his eyes and looking straight at Cagan. "It's better to talk in private. I never trust these office telephone lines."

"Good idea. I did try to call, though. Your line was busy."

Gaffner held up his hands. "My fault. The phone rang just after I'd signaled you. The call was brief."

"So what's up, boss man. I ran into Merissa leaving your office. She seemed upset."

"She is. So am I." Gaffner fingered a manila folder on his desk as he talked, flipping it up and down nervously with his thumb. "How well do you know her?"

The question of the hour. How well did he know Merissa Thomas? Intimately. Not at all. Both answers were accurate, but neither uncovered the truth.

"I got to know her a little at the lake before Jeff was killed," he finally answered.

"Right. But how much do you really know about her personal life?"

"Next to nothing," he lied. "Should I know more?"

"I'd like you to," Gaffner answered, reaching for a box, hand carved in some sort of Indian design. "Would you like a cigar?" he asked, flipping the top open to reveal a selection of imported brands.

"No thanks."

"Do you mind if I do?"

"It's your office."

Gaffner took his time unwrapping the cigar, snipping the end and sticking it in his mouth, then carefully lighting it and puffing until the glow grew red-hot. The lingering odor that had accosted Cagan's nose when he'd first walked through the door strengthened considerably. Cagan scooted over to avoid the smoke's direct line.

"I need you to do something for me," Gaffner said after he'd taken two long puffs on the cigar. "It's over and above the call of duty, but I'll pay you well for your time."

"How well?"

"A thousand dollars a week. Cash. No written record. No taxes."

"That's illegal."

"I talked to your supervisor in New York. He said you were known for bending the law, even breaking it, if it suited your purposes."

"They never proved a thing." Cagan leaned closer and didn't back away from Gaffner's accusing stare. "And they never will."

"That's what I like about you, Cagan. You know what you're doing."

"Count on it," he assured him. "Now what is it you want for your thousand dollars?"

"I want you to tail Merissa Thomas. I want to know where she goes, what she does and whom she does it with. And I want to know it twenty-four hours a day."

"No one can be on duty twenty-four hours a day. Besides, I have my work here at LPI."

"When you're not able to tail Merissa yourself, hire someone you can trust. Surely you have connections."

"I can handle it. But if you're so interested in what she does, why did you fire her?"

"Fire her? Who told you I fired her?"

"She did. In the hall, when I was on my way in."

"I didn't fire her. I *suggested* she take a leave of absence with pay until the scandal surrounding Jeff's murder is cleared up. Then, if she's still free to work, she can come back."

"So you think she killed Jeff Madison?"

"Thinking about that is the cops' job, not mine. And it looks like they have a pretty good case against her." Gaffner nodded his head, and for the first time since Cagan had come in, a smile parted Gaffner's fat lips.

"I still don't understand," Cagan said, leaning back in his chair and propping his right foot over his left knee. "Exactly what is it you think I'll find out by tailing Miss Thomas?"

"Just do what I said before. I particularly want to know if she leaves town."

"She's under orders not to leave town until the investigation clears her."

"People don't always follow orders. You know that as well as anybody," Gaffner returned. "Especially people who are guilty of murder."

Cagan nodded agreement. He'd be keeping an eye on Merissa with or without Gaffner's money, but he might as well see how much his services as a spy were worth to Gaffner.

"Two thousand," he said. He kept his voice steady and his face expressionless.

"What do you mean two thousand?"

"That's my price for tailing Merissa. Two thousand dollars. Take it or leave it. My ex-boss may have told you I played by my own rules, but I bet he didn't say I came cheap."

A scowl crossed Gaffner's face. Standing, he stuck his right hand in Cagan's direction. "You drive a hard bargain. I hope you're worth it."

"Oh, I'm worth it, all right. Take my word for it. I'll start as soon as I pick up the first payment. Two thousand dollars in hundred-dollar bills."

"Then let's make it tonight. Seven o'clock, Mardi Gras Lights, in my office. Come up the back way. There's a private entrance that avoids the hassle of the casino. Knock at the door that says do not enter. I'll let you in."

Cagan smiled and nodded his approval as Gaffner escorted him to the door. The adrenaline that always hit when action was imminent simmered in his veins. A murder, spying, wild parties, employee gossip and all kinds of rumors. The plot was thickening fast. All he needed now was for someone to panic and break. When they did, it would be his time to strike.

MERISSA RIPPED THE SHEET of paper from the tablet she'd been writing in and wadded it into a tight ball before hurling it to the most distant corner of her living room. She shivered in spite of the record-breaking heat that was crippling the city.

Slipping out of her black pumps, she stretched her legs and rested her feet atop her coffee table. Using a toe, she inched the plate containing her half-eaten sandwich out of her way. After two hours of scribbling notes, jotting down every minute detail she could remember about the trip to the lake, she was exhausted and no closer to any real answers.

Everything came down to only one logical conclusion. She was being framed for Jeff's murder. Other facts like why and by whom were still complete mysteries. Except that Jeff had been moody the last few weeks before his death. She'd associated his cranky disposition with his transfer to personnel, but maybe that wasn't the whole story. Maybe his new friend, Cagan Hall, had something to do with his moods. Now that she thought about it, Cagan had come along about the same time Jeff had started behaving so oddly.

Cagan Hall. She scribbled his name on her pad, not for the first time that night. She'd already gone over all the reasons to suspect Cagan was either Jeff's killer or else he was involved in planning the murder.

He had appeared from nowhere and latched onto Jeff like a thirsty leech. He had been snooping around the plant before and after the trip to the lake asking questions that had nothing to do with his job responsibilities.

And most importantly, Cagan had both opportunity and access to the murder weapon, and he had lied about arguing with Jeff. Reasons enough to be suspicious. She closed her eyes and tried to picture him as the villain.

It didn't work. It was the Cagan from the lake who filled her senses. Breathtakingly handsome, his easy smile softening the rugged features of his face. His hands on her skin, his lips locked with hers, the desire that had smoldered in his eyes.

She closed her eyes and took a deep breath. She had to face facts and put memories behind her. There was only one Cagan Hall, and she had no reason to trust him.

Flicking off the living-room light, she stopped to stare into the darkness. The night was bathed in the soft lights from windows. Windows of houses where people were getting ready to climb into bed for a peaceful night of rest.

There would be no rest for her tonight. Her insides were as settled as a drop of water in hot oil. She needed answers.

Answers. That was it. Jeff had been killed for a reason by someone who was setting her up to take the blame. She'd searched her mind for answers. Now it was time to search his apartment. It was forbidden territory, of course, still tied up in yellow police tape that said Do Not Cross.

But Jeff had given her a key long ago when she house-sat for him while he was vacationing in Aruba. Jeff never collected the key and chances were slim anyone would notice her this time of the night. Besides, why worry about getting busted for crossing a police line when she was about to be arrested for murder?

Grabbing her car keys and handbag, and a flashlight from the shelf, she opened the back door and stepped into the garage. She flipped the light switch, but no instant illumination dissolved the darkness.

Uneasiness washed over her. She paused, her hand on the door. A burned-out light bulb, that's all it was. Doing her best to overcome the shakes, she turned on her flashlight and cast a beam around the walls of the garage.

A sharp pain struck her arm, and the flashlight flew from her hand, crashing to the floor. She whirled around, but not fast enough. A heavy object crashed against her head and shoulder. Instinctively, she tried to turn toward the attacker, but her head swam dizzily, and her feet slipped out from under her, hurling her into endless darkness.

Chapter Five

Using her elbows for leverage, Merissa managed to raise her head above pillow level. Dizzying stabs of pain shot through her, sending the dimly lit room into orbit. Groaning, she dropped back to the soft cushions that cradled her body.

A minute ago, she had just gone into the garage. She forced herself to look around. Colors swam before her eyes. Not the dingy white paint of her garage but the pale mauves and blues in the muted pattern of her curtains, the sunset yellow and emerald green in the painting on the wall.

Running her fingers along the cushion at her elbow, she traced the rough lines of the fabric. She was on the striped sofa in her own living room. That was all she was sure of. That and the fact that she must be alive. Death couldn't possibly hurt this much.

She tried to think as unfamiliar sounds pulled her to a higher level of awareness. She was not alone. Someone was in the house. A man. She could hear his breathing, smell his masculine scent. Her own breathing all but stopped.

A hand squeezed around hers. Frantic, she jerked away as a face coalesced in the fog.

"Cagan?"

"Yeah. It's me. Just take it easy."

Adrenaline surged, bringing with it more fragments of memory. A burned-out light bulb, a blow to the head and shoulders. She struggled for coherence. "Wh-what are you doing here?" she asked, her voice shaky.

"Trying to take care of the wounded."

She worked her fingers to the back of her head and found an ice pack propped against a lump the size of a plum. She forced her body to a sitting position. It was a big mistake. The vertigo attacked with renewed vengeance.

Cagan wrapped an arm around her to steady her. She squirmed out from under it and fell back to the cushions.

"Take it easy, Merissa. I'm not the one who tried to kill you. If I were, I wouldn't be hanging around giving first aid."

He had a point. But she wasn't sure it was valid, not with her mind still swimming through muddy water. He plumped her pillows and slipped one arm under her shoulders, raising her head.

"Just relax and drink this," he urged, touching a steamy mug to her lips.

"I'm not thirsty," she mumbled, pushing the hot cup away.

The liquid jiggled in the cup, and a few drops spilled over the rim and slid down his fingers. He shook them off, spraying her arm lightly with the warm liquid.

"It's only hot tea with a taste of honey, my mother's favorite cure-all." He took a long sip. "This isn't as good as hers, of course, but it's strong and wet. It'll do you good."

Merissa pushed herself to a sitting position and this time managed to maintain it. She still wasn't sure what was going on, but it was hard to fear a man who was sitting beside her, nursing the lump on her head and coaxing her to drink hot tea.

"I'll try it," she said, relenting. She reached for the cup, but he didn't trust her shaking fingers enough to let go. Instead, he held it to her mouth while she sipped.

She swallowed slowly, letting the warmth fill her mouth and trickle down her throat while she appraised the situation. She had been standing in the garage when someone had come up from behind her and ... And that was all. She didn't remember going back into the house, and she was sure, or almost sure, she hadn't called Cagan.

"How did you get into my house?" she asked when the last of the tea was gone, and he hadn't volunteered any further explanations for his presence.

"I walked in through the open garage. The same way your attacker exited." The muscles in his face and neck grew tense, and his voice grew husky. "Who was here, Merissa? Who tried to kill you?"

"Do you think I know?" she asked incredulously.

"People generally do, whether they get a look at them or not. Or at least they have a good idea." He was staring at her, his eyes dark and penetrating, yet tinged with a warmth that left her more disconcerted than ever.

He was a puzzling combination of opposites. Hot and cold, nurturing and demanding, soothing and frightening. She couldn't possibly understand him, and this was no time to trust what she didn't understand.

"Believe me, Cagan, I have no idea who hit me. I opened the door to my garage and tried to turn on the light. It didn't come on. The next thing I knew—bingo! Something came from nowhere and nearly knocked my head off."

Worn out from the burst of words, she leaned her head against the back cushions of the sofa.

"How many fingers am I holding up?"

"Three," she answered, rubbing her blurry eyes. The old concussion-diagnosis routine. She'd seen it on a hundred TV shows. Evidently, Cagan had, too. "Do I pass the test?"

"I don't know. Let's see how good you are at answering the original question this time. Who hit you?"

"I fail the test. I have no idea, unless it was you."

"Are you telling me some stranger was waiting in your garage just in case you decided to come outside in the middle of the night? Which you did. That's a little hard to buy."

"I'm not trying to sell anything. That's what happened."

He shook his head and frowned, drawing his eyebrows into an almost solid line. "Maybe the attack was meant to be a warning, a preview of things to come if you don't cooperate? What do you know that someone wants to make sure remains a secret?"

"Cut the cop games, Cagan." Merissa pressed her fingers against her temples, massaging the throbbing that had resumed with almost paralyzing force. "I'm a design engineer, nobody important. What could I possibly know that anyone would kill for?"

"Maybe the same thing Jeff knew."

"I told you I don't know anything." Her voice rose and her hands started to shake. She struggled for control. "Besides, if I knew anything, the police would have already dragged it out of me. They've questioned me so many times I answer them in my sleep."

"That brings us to the next question. Do you want me to call the police?"

"No way. Absolutely not. I'll settle for a mere mugger any day."

"Okay. Take it easy. If you throw up or pass out, we'll have to go to the emergency room."

"I'm not going anywhere, and I don't want to deal with any cops. At least not tonight." She settled back on the pillows, the ones Cagan had apparently retrieved from her bed. The throbbing in her head and shoulder didn't ease and neither did the apprehension that tingled along her nerve endings.

"Look, it's obvious you were going out to deal with something a few minutes ago. You were in the garage with your car keys out."

"I was sleepwalking."

"Sure. With all your clothes on."

"Do you really think someone was trying to hurt *me*?" she finally asked, her mind frantically searching for answers.

"From the looks of that bump on your head, I'd say they did more than try."

"No. I mean me particularly and not just in a random burglary attempt."

"It looks that way. Your purse was untouched, and that expensive watch is still on your wrist. You were lucky, though. You must have dodged the blow. Your left shoulder took a lot of the force. Shoulder injuries are a lot less deadly than head blows."

"Lucky Merissa. That's me."

He was right. She had plenty of luck. All of it bad. Her friend had been murdered, she'd been suspended from a job she loved, and she was a heartbeat away from a jail cell. Now someone had nearly knocked her head off. And everywhere that trouble went, Cagan was only a few steps behind.

"You still haven't answered my question," she accused. "How did you know I was in the garage being attacked?"

"I didn't. For some reason, after the guy slugged you, he opened the garage door and ran. I took off after him, but he jumped a couple of fences and disappeared. He wasn't big, but he was damn fast."

The image of Cagan chasing the bad guy over and around fences danced surreally across her mind. "So you went after him? Just like Dirty Harry."

"No. Dirty Harry would have caught the rotten coward. In the movies the good guy always gets his man." He reached out and took her hand, tracing the top of her fingers with a roughened thumb. "And his woman."

A moan escaped her lips as spasms of pain shot through her shoulder. She rolled over and stared at Cagan, at the dark brooding that pulled his face into tight lines, at the set of his square jaw, like a fighter eager for his next bout.

"*Are* you the good guy, Cagan?" she whispered. It was a loaded question, but one that never stopped tormenting her.

His gaze bore into hers, and she trembled beneath his dark stare. "There are no good guys," he said, placing her hand back on the sofa. "Life isn't the movies."

Silence settled around them, thick and almost palpable in the soft glow of the lamp. Merissa shifted again, gently, taking care not to put pressure on her injuries. Her head was the most painful tonight, but she had a feeling the shoulder would be the killer tomorrow.

Cagan reached over and slipped the ice pack back into place. "Can I get you something? A glass of water, more tea, food?"

"A painkiller would be nice."

"Sorry, not with a head wound."

"Dr. Cagan Hall. The man of the hour. By the way, what is the hour?"

He glanced at his watch. "Ten before midnight. You were only out for a few minutes, though it was long enough for me to be concerned. Five more minutes and we'd have been on our way to the emergency room." He stretched his long legs and stood up.

"Before you go, I still have one question."

"Fire away."

"Exactly how did you happen to be outside my garage at the exact time my attacker opened the door and fled?"

"I told you earlier today. I wanted to see you." He began pacing between the front door and the faux fireplace. "When you didn't call me, I drove over uninvited. It seemed the only way I'd ever get to talk to you again in private."

"At eleven-thirty at night? That's an odd time for a visit."

"Evidently not for you. You had two of us on the same night. And apparently you were leaving yourself for some sort of late-night rendezvous."

"A world of coincidences," she said, not believing a word of his explanation. How could she? He'd all but admitted that he couldn't be trusted. Yet for some strange reason, she wasn't afraid of him, at least not at this moment. He wasn't here to hurt her.

The problem was that she had no idea why he was here, or why he had been outside her house, spying on her. Evidently, he wasn't going to provide any truthful answers.

"Do you have any eggs in the house?" he asked, stopping to look down at her.

"I'm not hungry."

"Really? I'm starving." He turned his back on her and headed toward the kitchen.

"There's an all-night diner on Government Street. Try it. You'll like it," she called to his disappearing back. "It's probably full of cops this time of the night."

"I'm not a cop. Not anymore. And I'm not going anywhere. I have a patient to take care of."

In no time, the odor of frying ham drifted into the living room. Merissa relaxed against the cushions Cagan had plumped as a low growl echoed through her stomach. Suddenly, she was ravenous.

CAGEN HALL MADE his early-morning rounds at LPI, but his mind was back on Coursey Lane where he'd spent the night watching over a woman who was driving him up the wall. He was doing exactly what he'd promised himself he wouldn't do again: Let a woman get close to him, let her make him feel instead of think.

He'd gone crazy for a minute when he'd found Merissa in the garage, slumped lifelessly on the concrete floor. And later, even when he knew she was all right, at least for the time being, his emotions had lunged ahead on their destructive course.

Something about her drew her to him, made him want to protect her as if... as if he were Dirty Harry. No, worse. Hell, he'd even made her tea. One more night like last night and his image as a tough ex-cop would be about as credible as a Louisiana campaign promise.

And he still couldn't read her. She had to be directly involved in the criminal goings-on at LPI or she knew something. Either way, she was in big trouble. And not necessarily from last night's mystery guest.

The person who had delivered the painful blow to her head had done so in a moment of panic. He had come to snoop, not to kill. At least, the evidence pointed in that direction.

When Merissa had settled down for the night, Cagan had done a little snooping on his own. After all, he was being paid to spy, and he liked to be thorough when he was on the job. Not that he was going to share his findings with Gaffner, but that was Gaffner's problem. When you hire someone to break the law, you can't expect them to be honest.

Cagan had found a stack of three cardboard boxes on the top shelf in Merissa's garage. They hadn't been there long. They had gathered almost no dust, unlike the other boxes that shared shelf space.

One of them had been left open, and it and one of the other two boxes were stuffed with files that had been crushed together in helter-skelter fashion, as if they had been rifled through by someone in a hurry. That someone had been last night's attacker, unless Cagan missed his guess.

Merissa had interrupted him before he had gotten to the third box. Startled by her sudden appearance, the snooper had apparently picked up an empty flowerpot and crashed it over her head.

The two boxes that had been ransacked still held broken remnants of sealing tape, and "Personal, Jeff Madison" had been printed across the top and sides of all three with a black marker.

He had skimmed the files, but found nothing except a hodgepodge of legal-size manila folders with records of LPI shipments. Still, it was strange that Jeff would have taken those records out of the office to store at Merissa's place.

Cagan finished his rounds, winding up at the front door. Yawning, he stretched his arms above his head. His sleepless night was getting to him. He'd have to watch that. This was no time to grow lax.

A key turned in the door behind him, and he spun on his heels.

"Don't shoot, Detective. It's only a working woman on the job a little early."

Lana Glass wiggled her way toward him, her high heels clicking on the tiles in the building's wide foyer. At six in the morning, she had already applied a thick layer of makeup and pinned her long red hair into a loose bun on the top of her head.

"I never shoot innocent people."

"That's not what I hear." She lightened her accusation with a sexy smile, the devastating variety obviously designed to tantalize the opposite sex.

Cagan wasn't impressed. "Don't believe everything you hear," he warned, adopting her teasing tone. "I'd agree this is a little early for a working woman. Or maybe it's a continuation from the night before?"

"I have no idea what you mean. I was in bed by eight last night."

"So what does a secretary do in the office at six in the morning?"

"I wouldn't know. I'm not a secretary. I'm an administrative assistant. At least I was. Since Jeff's death, I've had to take over all of his duties, too."

"That's right. You did work with Jeff," he commented casually, as if he'd forgotten the connection. "His death must have come as quite a shock to you."

"It did."

"Do you have any suspicions about just who the killer might be? I mean, working with him all day, you must have heard him complain if he had that kind of an enemy."

Cagan watched as Lana's expression turned from flirty to worried. Neither look concealed her usual hint of insincerity. She shifted from one foot to the other and fingered the clasp on her Gucci handbag, looking at the floor for long seconds before raising her head to meet his gaze.

"I have a couple of ideas," she finally offered, her voice soft.

"Do you want to tell me about them? It might make my job of security around here a little easier. We sure don't want anybody getting killed on the job."

She looked behind her and took a couple of steps forward, far enough so she could glance down the empty hall. "Yes, I'd like to do that. But not in my office."

"Why is that?"

She ran her tongue over her bottom lip and nervously slipped her fingers up and down the strap of her bag. "I think it's bugged," she whispered, glancing nervously around the empty room, as if someone might jump out and grab her at that admission.

Cagan stepped closer. "What makes you think that?"

"Gaffner. He seems to know everything before we tell him."

"Well, office gossip travels fast."

"No, it's more than that. Before he died, Jeff told me he didn't trust Gaffner at all. Everyone thought it was just office politics, what with the demotion and all, but now . . ."

"Whatever Jeff told you might help in finding his killer."

"Or it might get me killed, too." She took a deep breath, as if bracing herself for words she was afraid to utter. "I think Gaffner had it in for Jeff. Now I think he might be after Merissa Thomas, as well."

Anger pulled at Cagan's muscles and hardened his thoughts. He forced it away. He couldn't let feelings for Merissa interfere with what he had to do. He needed his mind clear of emotional entanglements. Those were the rules of the game.

"Gaffner involved in a murder and out to get Merissa Thomas. That's a pretty strong accusation, Miss Glass. Do you have some kind of proof to back it up?"

"Yes." She stood quietly, tangling her fingers into nervous knots.

"Did you tell the police about this? I know they've questioned you several times."

"I did. But they ignored my testimony. It's Gaffner. I know it is. He's paid them off like he does everybody who gets in his way."

"He must not have paid off Jeff."

"Jeff wouldn't be bought. I know that for a fact." Her voice quivered. "I'm scared, Cagan. Really scared, but what can I do? I need this job."

"You're right, Miss Glass, I think we need to talk. Let's go for coffee, somewhere where we're sure we won't be overheard."

MERISSA AWAKENED to an empty house. Cagan had slipped out while she was sleeping, leaving nothing behind but his lingering masculine fragrance. Reminder enough that he had been there last night, tending and protecting her in true lawman fashion.

After slipping off her clothes, Merissa stepped into the shower, letting the hot spray and steam envelop her. She leaned back to let the water soak her long hair, and pain shot through her shoulder and down her arm, the bitter calling card from last night's mystery visitor.

Apprehension churned inside her, filling her with an acute sense of dread. She felt as if she were wandering blindly through a maze that was being altered at every turn. Every time she found a new passage, someone erected a higher obstacle in her path. Her only hope of staying out of jail, or maybe even alive, depended on finding her way out of the maze.

The shrill ringing of the telephone cut through her thoughts. She grabbed a towel, wrapped it around her and ran dripping to catch it before the caller gave up.

Her breathless hello was greeted only by the sound of breathing. "Hello," she repeated again, her nerves taut, already strained to nearly breaking. "Who is this?"

"Merissa?"

She recognized Rod Lopen's voice at once. "Yes," she answered, suspicion settling in her stomach like lead. It was a relatively new emotion for her, but one that was fast becoming as familiar as hunger. Or fear.

"I need to see you, Merissa. As soon as possible."

"I'm busy," she lied.

"It's important. Some new information has come up. It's about Jeff. And about the money he stole."

Anger coursed through Merissa and threatened her self-control. "What makes you think Jeff stole money?"

"I'll tell you when you get here. I don't want to discuss it over the phone, but we need to move quickly, before the boys in blue show up to arrest you."

Her stomach lurched sickeningly, and the constant churning she'd almost learned to live with intensified. The last thing she wanted to do was see her so-called attorney, but her options were disappearing fast. If he knew anything about why Jeff was murdered, she needed to hear it. She'd decide later if she believed him. "What time do you want to meet?"

"As soon as possible, but not at LPI. It'll be better if no one at LPI knows about this meeting. Come to Mardi Gras Lights. Gaffner's office. I'm calling from there now. He's here, too, Merissa, and he wants to help you."

She hesitated, fighting new suspicions that played at the back of her mind. "Okay," she finally agreed, knowing only that she had to find answers somewhere. "I'll be there in half an hour."

Thoughtfully, she hung up the phone and walked to her closet. She'd been so angry with Gaffner yesterday she couldn't see straight. But maybe she'd misjudged him. Maybe they all had.

She dressed quickly, pulling on a pair of yellow linen slacks and a white cotton blouse. After brushing her hair back and tying it with a ribbon, she slipped on a pair of sandals. This was definitely not a panty-hose day. The temperature was supposed to reach a scorching ninety-eight degrees by afternoon, and the humidity was already nearing a hundred percent.

She switched on her answering machine, grabbed her handbag and headed for the back door. She stopped suddenly, her hand frozen on the knob. Last night when she'd started to leave, someone had been waiting.

Sucking in a steadying breath, she threw open the back door, half-expecting trouble. When none came, she opened the garage door and watched appreciatively as the sun sneaked in, washing away the gray.

All was clear. She might as well hit the road and get the meeting with Gaffner and Lopen over with. The melodic pealing of the doorbell stopped her in her tracks. She groaned inwardly. One more minute and she'd have been out of here.

She headed toward the front door. *Your arrest is imminent. Move quickly, before the boys in blue show up to arrest you.* The warnings that had been coming at her the past few days resurfaced in her mind, and she was tempted to forget the door and just climb in the car and make a quick getaway.

No. If the police were here to arrest her, she'd go without an argument. Running wasn't her style. Besides, she was innocent, and the police had nothing but weak circumstantial evidence to tie her to Jeff's murder. She had to believe the truth would win out. She took a deep breath and pulled open the front door.

"I have a registered letter here for Merissa Thomas."

The smile that curved her lips was genuine. She could have kissed the mailman. Instead, she signed the paper on the clipboard he stuck in her face.

"Is it hot enough for you?" he asked, grinning as he exchanged the clipboard for a letter-size business envelope. It was the standard summer question, asked thousands of times a day by people who knew the answer all too well. Usually she found it annoying. Today she welcomed the familiar mundaneness of it, feeling that the world hadn't really turned upside down.

"It certainly is," she answered. "Just about as hot as I can stand it." *In a lot more ways than you can imagine,* she added silently as the man went on his way.

The letter was from a law firm in New Orleans. Ripping open the top edge, she pulled out a typed letter, and a metal key dropped from the folds into her hands.

Without bothering to read the enclosure, she dropped the key back into the envelope and stuffed the whole thing into the side pocket of her handbag, then pulled the door shut behind her. It was probably some kind of stupid giveaway. She'd no doubt been given a chance at winning a new car. Send twenty-five dollars and try the key. The extremes people went to in order to con greedy suckers out of a few dollars was unbelievable.

She hurried back to the garage and got in her car. Tossing her purse onto the passenger seat, Merissa backed out to the street and turned west, toward the Mississippi River and a meeting with Lopen and Gaffner.

THE PARKING LOT OF Mardi Gras Lights was almost empty since it was only eight-thirty in the morning, but a few cars were scattered about the concrete sea, most too far from the door to be recent arrivals. Merissa pulled her Mazda up next to Gaffner's pricey red sports car and slid out the door.

She'd been to Las Vegas once. She'd enjoyed the shows and even dropped a few dollars in the slots, but she'd never been inside Gaffner's cruising monstrosity. At least, it sometimes cruised. Today it appeared to be securely docked. She hoped it stayed that way until she walked the gangplank back to land.

Reality vanished as Merissa stepped inside the wide glass doors. The carpeting was plush, the furnishings baroque and gaudy, the air thick with stale cigarette smoke. She stood for a minute, eyeing the huge crystal chandelier that hung above the wide, curving staircase and the huge vases of long-stemmed silk flowers that graced the lower posts of the banister.

The place was almost empty, yet a gaudy circus atmosphere prevailed, complete with flashing lights, clanging bells and shapely female attendants in short leather skirts and halter tops. One of the young women walked up to her, carrying a tray of Bloody Marys.

"Good morning. Welcome to Mardi Gras Lights, and I hope this is your lucky day."

"Thank you." Merissa was sure the friendly greeter didn't hope it half as much as she did. "I have an appointment. Could you direct me to Mr. Gaffner's office?"

"Certainly. It's up those steps," she said, waving her hand toward the winding staircase. "Just ask any of the cashiers. They'll point his office out to you."

Merissa murmured another thank you and made her way to the stairs between rows of gleaming machines bearing images of cherries, jokers and spewing volcanoes. A woman who looked as if she hadn't slept for days glared at Merissa as she walked by and offered her jaded assessment of the casino.

"The slots just aren't hot like they used to be. This place is a rip-off."

Merissa nodded and didn't bother to suggest the obvious, that the woman go home and get some sleep instead of continuing to feed the machines. Finally, she reached the cashier's booth. A thin blond woman sat behind the bars, counting a stack of dollar bills.

"I'm here to see Mr. Gaffner."

The blonde stopped counting and looked up. "Could I have your name, please?"

"Merissa Thomas."

The woman patted her hair and flashed Merissa a knowing smile, as if the two of them shared some secret. "Mr. Gaffner said to send you right in."

The woman stepped out of her elaborate cage, and Merissa followed her, walking past a row of card tables to the far corner of the casino. The woman stopped and shoved a heavy wooden door until it opened a crack.

Merissa peeked through it and down a long hallway lined with framed nondescript pictures and a host of other doors, all closed.

"Mr. Gaffner's office is the last one on the right. Just knock when you get there."

Merissa stepped inside, and the heavy door slammed shut behind her. The corridor was long and dark, at least it seemed dark after coming through the brightly lit gambling area. The only light here came from dim brass lamps that hung along the wall. She quickened her pace, anxious to see Gaffner and Lopen and find out what had prompted this emergency meeting.

Her footsteps were noiseless on the thick carpet, and no voices wafted into the hallway from behind the closed office doors. From clanging bells to silence. The drastic change seemed to signal that something dramatic was about to happen. An eerie uneasiness slithered along her spine.

Forcefully, she reined in her overactive imagination. The events of the past week were definitely taking their toll. When all of this was over, she'd take a long vacation, maybe to the bayou country where her grandparents had lived.

She hadn't been back since their deaths, hadn't wanted to experience the sorrow and loneliness of being there without them. Only loneliness now was everywhere. The sudden longing to return to someplace she'd felt loved and safe was almost overpowering.

Finally, she reached the last door. It was Gaffner's office all right. His name stood out in bold letters on the brass nameplate. She knocked loudly and waited.

Seconds dragged into minutes. She knocked again, this time using the brass knocker to add power to her pounding. Still no response. She fought the urge to turn, march down the hallway and out of the casino. She was tired of games. Gaffner's, the cops', even Cagan's.

Determinedly, she twisted the doorknob and pushed. The door opened easily, and she stepped inside, no longer caring about employee/employer protocol. That relationship had ended yesterday. Gaffner's choice.

"Mr. Gaffner." The last syllable of his name tore from a dry throat. He was sitting behind his desk, his arms and head slumped across the heavily polished wood.

For a second, she closed her eyes, willing the image to disappear. It didn't. Rushing toward him, her right foot slipped on a sticky puddle of something trailing from beneath his desk. She grabbed the corner of his desk for support, and her hand raked across a piece of paper.

Cagan's name was printed across the paper in giant, shaky letters. For a moment, she froze, her breath trapped in her lungs. Then slowly, gingerly, she touched Gaffner's wrist, feeling for a reassuring pulse. Nothing. Absolutely nothing.

She stepped back, her mind reeling in facts and images it refused to absorb. This was a nightmare. It couldn't be real, not again. She just had to wake up and she'd be back at home, drinking a second cup of coffee and perusing the morning paper.

Easing backward, she wiped the stain from her foot on a clean stretch of carpet. Her knees buckled under her, but she forced them to straighten. She couldn't think, couldn't deal with this. All she wanted to do was run, escape this horrible place, this horrible scene.

Now.

Before she could never run free again.

Chapter Six

Merissa slid behind the wheel of her car and yanked the door shut. She leaned her head back against the seat and closed her eyes. It didn't help. Her heart still hammered against her chest and her breath came in painful, jagged gasps. Shaking, she wrapped her hands around the steering wheel, grateful for something to hold on to.

Forcing her eyes open, she tried to assess the situation. She glanced into the rearview mirror, half-expecting to see a crowd of people chasing her. No one came. She was relieved that her exit had not aroused attention. It had taken every ounce of control she could muster to walk through the casino without screaming or breaking into a frantic run. She wouldn't wait around to be accused of Gaffner's murder. One was more than enough.

Finally, she managed to control her trembling fingers enough to fit the key into the ignition and start the engine. The car roared to life, the only thing still under her control.

Perspiration beaded on her forehead, and her clammy hands slipped on the steering wheel as she guided the car out of the parking lot and into the street. She loosened the clasp on her purse with one hand and rummaged for a tissue. The humidity was stifling, the air thick as warm syrup. Already her blouse clung to the leather seat and her hair hung limply from its ribbon.

Unable to bear the heat any longer, she turned the air-conditioning up higher. She had to think. Unfortunately, the cooler air did not lessen the feelings of nausea that threatened to swamp her. Gaffner was in his office, lying in a pool of his own blood. And all around him, women in leather minis were serving drinks and bells were clanging.

Gaffner was dead and only two people knew it. Her and the murderer. She turned at the corner. She wasn't sure why. So much was happening that she couldn't think clearly.

The image of Gaffner's limp body loomed front and center. She had seen him and run. Not for help. It had been too late for that. All vestiges of life had been stolen from his body by someone who had been there before her.

Fingers of ice traced a shaky path up her spine. She hadn't run when she'd found Jeff Madison's body, at least not intentionally. She had staggered away, confused and terrified. That's exactly what Cagan had told the police. They hadn't interpreted her actions that way. They had chosen to focus strictly on the facts. Cagan had found her in the woods, going in the opposite direction of the campsite.

She had to talk to a lawyer. *Her* lawyer. Fat chance Lopen would help. He was Gaffner's attorney and friend. At least he had been. No, she'd have to think of someone else, someone she could trust.

It definitely wouldn't be Cagan Hall. Not when his name was the one scribbled by Gaffner in his dying moments. Had he been trying to identify his killer?

New dread gripped Merissa and knotted her stomach. Even now, she almost expected Cagan to materialize, like a magician's rabbit. At the first sign of trouble, up pops Cagan Hall. Instigator or savior, his role had never been totally clear. But the role of savior had just lost a lot of credibility.

The traffic light in front of her turned from yellow to red, and she skidded to a stop. She had to get hold of herself, watch what she was doing. A minor mishap and the police would be on the scene checking her identification. They might be looking for her right now. She could almost hear the words of the news report that would soon hit all the airwaves.

Merissa Thomas, the prime suspect in the murder of her friend, Jeff Madison, is now being sought for questioning in the murder of her boss, Marshall Gaffner.

Her chest constricted, and she couldn't breathe. She had done nothing wrong, and yet her whole life was going up in smoke. Jumpy and growing more paranoid by the second, she studied a gray sedan in her rearview mirror. It had been following her for several blocks.

She slowed. The car slowed, too, then turned at the next corner. Still her breathing did not come any easier. The gray car hadn't been following her, but one soon would be. A police car with sirens and flashing lights.

In a matter of minutes, if not already, someone would find Gaffner's body, and there would be no doubt about who had been in his office last. And only one person would know she was innocent. The real murderer.

"Murderer." She said the word out loud, and the sinister sound of it exploded in her ears. Someone had killed Jeff, and now that same someone had probably killed Marshall Gaffner. But who? And why? Pick a question, any question. What did it matter? There were never any answers. At least, none she could find.

These things weren't happening by coincidence. They were planned, orchestrated by someone with his own agenda. Someone with brains and without a conscience.

And she had become a central figure in the bizarre plot, the patsy who'd go to jail for the crimes while the guilty party went free.

Locked behind bars with every type of criminal. The thought sent new shivers cascading through her body. She couldn't go on like this, couldn't keep running from people she couldn't see, from situations she couldn't control. And she wouldn't find the answers sitting in a jail cell.

A new fear settled like lead in her stomach as her brain finally flew into action. She had to get away, go somewhere she couldn't be found, at least for a day or two. Until she had time to hire a new lawyer, someone who would work for her. Until she had time to reason, to piece together the jagged edges of the puzzle that tied Jeff Madison and Marshall Gaffner together in someone's murderous scheme. Until she had time to find out if Cagan was as guilty as he seemed.

Merissa rounded a corner and pulled into her driveway, pressing the control that opened the door to the garage. She'd change into jeans and grab a few things—a toothbrush, underwear, a couple of changes of clothes and a sleeping bag. She'd have to make it fast.

Opening the back door, she stepped from the hot garage into the air-conditioned coolness of the kitchen. But there was no reprieve. A new shock assailed her senses as her mind slowly registered the havoc. Drawers had been flung open. Steak knives, kitchen utensils and silverware littered the tile floor. Even her few pieces of crystal had been thrown down and smashed to pieces.

In a trance, Merissa walked through the empty house. Each room seemed worse than the one before. In the bedroom, her silky nightshirts, her lacy underwear, her panty hose were strewn over the carpet and left dangling over the Tiffany lamp and an arm of the upholstered chair. An intruder had been here, walked through her house, turned her orderly existence upside down.

Whoever it was had been looking for something. That much was clear. Something he wanted badly enough to break into her house in broad daylight.

Had the killer who stuck the knife in Jeff's chest, who'd murdered Gaffner in his own office been here walking on her floors, going through her most intimate belongings? Were both murders even committed by the same person? Was she still the fall guy, or had she become the next target on his list?

Pulse racing, she willed herself to forget the paralyzing images. She gathered up a few necessities and stuffed them into the small duffel that had toppled from the closet shelf. Her sleeping bag lay nearby and she snatched it up, as well. Her legs had turned to jelly, but she forced them to keep moving, to propel her through the kitchen, where she stopped only long enough to grab a couple of bottles of water from the refrigerator and a box of cheese crackers from the cupboard.

A siren sounded in the distance. Quickly, Merissa took a last look around and headed for the car. This time, she was running for her life.

CAGAN UNBUTTONED his shirt and threw it on the couch as he entered his apartment. It was only midafternoon, but he was exhausted. He'd been up all night watching over Merissa, spying from the inside, so to speak.

And the morning had held surprises of its own. First Lana and her suspicions. Then murder number two. He still couldn't quite believe it. He'd have sworn Gaffner was one of the big boys. If so, the room at the top had just become a lot less crowded.

Cagan headed for the refrigerator and pulled out a can of beer. He'd talked to the police for over an hour, answering every question they could think of, most of them twice. His alibi was airtight. He and Lana had sat in the coffee shop on Florida Avenue for over an hour. After he'd returned to LPI, he'd called a meeting with the two new men he'd added to the guard detail. Every second of his morning was accounted for.

Evidently, Merissa hadn't fared so well. Cagan took a long swig of the cold drink and walked back into the living room. He stepped out of his shoes and pulled his socks from his feet, tossing them to the floor as he dropped to the couch.

The air conditioner was running like crazy, but it was still hot in his stuffy, cramped apartment. Too damn hot even to think. Not that it mattered. He'd been thinking for four weeks now. Thinking, questioning everybody who'd talk to him, and sticking his nose everywhere but in the roses. All of that had gotten him exactly nowhere.

The facts replayed in his head. Marshall Gaffner, fifty-eight years old, head of Louisiana Prosthetics, Incorporated, part owner of Mardi Gras Lights, and mortgaged to the hilt. He left one survivor—his widow. She would inherit his entire estate, or at least the part that she could locate.

She probably deserved it. From what Cagan had learned, she had put up with Gaffner's wild partying and running around with one woman after another for years. Now she could cry, or maybe laugh, her way to the bank.

Only Cagan was back at square one.

He picked up the phone and dialed Merissa's number as he'd been doing at regular intervals ever since he'd gotten the news about Gaffner. When the answering machine started its recorded spiel, he dropped the receiver back into the cradle.

If she didn't answer soon, he'd go looking for her. She wouldn't be hard to find, not with the electronic bird dog he'd attached to her rear bumper when he'd left her house at dawn.

Cagan stretched out on the couch and rested his head on a throw pillow. He had to get some sleep. And hopefully, this time, Merissa would stay out of his dreams. His apartment was way too hot already.

THE LOUD RINGING PIERCED Cagan's sleep. He reached for the phone before realizing it was the doorbell. Raking his fingers through his hair, he walked barefoot to the front door and looked out the peephole.

"Well, well, will wonders never cease?" Cagan whispered to himself, surprise dissolving the last traces of sleep. The good senator he'd been hearing about for weeks had apparently come slumming.

Cagan opened the door.

"Mr. Hall. I'm James Bracer, Louisiana senator. I'm a good friend of your employer, Marshall Gaffner. At least I was until this morning."

"Yeah. It's too bad about Gaffner. I heard you were the one who found the body. That must have been tough."

"I'm still in shock."

"I can imagine how you feel."

"I doubt that. But...may I come in? I hate talking in the hall like this."

"Of course. Forgive my lack of manners." Cagan opened the door wider and waved him inside.

Bracer gave the small apartment a quick once-over, then took a few steps toward the kitchen. "Are we alone?"

"Unless someone sneaked in while I was asleep, it's just the two of us. Can I get you a beer or something?"

"No. I only have a minute. So, I'll get right down to business. I have a proposition for you. It's a bit unusual, but I'll pay you well for your time."

"I like the sound of it already." Cagan tossed his shirt out of the way and dropped to the couch, motioning for Bracer to join him. Propositions were popping out all over. He couldn't wait to hear what this one would entail.

Bracer put down the briefcase he'd been carrying, then took a handkerchief out of his pocket as he sat, carefully wiping the sheen of perspiration from his brow. "I understand that you've been with the New York police force for many years," he said, his voice growing conspiratorial. "You must have learned a lot about chasing down law-breakers during all that time."

"I *was* on the force. Past tense. Right now, I'm head of security at LPI. I plan to stay there if the new boss lets me."

"I know. In fact, I know a lot about you, Cagan. I know that before you left New York, you broke into a suspect's house without a warrant and that you shot an unarmed man."

"You're just a walking encyclopedia, aren't you?"

"No, I'm just a businessman," Bracer finally answered. "A very thorough businessman." He let a smile wash over his face.

"Not thorough enough. Some of your facts are wrong. The charges against me were dropped for lack of evidence."

"I've also heard you're a very smart man."

"I like to think so." Cagan propped his feet on the edge of the coffee table. "Something tells me you're not here to swap compliments. So why don't we cut through the preliminaries and get down to business. Why *are* you here?"

"Do you know the whereabouts of Merissa Thomas?"

"On her way to jail would be my guess," Cagan answered, sure Bracer had ideas of his own.

"I'm disappointed in you. It was my impression that Gaffner had hired you to tail her."

"He did. I had someone watching her. She managed to slip away from him," Cagan lied.

"That's real unfortunate in light of what happened this morning." Bracer scooted closer to Cagan. "I want Merissa Thomas found."

"So do the police."

Cagan studied Bracer. His eyes were cold steel and his face was drawn into hard lines.

"Make sure we understand each other, Cagan. The police are not my concern. *I* want Merissa found. She was the last person to see my friend alive. If she killed him, I will make sure she stands trial."

"And what if she didn't kill him?"

"That will be for a jury to decide." Bracer reached for the briefcase at his feet. "All you need to know is that I want her. Delivered to *me*. Alive. Do you understand?"

"Loud and clear. Now about my fee."

"Five thousand dollars. Cash. Payable when Merissa is delivered into my hands."

"Five thousand dollars for someone whose return means so much to you doesn't sound quite fair to me."

"I can get someone else for less."

"You could. But you came to me. I'd say fifteen thousand would be about right."

"You're crazy, Cagan. I won't pay that kind of money."

Cagan got up and walked toward the door, pretending to be ready to usher Bracer out. "Too bad," he said, baiting the senator. "I have a good idea where she ran off to. I might have had her for you by nightfall."

"You said you didn't know where she was."

"Fifteen thousand, Bracer. Half of it now. The other half when she's in your hands."

"You drive a hard bargain."

"Yeah. But I deliver."

MERISSA TUCKED HER DUFFEL and sleeping bag under the seat of the small boat she had just rented. Following the winding bayou would be the safest way to reach her grandparents' cabin. There would be no police cars, no roadblocks, nothing to bother her except alligators and hungry mosquitoes.

She went back to the car and retrieved the bag of supplies she had purchased on the way south. A can of insect repellent, a tube of first-aid cream and batteries for her flashlight. She half closed the car door then stopped, reaching back inside for her purse.

The sun glared down on her head, and she pushed strands of humidity-dampened hair away from her face. If she hurried, she could make it halfway to her grandparents' cabin by nightfall. She'd stop for the night, rest in her sleeping bag and hit the bayou again at daybreak. By midday tomorrow, she'd reach the cabin. It would be deserted, but dry. And most of all, safe.

Grabbing the handbag in her right hand, she gave the door a shove with her left. It didn't quite catch, and she used her hip to push it solidly closed as the wizened old man who operated the fishing marina walked over.

"Remember, hide the car so that no one passing by will see it," she reminded him in the local version of Cajun French, her accent still perfect even after all the years she'd been away. She placed the keys in his hand.

"Don't worry yourself, *chère*. I don't have seen you none a-tall. I don't know you none a-tall. You never set your foot here in my place."

"Thanks," she answered, hoping his word was better than the beat-up boat she had rented.

Minutes later she was gliding down the Atchafalaya River, the small boat's motor pushing her along, filling the sultry air with its soft hum. She was miles away from her grandparents' home, miles upstream from the bayou she had explored as a child.

Nothing was the same, yet everything was familiar. The grayish green hue of the water, the tall grasses that carpeted the bank, the rustic cabins that sometimes appeared for a second between clusters of moss-draped cypress trees.

She had reentered the world that served as backdrop for her favorite dreams, and for the first time since Jeff's death, a semblance of calm began to wrap around her. The problem was she couldn't stay here forever. Soon she would have to go back to the world of chaos from which she'd just escaped.

And when she returned, she'd have to be armed with answers, explanations for all the events that threatened her freedom and safety. At the very least, she would have to clear herself of any suspicions that she was somehow responsible for the brutal murders.

The sound of splashing water startled Merissa and she twisted around in time to see a huge turtle disappear into the water as a second slid from the log where they had been sunning. The sound of her motor had apparently intruded in their afternoon quiet, frightening the peaceful creatures and sending them diving for cover.

One minute safe in the sun, the next dashing for your life. She knew the feeling all too well. She also knew the turtles had not necessarily escaped danger by diving into the watery depths. An alligator could come drifting by at any time, appearing as innocent as the log the turtles had just vacated.

Merissa shuddered at the thought and then stiffened her back and her resolve. She didn't know about the turtles' safety, but she was sure of her own. No one from the outside world would find her here once she'd made her way deep into this refuge of steamy beauty.

"No one." She said the words out loud, hoping the sound of them would convince her they were true. It *almost* worked.

THE SUN HAD DIPPED LOW in the sky by the time Cagan pulled into the marina. Merissa was nearby, or at least her car was. The small bird-dog device he had planted under her bumper this morning had paid off, that and the money he had dropped into the gas station attendant's hand back on the highway.

He opened his car door and slid out, patting the handcuffs beneath his bulky shirt. By dawn, they'd be wrapped around Merissa's pretty wrists. But it was dread, not satisfaction that balled in his gut.

So where was the thrill of the hunt now that he needed it?

A muttered curse slipped from Cagan's lips as he headed toward a dark-haired, muscular man who wasn't bothering to hide his suspicious scowl. The man wouldn't want to answer questions from a stranger.

That was fine. Merissa's car might be out of sight, but it was close by. That was reason enough for Cagan to be sure she'd taken to the water for transportation. He'd rent a boat and follow her. Somewhere in the darkness of the Atchafalaya wetlands, he'd find her.

And this time he'd call the shots.

Chapter Seven

Hours later, Cagan was still guiding his small rented boat through the still waters. He'd left the river, maneuvering now down a winding bayou, following the map Merissa would never guess he had.

It was nearing midnight, and he'd have to stop soon for the night. The prospect wasn't a welcome one. He had slept many nights in the open, under starry skies and in downpours, sometimes on ground as hard as rock. But he had never trusted his fate to the creatures of a boggy swamp.

Before dark, he'd watched alligators as long as six feet or more glide by his narrow boat, had watched slithery snakes slide from the bank into the murky water. These were not his choice of sleeping companions.

Something moved near the water's edge in front of him, and he stretched to see around the trunk of an overhanging tree. He saw it then, a small boat just like the one he was in. It was pulled onto the shore, nestled in the leafy fronds of a giant palmetto. He brought his boat to a sudden stop.

Dipping an oar into the water, Cagan guided his boat to the bank. He stepped out and his boots sank ankle-deep in the soft earth. With quick hands, he tied his boat to a cypress tree and carefully made his way up the slippery incline toward the other boat.

He was almost there when the sound of rustling grass caught his attention. He spun on his heels, his fingers instinctively flying to the pistol tucked at his waist.

For a second, he saw nothing but the shadowy mist that hovered like clouds over the steamy swamp. Finally, a shape coalesced in the fog, slender and female and racing away from him. The figure seemed more ghostly than human, with long, graceful legs and flowing hair. Cagan wasn't fooled.

"Merissa!"

He shouted her name, his voice cracking through the night like a gunshot. She had to hear him, but she didn't even break stride.

He didn't bother calling again. His breath was better used for running, and he was going at it full throttle. His stride was longer than hers, but he wasn't gaining on her. His heavier body forced his feet deeper into the bog, requiring precious seconds to pull them out again.

Humidity clogging his lungs, he rounded the tree where he'd seen her disappear and stopped, his breath shallow and rapid. He peered through bushy undergrowth and tall, straight trees. He couldn't see Merissa, but she was near. Her fragrance mingled with that of the blooming water hyacinths and damp earth.

Easing backward, one step at a time, he kept his hand poised on the gun at his waist. There was still the outside chance—way outside—that Merissa was totally innocent and running from pure fear, but he couldn't go in blindly. Not when two men who knew her well were already dead, and she was the prime suspect in both murders.

"Don't be afraid, Merissa. Just come out in the open. Slowly. Nice and easy, with your hands over your head." He turned slightly, still keeping his back to the trunk of a tree. "You know I won't hurt you."

Silence answered his request. He eased to the next tree, his eyes peeled for movement. There was none, except for a few fluttering leaves.

"I'll help you, Merissa. No matter what you've done. You can't run forever. Just tell me where you are, and move slowly. No surprises, and you won't get hurt."

The sucking sounds of footsteps came from somewhere behind him. Startled, he pulled his gun and twisted his body to face them. Too late. Merissa was off again, dashing away like a frightened fawn.

Damn. He'd almost had her, and he'd let her slip away. Without stopping to think, he took off after her, aggravation with her and himself urging him even faster than before. Luck was with him. The ground was dryer here, and she was no match for his speed. A step away, he lunged forward, wrapping his arms around her above the waist. An old football move.

"Let me go!" she snapped, straining to get away. She clawed at his hands, her sharp nails digging into his flesh.

"You're a little hellcat, aren't you?" He pulled her hand away. She used the rest of her body then, kicking his ankles and throwing all her weight into him in one forceful push.

His foot slipped, and he lost his balance. He fell to the ground with a squishing thud, pulling her with him. She squirmed from his arms, pushing with her legs and managing to deliver one well-placed knee kick before he regained control.

Gripping her wrists, he held her on top of him. Her breasts heaved beneath the thin fabric of her cotton shirt and her hips ground into him.

"You're hurting me!" she grated through clenched teeth.

"Good. Then maybe you'll calm down."

"So that you can kill me like you did Gaffner? Or maybe you have another knife on you. Of course, you'll have a much harder time laying the blame on me if I'm the victim.''

''If you kick me like that again, I can claim self-defense.'' He held her closer, trying to control her heaving body and read her reactions. She was a fighter, but she appeared to be genuinely frightened of him. Maybe she did believe he was guilty. Which meant *she* wasn't. At least not guilty of murder.

''Of course *you* didn't kill them,'' she taunted sarcastically. ''That's why the ridiculous cop duo is after *me*.''

Or maybe she was just a damn good actress, he decided, watching her fume. Doubts once more clouded his mind like smoke. They always did, no matter how badly he wanted to believe her. He couldn't help it. He'd been here before. Only the names had changed.

''If you're not planning to kill me, then take your hands off of me. Just leave me alone. You have no right to follow me.''

''I make my own rights.''

''Oh, sure. Mr. Macho Cop. You make all the rules.''

He rolled over, dumping her to the carpet of damp grass beside him but still not letting go of her wrists. She stared at him, her eyes wide and frightened, her hair tumbling about her face, her lips trembling. Did she have to look at him that way? So vulnerable. He longed just to take her in his arms and never let her go.

''Why did you follow me here, Cagan?''

''To find you and bring you back to Baton Rouge. Running won't solve anything.''

A piece of grass clung to her cheek. He let go of one of her wrists to wipe it away. It was a mistake. Using her newly freed hand as a wedge, she pushed against him as hard as she could. He grabbed her wrist again, this time so forcefully she winced in pain.

Her cry hit him like a solid right to the gut. "Don't make me hurt you, Merissa."

"I haven't made you do anything, Cagan. I certainly didn't invite you here." She shifted away, making sure their bodies didn't touch. "And I don't need you. All I want is a little time to think."

"Is that why you ran, Merissa?"

"Why ask me? You don't believe anything I say anyway. Even at the lake, you didn't believe me. Either that or framing me suits your purpose."

"What's that supposed to mean?"

"Exactly what it sounds like." She wiggled around in the grass until she managed to raise herself on one elbow. "You expect me to believe you didn't kill Jeff, but you lied about arguing with him at the lake. Innocent people don't have to lie."

Or run, he thought, though he didn't say it. Tears were already glistening in her eyes. He was tempted to wipe them away. He didn't dare. Not with her lips quivering in anger and her body trembling so close beside him.

He was losing the battle again. One minute he was ready to do whatever he had to, even pull a gun if necessary, in order to see that she didn't escape. The next he was ready to run with her, to forget everything but the crazy need she triggered inside him.

"I did argue with Jeff, Merissa, but I didn't kill him," he finally answered.

"And just because you say it, you expect me to believe it? After you lied before to me and to the police?"

Cagan stood up, pulling Merissa with him. He stared into her eyes. They were dark, shadowy pools in the moonlight. For two cents he'd forget the world and run away with her. Two cents. A paltry sum compared to the bounty of fifteen grand Bracer was ready to pay to get her back.

"I'd say we're at a standstill, Merissa. You don't believe me. I have no reason to believe you. And you're the one the police are looking for."

He started walking, pulling her along with him.

"Please, Cagan. You can't take me back. Not yet. Not until I know what's really going on and why I'm being framed for murder. All I ask is a chance."

The pleading in her voice came close to melting his insides. He cursed his weakness and ignored it. "I have to take you back."

"Why? What's in it for you?"

"I'd say that's none of your business."

"I'd say it's *all* my business."

She stepped closer, so close her thigh brushed his, so close Cagan could feel the heat from her body kindle the need he'd been trying so desperately to bury.

"I think someone's trying to kill me. I'm afraid. Not of fighting, but of not knowing who to fight or why."

He slipped his arm around her shoulders and pulled her into the safety of his embrace. He could feel the trembling in her body, hear the panic in her words. Her agony tore at him.

"I have to know about you, Cagan."

She looked up at him, and he turned away, knowing he couldn't look her in the eye and lie.

"Promise me you'll tell me the truth. You owe me this much."

"If I can." He couldn't promise more. He didn't dare reveal the whole truth, not even to her.

"Did you kill Jeff or Marshall Gaffner?"

"No." He wrapped her in his arms, rocking her to him. "No. That I can promise you." He tilted her chin and captured her gaze. "I'm not the enemy. Do you believe me?"

"I want to." She leaned into him again, burying her head against his chest. "I want to."

His heart buckled inside him. He knew exactly how she felt. As much as he wanted to believe her, trust her, the gnawing suspicions wouldn't quite go away. He'd been fooled by a beautiful woman once before. He'd staked his life and several others on her innocence. That time he'd been wrong.

And that one mistake would haunt him for the rest of his life.

Slowly, he led Merissa back to the boat and to his meager camping supplies. Tonight they'd get some sleep. Tomorrow would be soon enough to face the devil and the dilemma of what to do about returning Merissa Thomas to Baton Rouge.

THE PATCHY FOG was lifting by the time Merissa and Cagan reached the edge of the water where the two boats were tied. "I'll wait here while you get your things," she offered.

"Right. But just so you don't get any ideas about escaping..." He pulled a set of handcuffs from his pocket and locked the ring of hard metal around her wrist. "I really do hate to do this, Merissa, but it's the only way I can be sure you won't run."

"Once a cop, always a cop," she said, fighting the suffocating horror that made her want to scream and to cry at the same time. This was a preview of things to come, a firsthand experience of what it was going to feel like when she was a convicted criminal behind bars.

That's why she could trust no one, not even Cagan. He might not be the enemy, but handcuffs were not the trademark of a loyal friend. No matter what it took, she wasn't going back to Baton Rouge with him. Not until she knew exactly what was going on.

Merissa waited silently while he attached the other cuff to a low tree limb. Leaving her on the bank, he retrieved a plastic-wrapped sleeping bag and a black canvas backpack from beneath the seat in the rented fishing boat. The boat had the same markings as hers. She'd hoped the man at the marina would keep his word and his silence. Evidently, Cagan had made him change his mind. She didn't even want to imagine what kind of coercion he'd used to loosen the man's tongue.

Cagan removed the handcuffs before Merissa led him back up the incline and through a cluster of trees, but he never let her get more than a step in front of him. With or without cuffs, their relationship was clear. She was his prisoner.

"This is it," she said when they reached the clearing she had chosen to spend the night. The area was circled by trees, but the ground was dry, and she had beaten a small rectangle of tall grass into a thick carpet for her sleeping bag.

Cagan dropped his own bag next to hers. She pulled hers a few feet away.

"This will be a lot easier if we don't fight," he said, his voice husky from the heat and humidity that enveloped them.

"Nothing's easy, Cagan. Not anymore."

Cagan started to say something, but stopped. He knelt on the ground and began rummaging through the backpack. Organization was apparently not one of his virtues. He pulled out first one thing then another, dropping several to the ground.

A baseball cap, a pair of socks, a notebook and a pocketknife. Finally, he opted for some kind of energy bar and a bottle of water.

"Do you want a bite?" he asked, slicing the wrapper on the bar with his knife.

"No, I'm not hungry," she lied. She'd eaten about a third of her box of cheese crackers. She'd have the rest in the morning for breakfast.

Cagan took a big bite and chewed appreciatively. "It's not bad." He sat on the side of his sleeping bag, stretching his feet so that they rested on the ground between them and propping his back against a tree. "Are you sure you don't want a bite?" he asked again, poking the bar in her direction.

"I'm sure." She reached down and grabbed the edge of her sleeping bag, pulling it even farther away from his.

"We're together for the night. There's no reason not to at least act like friends," he said between bites.

"There's every reason. We're not friends, Cagan. We almost were. It didn't work out. Now we're just two people mixed up in some kind of bizarre crime spree."

An unexpected lump settled in her throat. Almost friends. Almost lovers. Things had started out so well between them—a couple of murders ago. Now she was running scared. She didn't dare trust anyone, especially a man who carried a gun and handcuffs.

It was too bad because she'd never needed a friend more.

"What were you doing on the riverboat this morning, Merissa? You don't seem like the gambling type, especially at that time of the day."

"I went there to see Gaffner and Lopen." She didn't have to answer Cagan's questions. She owed him nothing. But she needed to talk, needed to sift through what had happened and arrive at the truth. He would make as good a sounding board as any. And maybe, just maybe, she could convince him not to take her back to Baton Rouge.

"How did you know Gaffner would be at Mardi Gras Lights and not at LPI?"

"Rod Lopen called and asked me to meet them there. He said he'd found out something about Jeff and needed to talk to me at once. He was making accusations, saying Jeff stole some money."

"Did Lopen call himself, or was it a secretary? Maybe Lana?"

"No. It was him. Why did you think it might have been Lana?"

"I had coffee with her this morning before work. I ran into her at LPI and she insisted we go somewhere we could talk. She said she thinks her office is bugged, and she didn't want to talk there."

"When did she come to that conclusion? She talked openly enough in my office yesterday. And if anyone's office is bugged, it would be mine. I'm the one who got shown the door."

"She didn't mention talking to you. She did talk a lot about Jeff and Gaffner, though. She thinks Jeff was blackmailing Gaffner and that Gaffner thinks you know the whole story."

"Where would she get an idea like that?"

"I was hoping you could tell me. Anyway, after we'd been at the coffee shop for a half hour or so, she used the phone at the counter to make two calls. I used the phone after her and tried the redial button. It was to Rod Lopen's office."

"Well, her first call wasn't to me."

Cagan chewed on his energy bar and sipped his water. "I'm surprised you went to see Gaffner at the casino even if he did ask. You seemed so angry with him yesterday. And you indicated Lopen was no longer your attorney of choice."

"I was still angry with him this morning. But if he had heard anything about Jeff, I needed to know what it was. I'm trying to stay out of jail, remember?"

"Yeah. I remember. I'd like to help you."

"I can tell." She didn't try to hide her sarcasm. Not that it would matter with Cagan. Anger, sarcasm, knee kicks. Nothing dented his armor. He was still pretending they were friends.

Untying his hiking boots, he slipped them off his feet and tossed them beneath the tree. "Tell me exactly what happened when you got to the casino. Go slowly and try to remember every detail."

She closed her eyes. She'd tried all day to erase the gory images from her mind. Now she let them return, wash over her in dark waves. Her throat grew dry and she had to force the words from her mouth. "It was early when I arrived, about eight-thirty," she began.

Cagan listened without interrupting as she recounted every detail she could remember. Her voice sounded hollow and flat, as if she were describing the plot of some movie. It was the only way she could get through this ordeal.

"He was just lying there," she heard herself say. "His head was facedown, and when I touched his—"

The words caught in her throat and she could hardly breathe, let alone speak. Pretending it hadn't happened to her wasn't working any longer. The images were too vivid, too real. Silent sobs racked her body, shaking her so much she could hardly think.

Before she knew it, Cagan had covered the distance that separated them. "That's enough," he whispered, wrapping his arms around her trembling body and holding her against his hard chest. "That's enough."

"No, there's more."

"It doesn't matter. The rest can wait."

He rocked her in his arms, comforting her as if she were a small child with a skinned knee. Too bad her problems couldn't be solved that easily.

"Nothing can wait. Not now. I left the casino in shock, but all the police will know is that I ran from the scene." She closed her eyes, fighting the tears that pushed for release.

"You had your reasons."

"More than you know. When I got back to my house, it had been ransacked. Someone had been there, looking for something, maybe looking for me." Her voice broke.

Cagan slipped his hand under her chin and tilted her face upward. With rough fingers, he brushed loose wisps of hair from her face. A bitter tear finally escaped, and he wiped it away with his thumb.

She pushed his hand away. As much as she'd like his comfort, she couldn't fall into his trap. There was still more she hadn't told him, like the fact that Gaffner had scribbled his name before he died.

"I'm sorry, Cagan. I didn't mean to lose control."

"You didn't. There's nothing wrong with shedding a few tears. Not after all you've been through." His voice was tender now, and his fingers pressed into her shoulders, massaging through the thin fabric of her T-shirt. "I want to help you, Merissa, and I can if you'll let me. But you'll have to trust me."

Her brain screamed at her to pull away. His touch soothed her fears and dissipated her anger. And she needed her fears and her anger to keep her alive. They were the only way she could break the invisible cord that bound her to Cagan even while everything that happened tore them apart.

Another tear fell, rolling down her cheek. This time, Cagan kissed it away, his mouth soft at first, then growing hard as he moved from her cheek to her lips.

It was wrong. She knew it, but she couldn't pull away. Every muscle, every nerve in her body cried out for him. She didn't want to think about why. She didn't want to think at all. She only knew that the man who held her now could not be a murderer.

A low moan gurgled from deep in her throat, and she parted her lips, deepening the kiss. His tongue slipped inside her mouth, and she was lost in him. It would be so easy to forget all about the police and the murders and let the heat consuming them burn wild.

Too easy. And far too dangerous. Shaking, Merissa pushed Cagan away. "Please, Cagan. Not now. Not like this."

His arms tightened around her. She struggled, pressing her hands against his chest. His gaze burned into hers, dark, secretive, tormenting. Finally, he released her and turned away.

Passion still surged in her blood, but she forced her breathing to steady. She watched Cagan unbutton his shirt and slip out of it, letting it drop to the ground in a heap. The fog had lifted completely, and moonlight danced along the strong muscles of his chest, shadows dappling the bronzed skin and dark hairs.

Her world was falling apart, yet Cagan had the power to make her almost forget the dangers that threatened her without mercy. He was like summer lightning, electrifying and frightening, born of forces too fiery to be contained. It had been that way from the very beginning. And only one thing would be strong enough to put out the flames.

Finding out that he had lied. Finding out that he was Jeff's killer. Gaffner's killer.

A cold shudder shook her as she pictured the scrap of paper on Gaffner's desk. She took a deep breath and pushed the thought away. Cagan had his faults and his secrets, but he wasn't a killer. There had to be another reason Gaffner had scribbled his name, probably while gasping his last breath.

A killer could never make her feel the way Cagan did.

Cagan pulled his sleeping bag over, once again placing it next to hers. "I know. You don't want me this close, but I promise I won't touch you," he said, evidently reading the concern she felt at his nearness. "I'll just feel better if I know you're safe, in arm's reach all night long."

Safe...and right beside him. So that she couldn't run without his knowing it. The words were unspoken, yet Merissa heard them as clearly as if they had been.

"What about tomorrow, Cagan? Will you go back without me?"

Silence filled the night like a poison, destroying the intimacy that had bound them minutes before. He could hold her in his arms. He could kiss away her tears. He could ignite passion so intense, she ached for release. But it didn't change a thing. Tomorrow morning, he'd be taking her to jail.

"I have to take you back, Merissa. For your own protection."

"Is it because you used to be a cop, Cagan? Is that why you can't make one simple concession to someone who's fighting to find the truth on her own? Fighting to stay *alive?*" Her words were hard. She meant them to be. Passion, no matter how strong, obviously wasn't going to save her. "Or is it because framing me protects you?"

"No. It's not because I used to be a cop." Cagan lay on his back, so close to Merissa he could hear her breathing. "And I'm not framing you." But she was right. Her request for information was simple. Too bad he couldn't comply. And he couldn't tell her his reasons.

A mosquito buzzed around his head but didn't land. Evidently, the repellent he'd all but bathed in was still working. He swatted at the annoying insect and then ran his fingers along the edge of the sleeping bag.

The hard metal of the handcuffs was a bitter reminder of all the reasons he couldn't promise Merissa her freedom. But he wouldn't put them on her wrists again. He'd hurt her enough already. Now he only wanted to protect her. He just wasn't sure that option was within his power.

He watched as she snuggled into her sleeping bag. The old familiar longing settled like a dead weight in his chest. Everything he wanted was inches away. And miles out of reach. It was going to be a long night.

MERISSA OPENED HER EYES and stifled a scream. Something hairy and multilegged was crawling across her arm. Pulse racing, she flicked the ugly creature off her skin and into orbit.

She shook her head groggily. It had to be late, two a.m. or so. A slight breeze blew across her face, and the night seemed much darker than when she'd gone to bed. A quick glance at the sky told her why. Clouds heaved like rolling waves, blocking out the moon and stars.

Stretching, she let her limbs come slowly to life. She had been determined to outlast Cagan, but sleep must have finally claimed her in spite of all her efforts.

Turning her head, she checked the current status of her overnight companion. Cagan's chest rose and fell in a steady rhythm, and his eyes were closed tightly. She rolled over, and he didn't move. Sound asleep. She couldn't have asked for better.

What was it her mother used to say? If it seems too good to be true, it probably is. Sorry, Mom, she thought to herself. I'm not looking a gift cop in the mouth.

Merissa eased from the sleeping bag as quietly as she could. Somehow she was sure Cagan wasn't sleeping so soundly that a loud, unexpected noise wouldn't bring him jumping to his feet, ready for action.

He'd never let her leave without him. And the only place she'd be going with him was back to Baton Rouge to face jail on trumped-up charges. Or to face a killer.

The thought hurried her actions. *Just get your things and walk quietly to the boat. You can make it.* She followed her own silent commands, scarcely daring to breathe as she stuffed her flashlight and half-empty water bottle back in her duffel.

She started to zip it closed, then stopped suddenly as the soft scratching noise was magnified in the surrounding quiet. Heart pounding, she watched terrified as Cagan twisted in his sleep, the muscles in his face and neck tensing involuntarily.

Merissa held her breath for long seconds until Cagan relaxed again, his eyes still closed. The sleep he had lost the night before while taking care of her was reaping unexpected rewards.

She wasn't afraid of Cagan, not seriously. If he wanted her dead, he'd had ample opportunities to do the deed tonight and last night when he'd stayed with her until all hours. He'd said it was only to nurse her wounds, but now she believed it was more than that. He'd stayed to protect her, just in case the attacker reappeared.

Funny, she almost felt guilty, sneaking away from him in the dark, especially as she knew she'd have to leave him stranded. But there was no other choice. She'd have to untie his boat and tie it to her own. It was a shame to desert him in such wild surroundings, but if she didn't, he'd only catch up to her again.

Necessity made her push the guilt aside. She was only playing by the rules Cagan had initiated. She hadn't asked him to track her down. Besides, even though she couldn't believe he was the one who had murdered Jeff, she was still certain he had his own agenda. As yet, she had no idea what it was, but the roles he played were too contradictory for him to be on the level.

Bad cop. Dedicated head of security. Friend who argued and lied about it. Almost-lover whose twisted sense of justice could deliver her into the hands of someone who wanted her dead or at least wanted her found and framed for murder.

Will the real Cagan Hall please stand up? No, she reneged quickly, praying that her next request would be the one answered. Will the real Cagan Hall stay asleep for at least five more minutes?

She tiptoed toward the edge of the clearing in her bare feet, waiting until she was out of earshot to slip into her heavy hiking boots. She didn't dare make the boggy trek to the boat without shoes. Anything might cross her path. Snakes, alligators, spiders big enough to cover a dinner plate.

Shivering in spite of the heat, she looked one last time at Cagan, and her heart constricted. Asleep, like awake, he exuded rugged power like an aura. Someday she'd have to finish a kiss with him, she promised herself.

Finish it to the very end.

Chapter Eight

Merissa made her way back to the boats, cautiously watching for any sign of movement before placing a foot to the ground. The bayou was far too heavily populated for her to be truly alone. Already her stomach had slid to her boot tops several times as various unidentified nocturnal creatures skittered out of her path.

Finally, she heard the faint sounds of water lapping against the bank. Only then did she dare flick on the beam of her flashlight. If Cagan awoke and found her gone, he'd be up and running. A flash of light in the midst of darkness would guide him to her like a beacon.

Even this close to making her escape, the thought quickened her already-rapid pulse. Directing the beam toward the water's edge, she went over her plans one more time. She'd tie Cagan's boat to her own. The extra weight would slow her down a little, but that way she would be sure his boat couldn't wash ashore a few yards down the bayou, just waiting for him to find it and give chase.

It would be daylight in a few hours, but he'd wake before that. The man had a sixth sense about her. Any minute now, it would kick in and tell him she had flown the coop. The first thing he would do would be to check and see if her boat was missing. When he found his was gone, too, he'd be furious. But helpless.

Well, describing him as helpless was probably being a little optimistic. She couldn't imagine Cagan Hall helpless, but still he'd be stranded. He'd have to set out on foot through the boggy swamp in hopes of finding a highway or an inhabited cabin where he could recruit help in chasing after the escaped criminal.

Only she wasn't a criminal. That was the main problem. She was totally innocent. To prove the fact, she needed time to think, to plan her next move. She'd need a decent lawyer, one that wasn't in on the plot to have her framed. Or worse, in on the murders themselves.

But even the smartest lawyer in Louisiana might not be enough to save her. Not with bodies dropping like flies everywhere she went.

Her mind boggled beneath the weight of confusion and fright. Forcing the unsolvable problems from her mind, she focused on the one at hand. She started down the incline, using the multitude of cypress knees as handholds to keep herself from sliding in the slippery mud.

Her right foot sank into the soft earth, and she pulled it out, testing the next spot of ground before she put her weight on it. The narrow beam of light was focused on Cagan's boat. With a steady hand, she worked the light up the rope to the tree it encircled. Unlike Cagan, she hadn't come prepared with pocketknife in hand. Tucking the flashlight under one arm, she slid her finger into the loop, loosening the knot.

A new noise caught her attention. It wasn't an animal's grunting or foraging, but more like a half cough. One that had been stifled. Her heart pounded against her chest like a boxer's fist, and she spun around. She couldn't see a thing, but she knew Cagan was out there in the darkness, searching for her.

But the beam of light told her she was wrong this time. In the split second the light had flashed across the water, the realization of what she saw struck a new blow. Her boat was there. So was Cagan's. But they were not moored alone. A third boat was there, bigger, sleeker, with a motor far too big for fishing these waters.

Untying Cagan's boat lost all its urgency. Instead, she dropped her bags at her feet and worked on her own nearby craft, undoing the knot that held it fast and stepping toward it.

She had to move quickly, before her latest uninvited guest returned to his boat and found her. Even now, the man must be trekking though the swamp in the formidable blackness, looking for her, ready to take her back to jail. Or maybe just to kill her here in the dark. It would be so easy. She was much smaller than Jeff, and even he'd been no match for a man wielding a knife.

Without warning, a gloved hand wrapped around her neck, pulling her backward and against a muscular body. A new stench assaulted her nose. Sweat, stale beer, a too-sweet after-shave. And the smell of her own fear.

A scream gathered force in her throat but barely escaped before the hand slapped across her mouth. "Don't even try it. You yell, and you and your stinking cop friend are dead meat."

The voice was low and hoarse, probably disguised, but even in her fear, Merissa knew she'd heard it before. She tried to twist around to see his face, but the arm around her neck was choking tight, preventing any movement.

The man pulled her backward, half carrying her, half dragging her away from her boat. Her air supply was severely limited, but she willed herself to stay calm, to think of a plan. She had to find some way to alert Cagan, some way to escape the brutal hands that held her.

"You had to be nosy." Her captor spit the words at her, his tone as demeaning as his words. Again she tried to place the voice, but it was no use. Something was changing it, twisting it into bizarre sounds that barely sounded human. "You're not cutting in on the action now. Better crooks than you have already tried that. They're both dead."

Mud oozed above her boots as her abductor stepped into a low-lying patch of ground. Violent obscenities flew from his mouth, and he tightened his grip.

"You'll cough up the goods, sweetheart, or I'm gonna slice ya. You'll be so disfigured by this hunting knife, no man will ever look at you again. Not even that lyin' piece of cop crud that's following you around. Then you'll talk."

It was then she felt the blade of the knife sticking into her back. Struggle was useless now. One wrong move and the knife would be buried between her shoulder blades. At least, that would be its first destination. From the sound of the threats, her attacker planned to use his weapon liberally.

"Over here," he called as they reached the bank. "Easy as trappin' a rabbit. I'm sure Hall's up there, too, but I want Merissa tied up securely before we go looking for him. She's the one we came for."

So there were two of them, Merissa noted, still struggling for air. She listened intently, hoping the other one would say something and give her a shot at identifying the voice. No such luck. The second person remained speechless and out of view.

"She just walked into my arms like she needed a real man. Probably does, too. How long has it been, sweetheart, since you had yourself a *real* man?"

A sick dread crawled over Merissa's skin. She longed to spit in his face, but she couldn't even open her mouth to protest. Finally, she caught a glimpse of his companion. He was standing about ten yards away. She couldn't make out much from that distance, not in the mist-shrouded darkness, but the figure was shorter than the man who held her captive, and much thinner.

The mouthy man stepped into the bayou and toward his boat, pulling her with him. The water swished suddenly at their feet, becoming a whirling mass of dark froth. Merissa stood perfectly still, her eyes staring into the churning water, knowing they had invaded some creature's turf.

She saw the shimmery blackness of the snake's back at the same time she felt it wrap around her leg. Panic fell like rain, washing over her in terrifying sheets.

Her abductor's right hand fell from around her, flying instead at the attacking reptile. It was a big mistake. In instinctive response, the snake held his head high and then struck. It was a direct hit, the fangs piercing the flesh of the man's leg. A string of curses flew from his mouth as he swung his arm, burying his knife blade into the head of the striking snake.

The man fell backward, and his left hand finally dropped from her throat. Air rushed into her starving lungs like hot lead, all but knocking her to her feet. Gasping, she struggled for balance and for a plan of escape.

Her legs worked before her mind. She propelled herself out of the water. The men were behind her, their curses low but threatening, their breathing much too close. "You better forget me," she cried, sloshing through ankle-deep water, "and help yourself. With all the poison that's in your veins, your heart won't be beating long." The footsteps slowed behind her, and she ran all the faster, knowing her lie was doing its work.

Suddenly, the air crackled with the sound of gunfire. She flew now, dodging overhanging branches and treacherous roots. Speed made her body skid instead of sink into most of the watery puddles that blocked her path.

She stopped for a second, sliding behind a tree. A second. That was all she'd take, just to ease the jagged pains that struck at her lungs. But once again, the night air was shattered by gunshots. Her arm stung as if she'd been attacked by a giant bee. She swatted the air and then she saw the blood, dripping from the sleeve of her shirt.

"Cagan."

She called his name in warning, but her voice didn't ring out through the air. Instead, it seemed to echo inside her head, mocking her helplessness.

The stinging in her upper arm grew worse and she wrapped the fingers of her left hand around it. It felt wet and sticky. The fireworks exploded again somewhere in the distance, but she couldn't worry about them anymore. She was tired and dizzy and suddenly weak. Still, she ran, too dazed and afraid to stop.

THUNDER CRACKED THROUGH the night sky, and Cagan sat up straight, instantly awake. His hand flew to the empty sleeping bag beside him.

Anger and agitation fizzling from his short fuse, he shoved himself out of his sleeping bag and stuffed his sockless feet into his wet boots. With steady hands, he unzipped the bag at his waist and snatched up his pistol, tucking it in his waistband in one smooth motion.

Damn. One mistake. That's all it took. Kicking aside his sleeping bag, he grabbed the handcuffs and cursed the unprofessional softness that had made him leave them under his bag instead of on Merissa's wrists where they belonged. If he had just played by the rules ingrained in his mind, he'd know exactly where Merissa was and what was going on.

Emotion. That was the killer every time. Start to care about someone and the brain went on vacation. What was it going to take to make him learn?

The quiet was shattered again, this time by a series of short, sharp explosions. Definitely not thunder. Adrenaline surged, charging Cagan's brain. Rushing from the clearing, he moved through the trees, alert for any sound, any movement. Merissa was out there, but he'd be willing to bet she wasn't the one who had fired the shots.

He'd been through her things while she slept, and the closest thing she had to a weapon was a package of needles tucked away in her duffel. Unless, of course, she'd had a gun hidden under her sleeping bag.

But a machine gun? Not likely. Which meant someone else had arrived on the scene. Several possibilities darted through his mind, none of them good.

Cagan stuck to the areas of dense vegetation, darting from one palmetto bush to another, from one moss-draped cypress tree to another. He was all but running now, and always in the direction the shots had come from.

A boat motor revved into action at the same time Cagan reached the bayou. He turned quickly but his foot slipped and he almost fell headfirst into the murky water. Too late, he saw the boat curve sharply and head back the way he and Merissa had come. He cursed as the wave left by the departing boat added insult to injury, propelling the bayou water up and over his feet and pants legs.

He scanned the area. It was the same spot he and Merissa had moored their boats. The two ropes were still tied to their trees, their cut ends dangling against the bark. But the boats were gone. Both boats.

Fear consumed him as he stepped away from the water. Somehow, someone had found Merissa and carried her away without his knowing it. Stolen her right from under his nose as if he hadn't even been there. He kicked at a fallen limb and sent it sailing through the night. All he'd had to do was keep her safe until he could get her back to Baton Rouge, until he could finish what he had to do.

The man who had her now wouldn't be carrying her to jail. He knew that even if Merissa didn't. The stakes in this game were too high to take a chance on her spilling her guts to the district attorney. And she obviously knew something she could spill. Something that was worth fifteen grand to Bracer. And if it was worth that much to Bracer, it was probably worth a lot more to Cagan.

Cagan pulled his flashlight from his pocket and used it to illuminate his path. No use stumbling in the dark when there was no one around to see his light anyway.

His foot hit the edge of something stationary, and he twisted the bright beam downward. Merissa's duffel met his gaze. And a few feet farther along, her leather handbag lay half-open.

He hit the handbag with the beam from his flashlight, and an envelope with a registration sticker caught his eye. Funny, he hadn't noticed it last night when he'd gone through her purse. Another mistake. He pulled it out of the side pocket. No wonder he hadn't seen it. It had gotten caught between a torn section of lining and the leather.

Crouching low to the ground, he studied the date and the address. The letter was addressed to Merissa from Ralph Goetz, attorney-at-law. Cagan recognized the name at once. Goetz was Jeff's lawyer. Cagan had talked to him two days ago, at least he'd tried to. Goetz had been unwilling to discuss any of Jeff's business without a court order.

Cagan slipped the letter from the envelope and a small metal key fell out, bouncing from his boot to the soggy earth. He picked it up, wiping it across his pants before rolling it about with his fingers. Then, his flashlight aimed toward the paper, he read the letter.

Anger—or was it hurt?—knotted inside him as the words burned into his brain. In the event of Jeff's death, Merissa was to use the enclosed key to open a storage locker at the bus station in downtown New Orleans.

Damn. Keys, letters, storage lockers—the whole thing smacked of amateur bungling. And his Cajun princess was looking more guilty by the second. She and Jeff against the big boys. No wonder she was afraid.

This had likely been Merissa's plan all along. Have someone meet her here and take her down the bayou. A quick flight across the Gulf of Mexico and she would be safely out of the country, the stolen money in hand. Only the money wasn't in hand. He might have overlooked an envelope, but not a huge stash of money. That meant someone else had picked it up for her. Another accomplice to worry about.

He turned the key over in his hand again. His theory was flawed. The letter was dated. The key had only arrived at her house this morning, and it was still in her purse. Frustration tore at his mind. This was no time for fretting. He had to think and plan. Merissa had disappeared, and he was stranded in an alligator-infested swamp with his feet as the only means of transportation.

Sluggishly, he made his way back up the incline. He was wide awake now, but he wasn't about to set off in the dark. Daylight would be soon enough to start finding his way back to civilization. Even then, his options would be limited.

"Blinded by the light." The words to the old song taunted him. But it wasn't the light that had blinded him. It was Merissa. Once again, he'd let his heart do the thinking, and once again, it had sold him a bill of goods.

Only this time, it wasn't too late. This time, he'd be able to do something about it. He'd come out the winner this time, and Merissa Thomas would rot in jail. He'd see to it himself if it took him the rest of his life.

Why not? he asked himself as he trudged through water several inches deep. The rest of his life. Forever. By then, he might even be able to forget her. The bitter truth tasted like gall in his throat.

Not that it mattered. Not that feelings ever mattered a hell of a lot in his life except to bring more grief. He dropped onto his sleeping bag, dreading the rest of an already miserable night.

PRISCILLA GAFFNER TAPPED her manicured nails on the antique desk in her study and stared at the diamond ring on her left hand. She'd insisted Marshall upgrade it just last year. It was positively embarrassing for a woman of her means to go to social functions in that little one-carat trinket he had given her thirty years ago.

She should have insisted on a whole lot more. He owed her plenty for sticking with him while he played overage tomcat to every shapely airhead that walked into his life. Oh, well, she shouldn't be so hard on him now that he was dead.

Actually, dying had been one of his most thoughtful acts in a long time, even if it hadn't been his idea. He'd gotten himself mixed up in so much garbage he was bound to get it sooner or later. And sooner was much more convenient. Divorcées tended to be frowned on in her social circle, but widowhood was next to sainthood.

She picked up her phone and punched the numbers for Bracer's office with the eraser end of a pencil. She hated to chip her nails. A busy signal again. Well, sooner or later, she'd get past the sweet-talking secretary who kept lying for him. And she'd much rather talk to him in his office than at the funeral. Talking money at funerals was so tacky. The type of thing that offended her sense of dignity.

Besides, it was stupid for him to be avoiding her anyway. She planned to be totally reasonable. Not a pushover like Marshall had been, but reasonable nonetheless. She only wanted her part of the money—nice, clean money that had been laundered, just like the funds he had played with.

After pressing the redial button, she finally got through.

"James Bracer's office. May I ask who's calling?"

"Just tell him it's a poor widow who needs comforting."

"Oh, Mrs. Gaffner. I'm so sorry. I left your message on his desk, but he hasn't been in all day. I'm sure he'll call you the very first chance he gets."

Like hell he will. "Listen, darling, save your manners for the constituents who put him in office. I never voted for the crook and never will. But you tell him to call me, *tonight.*"

"I'll tell him if I talk to him, but like I told you, he's out of town, and I'm not sure when he'll be back. But in case I talk to him, what should I say your call is in reference to?"

"The laundry."

"The laundry?"

"Just tell him. He'll understand."

Priscilla dropped the phone into the cradle and picked up her half-empty glass of Scotch, downing it in a single gulp. Standing in front of the floor-to-ceiling mirror that graced one wall, she admired her figure. Still trim, and with the face-lift she'd endured last summer, she could easily pass for ten years younger than her forty-eight years.

She might opt for a whole new setting. One not quite as conventional as the Baton Rouge Country Club life. The south of France might be a pleasant change. Or maybe a year or two in the islands first. It didn't really matter. With enough cash, she could create her own life-style.

Hands trembling from the booze, she picked up Marshall's photograph from her desk. "I'd like to say I'll miss you, dear," she crooned into the silver-bordered image of the man she had lived with for the past three decades. "But I was never as good as you at lying." She refilled her glass with the amber liquid she'd learned to drink on the lonely nights when Marshall had first started "working" all night with one of his bimbos. "Cheers," she whispered, toasting the picture with an uplifted hand. "And thanks for the memories. It makes what I have to do so much more enjoyable."

Setting down the empty glass, she stood and crossed the room, pausing only a second before shutting the light in her study and on life as she used to know it.

CAGAN WATCHED the first rays of light filter through the trees. He'd been up half the night. The wrong half. No use going through that again. He'd done enough self-recriminating in the wee hours of morning when dark had held him prisoner. Now it was time for action.

Digging through his backpack, he pulled out a pair of dry socks, though they probably wouldn't stay that way for long. He could walk the banks of the bayou and maybe catch sight of a fisherman out running his lines.

But more likely, he'd only run into more of the swampy undergrowth that often camouflaged a foot or two of water and a horde of snakes, alligators and those giant rats that Merissa called nutrias.

Better to stay away from the bayou. He'd head out where the ground was still boggy but at least dry in spots. He would follow his compass, walk north, back toward the spot where he'd rented the boat. Maybe he'd even come to a highway. Surely someone down here would pick up a hitchhiker.

Cagan went through his backpack again, deciding what, if anything, he could discard. He'd wash off in the bayou and then put on his clean clothes. The dirty ones he'd leave here with half the stuff in his bag. Hopefully, he'd be out of this miserable swamp by nightfall and in a real bed. Alone.

He'd go through Merissa's stuff, too, just in case she'd left something he could use. Extra water would be nice and something to eat besides the energy bars and overripe apple he'd grabbed off his counter. After all, he'd never planned on a lengthy hike through a swamp.

The sun beat down on the path to the bayou. Cagan walked quickly, searching for any signs of last night's intruders. There were three sets of footprints. Two going toward the water. One leading away. Stooping over, he studied the set leading into the swamp. It was Merissa's. He knew the curved pattern on the soles of her hiking boots.

Confusion toyed with his reasoning. She'd been running when these footprints were made. Her feet had slid as she made heavy contact, making the prints appear longer than the actual size of her feet. He followed the path back into the trees.

His heart sank. The trail here was dotted by patches of dried blood. Fear rattled his composure as his gaze swept the area. He'd heard shots last night. He's assumed they'd been to frighten him away, or maybe aimed at some animal that had jumped into their path.

But it was Merissa who'd been shot. That was the only explanation for the blood and smudged footprints. He followed the prints for a few feet, a very few. They led into a bog and then disappeared in the standing water. He circled the area until he picked them up again.

Damn. He was a fool. He knew Merissa was in real danger, yet last night when she'd disappeared, he'd been willing to believe the worst.

Grabbing a few necessities, he started through the swamp with nothing to guide him but footprints, dried blood and enough guilt to last forever.

IT WAS TWO HOURS LATER before Cagan sat down to rest on a rotting stump. Sweat dripped from his forehead in a steady stream, sticky and salty, falling into his eyes and mouth and catching the gnats that swarmed about his face and set up housekeeping in his eyelashes.

He'd followed Merissa's footprints for as long as he could, finding them only to lose them again repeatedly in standing water and heavy vegetation. But he hadn't seen any sign of her for over an hour. What he wouldn't give to have Tommy and Luke here to help right now. But his partners had their own jobs to do. Hopefully, they were more successful.

Pulling out a bottle of water, he sipped slowly, letting a few drops of the soothing liquid trickle down his throat. He'd have to go easy. There were only two bottles left, one of his soft-drink-size ones and one of Merissa's larger ones.

Obviously, she knew more about the swamp than he did. Of course, she should, having visited here frequently when she was growing up. Another one of the interesting tidbits of information his investigation had uncovered. In fact, it would probably be safe to say he knew everything about her except the things that really mattered.

Stretching his feet out in front of him, he put the bottle of water to his mouth and took one long, satisfying drink. He could have easily downed the whole thing in a gulp. He was hot, tired and hungry. And without even a remote idea where to search for Merissa.

A sound caught his attention. It was soft, a bird's cry. Or maybe a woman's. Movement behind him jarred him to action. He jumped to his feet and turned around. Merissa stumbled toward him, her face ghostly white and painted with brownish red streaks of dried blood.

He grabbed her just as she started to fall, her hands reaching out and wrapping around him. "Merissa, are you all right?"

"Sure. I'm just waiting for you." She lifted her face from his chest and looked him in the eye. "What took you so long?"

Chapter Nine

Cagan cradled Merissa in his arms. She trembled against him, and the shock of seeing her weak and reeling with exhaustion ripped away his crumbling defenses.

Carefully, he trailed his fingers along the outer circles of the wound on her arm. She winced, and he lightened his touch still more. The bleeding had stopped, but her arm was swollen and discolored. "What happened?"

"There were two men. With guns." She spoke in short bursts, her breathing shallow and ragged. "My arm. Just grazed, I think, but it bled like crazy."

Cagan half led, half carried her to the spot where he had left his supplies. Easing her to the ground, he propped her against the stump. "Are you in any pain?"

His throat closed around the needless words. Seeing her like this, pale, fearful, her disheveled hair tumbling about her delicate face and wide eyes, was almost more than he could take. Almost enough to make him forget his real reason for being here.

"I'll be okay," she finally answered, her voice scratchy.

Reaching into his bag, he took out the limited first-aid equipment he'd brought with him. "This is going to smart," he cautioned, gently swabbing her wound with peroxide.

She grimaced, but didn't cry out. For all her softness, she was tough as nails when it counted. Fortunately, she was also right. The injury was only a flesh wound. The bullet had torn off a few layers of skin, but hadn't penetrated the muscles or joints.

"Looks like you lucked out. A half inch more and you'd be in real trouble."

"Lucky me." Her voice rose. "I've had all the luck I can stand, Cagan. Had it up to here." She raised her uninjured arm to the top of her head. "My friend was murdered. And now, my boss. Now the killer is after me."

"It seems—"

"No," she interrupted. "Don't tell me what it seems. You can't possibly know. And don't make it sound like I'm responsible in some way. I'm not. And I can't handle any more insinuations." Tears pooled in her eyes, but she held them back, her fierce determination winning over her temporary fragility.

Bandaging the wound as best he could with adhesive tape and a cotton pad, Cagan took out the bottle of water. "How about a drink?"

She nodded, silent now that she'd voiced her fears and frustrations. He unscrewed the bottle cap and dampened his fingers, touching her dry lips with the moisture. Then, holding the bottle of water to her lips, he watched as she gulped down a healthy swig, drinking as if she'd never get enough.

He lowered it from her mouth. "Let that settle. You don't want to get sick to your stomach on top of everything else."

She rested her head against the stump, using her hand to ward off the burning glare of the sun. He lifted the bottle to her mouth again. She sipped slowly this time, as if savoring every drop.

"How much water is left?" she asked, wiping her hand across her mouth and letting her damp fingers linger on her lips.

"The rest of this bottle and the one you had left in your bag."

"So you found my bag. I must have left it near the boats when..." Her voice grew shaky.

"When you took off on your own?"

"I tried," she admitted. "Nothing personal, but like I told you, I'm not too keen on going to jail."

Her feeble attempt at humor was lost on Cagan. It was impossible to find anything funny when he was staring at the spot where a bullet had grazed her skin. "Someone almost made sure you didn't have to." He cupped a hand under her chin and forced her to meet his gaze. "Who came to the bayou after you, Merissa?"

"I don't know." She cocked her head defiantly, her eyes dark with a fury he'd never seen there before. "But I plan to find out."

"Then the men who showed up weren't the ones you were expecting?"

Irritation pulled new lines into her tired face. "I wasn't expecting anyone." She shook her head, causing loose strands of hair to fall over her forehead and the side of her face. With a steady hand, she raked them back. "I was going to the boat alone," she said, adding, "getting away from you."

"So you just planned to escape through the bayou without help?"

"Do you find that so hard to believe? I'm not fleeing justice, Cagan. I'm only trying to find a little. With everything happening so fast, I haven't had much time to think things through rationally." Batting at a dragonfly that had lighted in her hair, she scooted to a more upright position.

"Not that I expect you to believe me now any more than you did before." Disappointment dragged her tone to a dismal low, and she looked away from him, staring off into the sameness of their surroundings.

"I'm not against you, Merissa. I'm just looking for answers, the same as you." He settled into the grass beside her, crossing his legs, then knocking a hairy spider off his boot. "You said two men attacked you. Would you recognize them if you saw them again?"

"I didn't get a good look at either one of them, but one of the voices sounded familiar."

"Was it someone from LPI?"

"I'm not sure. It was familiar, yet strange, as if he had something in his mouth to disguise his voice. I can't quite place where I've heard it before."

"What did he say?"

"Nothing that made any sense. Except that they knew you were with me. But it was me they wanted." She massaged her right temple with her fingers. "Something about better crooks than me are dead, and a few disgusting remarks I'd just as soon forget."

Cagan fought the urge to kill that welled inside him, instead calming himself by brushing a sticky wisp of hair away from Merissa's eyes. "Have you had anything to eat?" he asked, wishing he had something more sustaining than his meager rations to offer before they had to set off again.

"Sure. Just yesterday I had some cheese crackers." She managed a smile, and his heart took another plunge.

"Today you get variety." Reaching into his bag, he opened the next-to-last energy bar and sliced off a piece. "Power and taste to spare," he read out loud, turning the bar in his hands to get the whole label in view. "Protein, vitamins and carbohydrates in a healthful snack."

She chewed the first bite he handed her with relish, and he sliced off more, placing the bite-size piece between her lips.

"How did you find me?" she asked after she'd chewed and swallowed.

"Pure talent," he lied. "And fate," he added, wiping a crumb from her mouth. Here he was taking care of her again. He'd never thought he had a nurturing gene in his body. Obviously, he'd been wrong. Too bad he had to find out like this. He trailed his hand across her chin, and a new kind of warmth filled him like wine.

He continued to feed her, slicing off the almost tasteless pieces and sliding them between her lips. She finished off about half the bar before insisting she'd had enough. He knew better. She was preserving rations. Hopefully, they would be out of here soon, but Cagan knew there were no guarantees.

"I just wish I could make sense of this, Cagan." Merissa's words broke into his thoughts. "I know all of this has to do with Jeff and with Gaffner. But why me? What is it I'm supposed to know that can help or hurt anyone?"

Cagan stuck his hand in his pocket, fingering the key. "That's what I'd like for you to tell me."

"I just told you. I have no idea." Frustration edged her voice. "Can't you just believe me for once without putting me through the third degree?"

"I want to believe you, and I want to help you. You're in serious trouble, Merissa. If someone doesn't help you, your chances of staying alive to see the next new moon are slim to none." He kept his voice steady. Somehow he had to get through to her. "The only way I can help you is if you tell me the whole truth."

He reached out to her, but she shoved his hand aside, cringing and pulling away from him. "I *have* told you the whole truth. I've told everybody the truth. And I don't need you to tell me my chances of survival. I'm the one who just got shot, remember?''

''Then tell me what's in the locker at the bus station, Merissa?'' He took the key from his pocket and dangled it in front of her. ''The truth this time. It's the only way I can help you.''

''Where did you get that key?''

''From your purse. Obviously, the gunman didn't give you time to take it with you.''

''I don't know what you're talking about. That's not my key.''

''It was in an envelope addressed to you, registered, from Jeff's lawyer. You signed for it and you opened it, so don't act like you've never seen it before.''

''So that's what this is about. You snoop in my things and then make accusations.'' Her eyes grew dark and fiery. ''I do remember the key now. The letter came just as I was leaving for Gaffner's office. I opened it, but I didn't know it was from Jeff's lawyer. I stuffed it in my purse to read later. But then . . .'' Her voice grew hard. ''Where's the letter, Cagan?''

He took it from his backpack and placed it her hand. She read silently, shock evident in her eyes and the grim set of her mouth. Muscles taut, she folded the letter and laid it across her lap.

''When did you find this, Cagan?''

''Last night, after you disappeared.''

''After you read it, you immediately jumped to the conclusion that I had been lying. That I was involved with Jeff in some criminal activity. What is it about me, Cagan, that makes everyone think I'm guilty?''

''It's not you. It's the situation.''

"No. It *is* me. It must be. You, Gaffner, the police, half my co-workers at LPI. Everybody's ready to believe in my guilt, but no one's willing to believe in my innocence." Her voice cracked and one lone tear started down her cheek.

"Merissa—" His voice curled around her like an endearment.

"I know," she interrupted. "All you want to do is help me. If *I* tell the truth?" Her eyes bore into his, shooting arrows of fire. "But I'm not the one playing games. As for your help, thanks, but no thanks, *Officer* Cagan Hall. I'd sooner take my chances with enemies who admit they're out to get me than rely on some forked-tongued cop posing as a friend."

Her taunts hit their target dead center, tearing into him with the force of a cannon. He was never what he pretended to be. Yet he made everyone else prove their innocence as if he was judge and jury.

"You're right," he responded, picking his words with care, stumbling over feelings that were too dangerous to accept, too intense to ignore.

"And . . . ?"

He knew what she wanted to hear. She needed assurance that he believed her. He could just lie about it, tell her whatever she wanted to hear. Heaven knew he lied about everything else in his life. He opened his mouth, but this time the lie just wouldn't come. Not to Merissa.

"Forget it, Cagan. You do what you think you have to, play your holier-than-thou lawman routine." She rose from the grass and stood over him, tugging her shirt down around her shapely body. "But don't expect me to fall into your arms in gratitude."

She turned and started to walk away.

"Where do you think you're going?"

"I'm getting out of here. Not alone, of course. I'm sure you'll be right behind me." She stopped and stuck her hands in his direction, turning them over so that her palms faced the sky. "Or do you want to put the cuffs back on me," she challenged. "You can't be too careful when you're dealing with a murdering scoundrel like me."

"No, you go right ahead and lead the way. After all, this is your native habitat, not mine."

She stopped and stared, her eyes ice-cold. "So nice of you to have checked into my past. Just another way of trying to help me, I'm sure." With an angry toss of her head, she headed south, toward the still waters of the bayou.

Cagan gathered his things quickly and took off after her, watching his step as he waded through a half-hidden pool of stagnant water that mounted to the top of his hiking boots.

"Don't you think it would be safer to try the other way?" he asked when he finally caught up to her. "It seems we'd be a lot more likely to find a road if we left the bayou."

"You go any way you'd like, *Officer*. Through snakes, alligators, bogs where you sink six feet to the bottom without warning. Nothing at all to a tough guy like you."

She'd made her point, Cagan decided, walking as fast as he could to keep with her. "Take it easy, Merissa," he warned, jumping out of the way of a rabbit Merissa's determined steps had frightened out of hiding. "You've had a rough night. Running through the swamp in this heat is not going to solve a thing."

"So what is, Cagan?" She stopped and waited for him to catch up, the fury in her eyes dark and powerful. "Listening to you pretend you have no idea what's going on? You wouldn't be out here in this swamp if that was the case."

"If I knew who was trying to kill you, don't you think I'd tell you?"

"No. I think you'd continue to play your cop games with your own special twist on the rules. I'm just a new challenge. Something to add a little spice to the game. As a suspect. *And* as a woman."

She all but spit the words at him and then whirled around, stamping away from him. Without thinking, he grabbed her around the waist and jerked her to a stop. Anger riding hard on the desires he'd fought to keep repressed, he pulled her into his arms.

She tried to push him away, but he couldn't let her go, couldn't stop himself any longer. He pressed his lips on hers, hard and demanding. Feelings that had tumbled inside him for days burst out, screaming for release. He was tired of fighting, too weary to do anything but give in to his body's demands.

Merissa struggled, the force of her resistance driving the tempting curves of her body against his. He didn't back down. If she wanted to play with fire, she had to face the heat.

His arms drew her closer, and all of a sudden, she wasn't fighting his kiss. Her mouth had grown greedy, opening, tasting, tugging on his, rocking him back on his heels. Purpose, motive, integrity. They were nothing now. There was no room for them in the hunger that ripped him apart.

Finally, he tore his lips from hers. "Is that what you want, Merissa? To know just how much power you possess?" His voice was ragged, raw with passion. He didn't try to hide it.

Merissa reached a trembling finger to her mouth, tracing the red and swollen lips that had fondled and fed his fierce hunger seconds before. There was no condemnation in her eyes, no anger or bitter rebukes. He wished there had been. Anything would have been better than the disappointment he read in the dark, misty reflections.

"No, Cagan. That's not what I want," she finally answered. "Not like that. Passion without trust is empty." Back straight and shoulders squared, she turned and strode away.

He followed a step behind, feeling the emptiness she'd talked about clear to the soles of his water-soaked feet.

HOURS HAD PASSED, and still the air was so thick with humidity Merissa felt each breath. She had forgotten about the stifling heat of summer afternoons along the bayou, or maybe she'd just grown too accustomed to air-conditioned environments to be able to take the heat anymore.

Either way, this was not the comfortable hideaway she had envisioned when she'd left Baton Rouge yesterday. If she'd driven straight through, or at least as far as she could have gone by car, she'd have been at her grandparents' cabin before dawn. Even by boat from the spot where she'd left her car, she'd have made it by now. But on foot, it would take forever. That's why they were going in the opposite direction now, back toward the spot where she'd left her car.

Not that her grandparents' cabin would have offered a lot of material comforts. It was deserted and probably crawling with bugs. But at least she would have had a dry bed and protection from the sun. Best of all, there would have been neighbors nearby, a family she could trust. Unlike her present company.

Her grandparents' friends would have showered her with food and water and emotional support. All items presently in short supply. Now she was tired, thirsty, hungry, and as confused as ever. She should have stayed in Baton Rouge and dealt with the charges, as she would have done if she hadn't panicked.

A slow change in the water caught her attention, and Merissa stopped and stared. The sun bounced off the rough back of an alligator, gliding by not two feet from where she stood. His body was as still as a log, but a steady swell of water followed in his wake.

"Time for a break," she said, stopping to lean against the trunk of a tree to watch the alligator pass. After stamping down an area of high grass, she sat on the bank of the bayou, taking off her boots and dangling her feet in the water.

Cagan sat beside her, eyeing her carefully as she splashed her bare feet beneath the murky surface. "Aren't you afraid to put your feet in there?"

"No. It feels wonderful." She cupped her hands and dipped them into the water, splashing a handful over her face. "The animals are much more afraid of humans than we are of them," she assured him. "As long as you splash to let them know you're around, they won't bother you. Take off your shoes and see for yourself."

"I'll take your word for it."

"That's a first."

"Then we're making headway. I say we call a truce, Merissa. Like it or not, we're in this together."

"I appear to be in a lot deeper than you. So, you win. I'm ready to give up, Cagan, just to quit running and turn myself in to the authorities in Baton Rouge."

"I'm not sure that's a good idea anymore."

Merissa leaned back on the grass, folding her hands to make a pillow for the back of her head, but she didn't relax. Her thoughts were tying her into knots. "Then how about your answering a question for me, Cagan? Truthfully, this time. Just like you got from me."

"I'll try. Shoot."

"What did you and Jeff argue about on that last night at the lake?"

Cagan stared into the water. "Jeff had something on Gaffner. He was considering using what he had to blackmail him. I was trying to convince Jeff not to do anything stupid."

Merissa drew a ragged breath. "Why didn't you tell me that before?"

"Jeff swore me to secrecy."

"Jeff was dead. He couldn't hold you to your promise."

"It's not important why I didn't tell you before. I'm telling you now. Jeff had something on Gaffner. I think Gaffner knew it. Someone else might have known, too."

"The something that's in the locker in New Orleans."

"That would be my guess."

"It doesn't make sense. Why did he go to the lake at all if he was holding something like that?"

"The trip was already planned. I think he decided to go through with it so that he could use the time to consider his options."

"And you believe he really found evidence like that?"

"I believe he knew enough to get him killed."

"Why didn't he tell me? We'd been good friends for years. Surely he knew he could trust me."

"Maybe he was afraid of involving you in something he thought was dangerous." Cagan picked up a stick and tossed it into the water.

"Evidently he wasn't concerned enough. He left his deadly legacy to me. A tiny key that someone is ready to kill for."

"But only as insurance, just in case the worst happened. I'm sure he didn't really think he'd be murdered before he could retrieve the evidence. And he transferred it through his lawyer. Secretly. Probably not even Goetz saw the contents of the letter. He had no reason to suspect someone would find out it had fallen into your hands."

"But obviously someone did find out. Do you have a theory for that, too?"

"I have an idea. The truth is I don't think they did suspect you of knowing anything, at least not until you ran. Before that, you were being set up as a patsy. You were at the lake, you'd had a past relationship with the victim, and your fingerprints were found on the knife."

"I explained that to the police. Jeff had used the knife to clean and fillet the fish the night before. When he finished, I washed and dried it for him."

"True, but you were still the perfect person to take the rap."

"If I was only supposed to be the patsy, then explain why my house was broken into. Twice!"

"Someone's getting desperate. That's why we have to get back to Baton Rouge. Not to take you to jail, but to retrieve the contents of the locker before the killer finds you."

Fearful shivers raced along Merissa's nerves. Struggling for calm, she sat back and watched while Cagan pulled his canvas backpack in front of him and rummaged inside.

"How about another sip of water before we start up again?" he asked, unscrewing the lid.

Water. Funny, it was all around her, soaking through her shoes, lapping at her feet. The humidity even made her skin clammy and her hair cling to her nape. Only her throat and mouth were parched dry, burning from thirst that couldn't be quenched.

"Just a sip," she whispered, reaching for the bottle. She touched it to her lips and let the liquid fill her mouth, swishing it over her tongue for precious seconds before letting it slide down her throat. "Your turn," she said, slipping the bottle into his hands.

"I'll wait," he said, screwing the top on without even a glance at the tempting contents.

"No fair. I drank. Now it's your turn."

"Later," he said, stretching his long legs and rising to his full six-foot-plus height. "I'm not really thirsty yet."

Merissa eyed the perspiration that dripped from his brow and dampened the yellow headband above his eyes. He was beyond thirst. They both were. He was saving the water for her, just in case they didn't find help before dark.

Once again, he was a complete mystery. She mentally listed his contradictory activities of the past few days. He had followed her through a swamp to take her to jail only to change his mind, he had stayed up all night to nurse her busted head, then circled her hands with handcuffs to make sure she didn't escape and now he had gone without water in unbearable heat to make sure she didn't have to.

"You're a strange man, Cagan Hall. Very strange."

"Yeah, so I've been told." He took her hand and pulled her to her feet. "Now let's see if you can get us out of this place. I have dinner reservations at seven."

Merissa started to walk away.

"Wait." Cagan's word was more command than request. She stopped and stared back at him. Cagan cocked his head, staring into the blueness of the sky. "Do you hear something?" he asked.

She listened carefully, stepping a few feet upstream so that the shade of a cypress tree fell over her face. "It sounds like a motor," she said, relief flooding her voice. "It's about time. I knew sooner or later a fisherman would pass."

The sound grew louder and less familiar. Cagan shaded his eyes with his hand and studied the sky to the west of them. "It's a helicopter," he said, taking her hand and pulling her into a dense bush that tumbled over the muddy bank. "Duck in here and don't move."

Merissa struggled, but she was no match for Cagan's strength. "I told you, I'm through running," she argued, kicking at him with her feet. "Let them take me to jail in a helicopter. It's better than walking all the way back to Baton Rouge. Either way, I'll be stuck in the same cell."

Finally wrestling one hand from his grasp, she stuck it through the top branches of the bush and waved it about wildly.

Cagan pulled her arm down to her side and held it firmly. "I told you to be still," he barked.

"You're hurting my arm."

"Good. Maybe that will remind you what type of rescuers showed up last night," he hissed in her ear. "Didn't it ever occur to you that the guys in the helicopter are probably the same guys who shot at you?"

Dread skittered up her spine as recollections of her foulmouthed abductor came rushing back. The last thing she wanted was to be at his mercy. She scrunched lower to the ground, not daring to move. Together, she and Cagan waited as the chopping sound grew louder.

PRISCILLA GAFFNER OPENED the wooden door and ushered James Bracer into and through her marble foyer. "Have a seat," she said, motioning to the rose-colored sectional sofa that dominated one corner of the living room. He glanced nervously around him, and she knew he had to be impressed. Everyone always was on their first visit to her home.

The living room was large, carpeted in a plush fabric the color of café au lait and lit by a crystal chandelier that had once hung in one of England's famed stately homes. She had wonderful taste, that's what her friends said. Actually, they were wrong. The decorator had taste. She had money. At least, she used to have money.

"I can only stay a few minutes," Bracer said, propping himself on the edge of the couch. "I have a news conference at six tonight. I plan to throw my hat into the ring for governor."

"How fortunate for the citizens of Louisiana. It will be so comfortable for them, having graft as usual the order of the day." She sat down beside him.

"Sarcasm doesn't become you, Priscilla."

"Neither does poverty."

"I'm quite certain you're not poor, Priscilla. Perhaps not as well off as you were, but surely Marshall was insured. And you know how sorry I am about his death. He was a good man."

"Cut the garbage, James. He wasn't a good man. He was the same sort of sordid trash you are. That's how he ended up in business with you. He just wasn't as smart as you. And that's what we have to talk about."

"My business dealings with Marshall were all aboveboard. He wanted money to invest in Mardi Gras Lights, and he put up his interests in LPI for collateral. One of my companies lent him the funds. It was a sound business deal, conducted in good faith. I'm sure your lawyer told you that."

"And now you're foreclosing on the loan. Just like that. Strip the poor widow of everything she owns and toss her into the street."

"This doesn't look like the street," he commented, letting his eyes scan the room. "If you're truly in financial straits, Priscilla, you might consider selling the house and moving into something smaller. This place must be worth a mint."

"Mortgaged from foundation to gabled roof. But then I'm sure you know that, too, don't you? Marshall talked over all his business dealings with you."

"No, he didn't tell me about the house. I never would have advised such a thing." Bracer laid his briefcase flat on his lap and drummed a nervous tattoo on the expensive leather.

"Since you're obviously in a hurry, I'll make this as simple and as direct as I can." She turned to face him, waiting until he made eye contact before continuing. "I need money, James. Lots of it. I stayed with Marshall and let him make a fool of me for thirty years. I will not stand by now and let you rob me of what should be mine."

He dropped his gaze to the stitching on his briefcase. "I'm sorry to hear about your problems, Priscilla, really I am. I have to go now, but why don't you call my secretary and set up an appointment for one day next week. Perhaps we can work out a low-interest loan through one of the companies I'm associated with."

"Not a loan, James. Cash. Lots of it, and without strings. If not, I'll go to the authorities and tell them all I know about your money laundering. You used my husband, and then you killed him."

Bracer's mouth twisted in anger, and his face turned bloodred.

"You see, your secrets were not as well kept as you thought. My husband was a foolish man. He couldn't resist bragging to me about the little schemes the two of you shared. I was the only one he could talk to, the only one he trusted not to talk. After all, if he went to jail and lost his business, I would be broke, just the way I am now."

"You must have misunderstood Marshall, Priscilla. We've never shared schemes, as you call it. You must stop talking like this. It's cruel to spread lies about your dead husband and useless to spread them about me."

"They're not lies, and you know it."

"Of course they are. My reputation is flawless. No one will believe such accusations against a man who's practically a legend in this state."

"I think they will, once they check your bank accounts. But don't worry, *Senator*. I won't do anything to upset your political dreams, not as long as you take care of me."

Bracer shook his head. "You're a pitiful old woman, Priscilla, overcome with grief. Even if what you say is true, which it isn't, no one would believe you." He reached over and took her shaky hand. "Especially when I let the cat out of the bag about where you really were last year when you were supposedly out of the country on a vacation. When I let it slip that you were in a little hospital in upstate New York, recuperating from a nervous breakdown. Or was it just too much booze and too many tranquilizers?"

He gave her hand an extra squeeze and then dropped it.

"Poor, pathetic Priscilla Gaffner," he taunted. "Your friends will see your shame. They may even doubt your sanity. Some of them will wonder if it was you who took your late husband's life."

She pulled away from him, stiffly stood up and headed for the bar. She hadn't planned to pour another drink tonight, but then nothing was going as planned.

"And even after all the trouble I've gone to for you today," Bracer added, a touch of satisfaction lightening his tone as he watched her.

"What have you done for me now?" Contempt hardened her voice and dried her mouth. She took a long sip of the Scotch, savoring the burn as it slid down her throat.

"Let's just say you won't have to worry about justice in the case of your husband's murder."

Priscilla returned her glass to the bar with a heavy thud. "What do you mean?"

"Exactly what I said. Merissa Thomas is obviously guilty of his murder, and she will pay for her crime." Bracer got up from the sofa and walked toward the door. "I have to go now, but you can call me next week about that loan." Priscilla watched his mouth curl in a smug smile as he walked right past her without even glancing her way. "I have a very busy night," he said, touching a palm to his heavily sprayed hair. "Very busy."

The door slammed behind him, and Priscilla dropped to the bar stool. With trembling hands, she poured herself another drink.

Chapter Ten

Merissa forced her legs to keep moving, even though her body told her it had reached its limits. She and Cagan had stayed crouched low as the helicopter made its first flyby. Then he had dragged her from one hiding spot to another, moving away from the bayou and the helicopter search party.

But now it was Merissa who was leading the way. Thankful for every tidbit of bayou knowledge her grandfather had taught her, she led them steadily west, searching for higher ground, a place where they could rest without sinking into the bog.

For the most part, they had been slogging through a watery maze, thriving with snakes, frogs, turtles and insects of every description. But at least the sputtering beat of the helicopter had been left behind.

Merissa took a deep breath and patted the earth with her foot. For the first time since they'd left the bayou, there was no squish. "Looks like we finally reached a dry spot," she said, turning to find Cagan right behind her. Exhausted, she dropped to the carpet of green moss that grew beneath the overhead tangle of swamp willows and sweet gums.

Cagan sat down beside her. "Dry ground. Who ever thought it could look this good? Now I know how Noah must have felt after the flood."

"Don't get too comfortable. This is just a rest stop. Hopefully, we can find a cabin before dark. Dry or not, this is not an area you'd want to spend the night in. Especially since I don't even have a sleeping bag."

Cagan untied his hiking boots and slipped them off, turning them upside down and letting the water pour out. "I'm still praying there's a Holiday Inn with a comfortable bed around the next corner."

"I'd settle for a fishing shack, dry, with a stock of canned goods and a supply of bottled water." Merissa removed her own shoes and stretched her wet socks across the feathery fronds of a giant palmetto.

"While we're dreaming, I'd like a telephone, too," Cagan added. "We could call for a pickup. Do you think a limousine company serves this area?"

"Sure. It's *our* dream. And someone's already sent a helicopter." Reality prompted an icy shiver in spite of the heat and humidity that dampened her clothes and skin.

Cagan scooted closer as if sensing her darkened mood. "Let's have a look at that wound," he said, pushing her shirtsleeve up and out of the way.

"My arm is not the problem."

He examined it anyway. "It's still red and patchy, but it doesn't look bad. No thanks to the cowardly rats who jumped you." Anger hardened his words.

"I've thought about them and what they said all day, Cagan, but I can't put the bits and pieces together into anything that makes sense. And I can't imagine how they found me."

"A quick background check and a few paid informants. Information is easy to come by. The Atchafalaya Basin is an area you know that most people don't, a natural place to run. It's the first place I thought of to look for you."

Cagan unzipped his bag, taking out the tube of first-aid cream and a packaged antiseptic towel. He swabbed her wound gingerly and then used the tip of the towel to spread a generous layer of the cream.

"I told the man at the marina to hide my car. I even paid him fifty dollars not to talk. He obviously didn't follow my instructions. You had no trouble following me."

"He hid your car. At least it wasn't in plain sight when I was at the marina, but that doesn't mean he wouldn't talk if someone topped your fifty-dollar bribe."

"Is that how you found me, paying off the man?"

"No. I got off cheap. I planted an electronic bird dog on your bumper before I left your house yesterday morning. It doesn't carry but a few miles, but once I got to the marina, it told me your car was close by. I probably would have found you anyway, though. A gas station attendant where you bought gas let me know you'd come this way."

"So from there you just followed the river."

"Right. Choosing the right bayou to take off the river was the tricky part."

"Looks like you made the right guess."

"Not exactly. I have a map to your grandparents' cabin, courtesy of an agency they dealt with. Everyone has records in one government file or another. A good investigator can find whatever he wants, as long as he knows where and how to look. Too bad the map isn't doing us any good now. With all the desperate running we've done, I have no idea where we are."

A good investigator. Good enough to track down a map to her grandparents' deserted cabin. Doubt surfaced again, and with it a new bout of uneasiness. "Why were you spying on me, Cagan?"

"I wanted to help you. I still do. And from the looks of things, you need all the help you can get." Cagan took out the bottle of water and unscrewed the top, poking the opened bottle in her direction.

"No, I'll wait. That may have to last us until morning."

"You have to keep up your strength. After all, you're the guide. Just a sip," he urged.

Concern burned in his dark eyes. He was a man of hard steel, but it was not his toughness that pulled her to him, that drew them close in spite of everything that tore them apart.

"One sip," she agreed, "but only if you take one, too."

He smiled and traced a finger down her cheek, pushing back a strand of hair that had pasted itself against her skin. "That's a deal, partner."

She took the bottle from him and touched the mouth to her lips, letting the liquid drip deliciously down her throat. It was amazing how wonderful water could taste and how difficult it was to settle for so little when she longed to drink until her thirst was quenched. "Your turn," she said, pushing the bottle toward him.

Fatigue overtook her then, and she dropped her head to the moss-covered earth and closed her eyes. So much had happened the past few days, and strangely enough, Cagan had become her rock. He was always there when she needed someone, not only tending her wounds but risking his life to protect her.

He would never hurt her. She was sure of that much, no matter how peculiar his lawman tactics seemed. But neither was he being totally honest. She was more convinced of that than ever.

Cagan lifted her head and slid his backpack under it to serve as a pillow. His fingers cradled the back of her head as he lowered it to the bag. She opened her eyes, and her gaze locked with his. Everything between them was there in his eyes, reflected in the their dark depths, almost palpable, consuming.

"Do you believe I'm innocent, Cagan?" Her voice quivered, but she had to know.

"I don't believe you killed anyone. I don't believe you could." He whispered the words huskily, his eyes mesmerizing. And then his lips were on hers.

Merissa trembled, dissolving into his kiss. Dream or reality, she didn't really care anymore. All she knew now was the feel of Cagan's mouth, the taste of him, the passion of him. She parted her lips, hungrily deepening the kiss, taking from him and giving back.

He rolled her toward him, and she felt his body, hard and firm, stretched out beside her. His left arm encircled her, his fingers pressing into the hollow of her back, circling, massaging, burning through the thin cotton fabric of her shirt.

The fire inside her grew hotter, licking its way through every part of her being. With each stroke of Cagan's fingers, each thrust of his tongue, her body arched toward him, begging for more.

They were in a world of dark dangers, a place where every emotion was magnified. But nothing she had seen or felt in the past two days compared with this. Passion rocked her, charging every erogenous nerve, bubbling inside her like molten gold.

Cagan pulled his mouth from hers. His control had vanished, lost to desires that had intensified steadily since the day Merissa had walked into his life. He touched his lips to her eyelids, her nose, her chin, sliding slowly down her neck, not stopping until his lips rested in the crevice of heated flesh between her breasts. Fumbling, he pulled off her T-shirt.

Her breasts were perfect, delicate pink buds, firm mounds of soft flesh. Tempting and teasing. Cagan encircled one in his hand, his thumb massaging and pebbling the nipple. "So beautiful, like everything about you," he whispered, wrapping his warm mouth around first one aroused peak and then the other, tugging, sucking, devouring.

A throaty groan escaped his lips, and Merissa cuddled closer, pushing against him, grinding her gentle curves into the tautness of his thighs and groin.

"Merissa." Her name was a cry, tearing from his throat as his hands slipped beneath the waist of her jeans. Tugging the snap loose, he eased the zipper down until his hand could reach inside her silky panties. Desire rocketed through him as his fingers found new areas to explore. He traced a path down the smooth, firm skin of Merissa's belly. Her body arched toward him, hot and wanting, and the passion he'd held inside for so long seemed to rip him apart. "I want you so much," Cagan groaned. "I have since the day I met you."

"I know." A soft moan escaped her lips, but she bit it back almost before it began. "But not here, not like this," she whispered.

"Yes. Now. Here. Swamp, alligators...I don't care. I only care that you want me the same way." He kissed her again, wild and unbridled, like the strange land they were in, his unleashed desires ravaging his mind and body. Finally, he tore his lips away. "Tell me you want me, Merissa. Let me hear you say it."

"I want you, Cagan. So much."

She'd whispered the words, but they echoed like thunder in Cagan's ears. He'd dreamed of this moment since the day their paths had crossed. Dreamed of holding her, touching her just like this. Dreamed of making her burn with the same fire that consumed him. Now that it was happening, his body was exploding.

His jeans pulled against his aroused body, all but cutting off circulation. Shaking so badly, he could barely function, he fumbled with the metal button at his waist.

Merissa wrapped her fingers around his, pushing the button through the hole and easing the zipper down the rough denim. Then, with fingers of fire, she reached inside and wrapped her hand around him. His body shook with desire so intense he ached.

Struggling for breath, he slipped a thigh between her legs as she wiggled out of her jeans and panties. He longed to touch her in every place that would bring her pleasure, to make her writhe with desire and ecstasy, the way she was taking him to the brink.

He couldn't, not with her fingers stroking him, pulling him inside her. Not with her body wrapping around him, squeezing, burning, bathing him in rivulets of liquid fire.

"Oh, Cagan." She swallowed his name as soft moans of pleasure escaped from her lips. The sounds urged him onward and he thrust inside her over and over until he couldn't hold back. He thrust one last time before he rocketed skyward, passion shooting through him like dynamite, blowing away all vestiges of control.

He lay still for long minutes after that. His gaze fell on Merissa as she cuddled in his arms, her soft breath warm on his chest, her delicate skin caressing his.

A new feeling washed over him, unfamiliar and far more frightening than the environment. He was a man of action, a man who'd learned the hard way not to trust emotions and feelings. Yet here he was, relying totally on feelings he couldn't understand. And nothing had ever felt this right before.

"Merissa." He whispered her name, but she didn't move. Passion spent, exhaustion had taken hold. He cradled her closer, and a longing such as he'd never known stirred deep

in his gut. He closed his eyes and pushed it away. He was
who he was, and nothing could change that.

THE SUN DIPPED LOWER, lengthening shadows and prom-
ising nightfall. Merissa quickened her pace, the warm afterglow of the afternoon's intimacy giving over to urgency.
For a while, right after Cagan had awakened her with a kiss
and urged her on, she had walked with light steps. She had
been certain everything had changed, the way she had
changed. The way Cagan's trust and passion had changed
her.

She'd expected to walk up to an inhabited cabin any minute and be greeted by half a dozen people offering their as-
sistance. Now that confidence was fading as fast as the day.

"Look," Cagan said, grabbing her arm and pointing
ahead of them.

Merissa stopped and stared into the gathering darkness.
The battered cabin he'd spotted was shrouded by fog and
moss-draped cypress trees, more ghostlike than real. For a
second, she feared it was a mirage and blinked. She studied
its dilapidated shape, thankful that it wasn't disappearing.

"Not quite the luxury hotel I'd hoped for, but it sure
looks good to me," Cagan said. "Do you think they'd like
to have company for the night?"

"If they buy our story."

"Two city slickers out for a self-guided swamp tour. We
left the boat behind when we hit a bayou clogged with water hyacinths. Next thing we knew, we were lost." Cagan
repeated the story they had agreed on.

"Let me do the talking," Merissa said.

Cagan arched an eyebrow.

"Your male ego will recover," she assured him. "And
we'll get a warmer welcome if I throw in a few Cajun ex-
pressions. These people take care of their own."

"You got it," Cagan said, stepping over a fallen tree limb and holding the low-hanging branch of a willow back so she could pass. Their shoulders brushed, and she trembled from the unexpected contact.

They hadn't spoken yet of what had happened between them, but their whole relationship had been transformed. They were no longer enemies bound by the dangers of the environment. They were lovers, bound by trust and emotion. And by purpose.

She ducked under the tree and hurried toward the cabin, her apprehension mounting with every yard gained. The place was in shambles, one side leaning to the right, and several windows boarded up.

"It looks like the story we concocted won't get told tonight," Cagan said, agitation edging his voice as he stopped at the foot of the rickety steps. "No one could possibly live here."

"Not anymore," Merissa agreed. "But they still may use it for fishing and hunting. And they may have left goodies," she added, faking a confidence she didn't feel. "A dry bed and some water would be good enough for me."

The steps creaked under her feet, and something rustled the leaves beneath the house. For a split second, her breath caught and held. Cagan took her arm and led her to the porch. Breathing deeply, she forced her nerves to a state of semicalm. The swamp was alive with sound and movement, and she couldn't start panicking at every one.

Cagan banged on the door and waited. It was a wasted effort. Stepping over a gaping hole where the porch boards had rotted away, Merissa peered through a narrow window. Gray shadows and the dark outlines of a couple of chairs and a table were all she could make out.

"Looks empty," she said, "but dry. Try the door."

Cagan twisted the doorknob and pushed. "The place isn't even locked," he said as the door swung open.

"They usually aren't. Anyone wanting inside could break in easily enough. Besides, most of the owners would be glad to share with you anyway if you were in trouble, so why bother with locks?"

Cagan stepped inside, using his flashlight to shoot a beam of light across the floors and over the walls. Merissa scooted closer to him as several cockroaches and unidentifiable multilegged bugs scattered to the four corners. Taking a step backward, she gasped for fresh air. The house reeked of mildew and decay and the stench of dead fish.

"Sportsman's paradise," she said, holding her nose.

"Good. Maybe the fishermen left a few of those goodies you talked about." Focusing the light on a gas lantern in the corner, Cagan crossed the room and picked up a book of matches from the table. He scraped one of the matches across the sandpaper strip and touched the wick. New shadows emerged as a dim circle of light spread over the room.

The floors were unfinished cypress, marred from layers of tracked mud and the battering of heavy boots. There was a wooden table in the corner, stacked high with yellowed copies of fishing and hunting magazines, a makeshift ashtray fashioned from a cypress knee and a slightly rusted hunting knife.

Merissa walked from the table to the far side of the room. "Here's your comfortable bed," she said, easing down to sit on the side of a lumpy bed with a creaky metal headboard. Pushing back the edge of a faded quilt, she stared at a sagging mattress and its various patterns of stains. "I hope clean wasn't one of your requirements."

"Just so there are no snakes or alligators lurking under the springs, I'll be happy."

She bent over and looked. "No, just a couple of oars. Oh, and a wicked-looking spider."

Cagan turned and walked through an opening where a door probably used to be. Merissa followed him into a square room about eight by eight. There was a butane range and a sink on one wall. She twisted the faucet and a brownish liquid sputtered out. Her stomach lurched sickeningly, and she felt the disappointment down to her toes.

"It's a good thing we saved a little drinking water," Cagan said, coming behind her to turn off the tap. "That looks like day-old coffee." He sniffed disgustedly. "And smells a lot worse."

Afraid to look, but knowing she had to, Merissa swung open all the cabinet doors, leaving them ajar so that Cagan could share the sight of her meager findings. A box of salt with half a label missing, a couple of jars of spicy seasonings, a big box of crab boil and a can of vegetable soup.

"Mmm, mmm good," Cagan said, mimicking a familiar commercial. "What's this stuff?" He held a package of the crab boil in his hand and sniffed it. "It looks weird, but it smells good." Without waiting for an answer, he continued his search, yanking open a bottom cabinet and pulling out a cast iron skillet and a huge pot.

"Okay. It looks like decision time." Merissa took the can of soup from the shelf and placed it on the table. "Is it soup for dinner or soup for breakfast?"

Cagan walked up behind her and circled her waist with his strong arms. "It's not so bad," he said, nuzzling his mouth in her hair. "We have a dry bed, enough food for a couple of meals, half a bottle of water and..." He twirled her around to face him. "And we have each other."

"You're right. I shouldn't complain. I'm probably safer and more comfortable here than I would be back in Baton Rouge right now."

Cagan felt the cold fingers of truth clutch and wring his heart. He could make promises of safety and happily-ever-after until the swamp dried up, but this time he couldn't necessarily deliver. He knew that better that anyone.

Keeping his arm about her slender waist, he led her to one of the two straight-backed chairs near the table. He held one for her and then straddled the other, wrapping his long legs around the back. "I know how hard all of this is for you, Merissa."

"I don't know what I'm up against. That's what makes this so difficult. I thought I knew Jeff pretty well, but now it seems I didn't know him at all. What could he possibly have taken that—"

A scraping noise interrupted her question. Cagan's hand flew to the innocent looking pack about his waist, his finger clutching the zipper. The noise started again. Fingers flying, he grabbed the silver pistol from the bag.

"Go to the other room," he whispered, gripping the knob of the back door.

Stepping out of firing line, Cagan swung the door open. All was quiet. Warily, he walked out onto the remains of a back porch. Something stirred at his feet. Cagan jumped back, stumbling over a knee-high cardboard packing box. Grabbing the door for support, he righted himself and stared at the intruder.

Damn. He'd almost broken his neck over a trapped raccoon. "Here's our visitor, Merissa," he called, sticking his head through the back door. "Come take a look."

She ran outside, then stopped, dropping to her knees on the rough wood. "Poor baby, you're in trouble, too," she crooned, leaning over to get a closer look.

Frantic, the raccoon rolled onto his back, his feet flying, tangling him even more into the fishing net that bound him. Cagan watched while Merissa worked to free him, all the time softly reassuring the frightened animal as if it was someone she had known all her life.

Cagan tried to help with the rescue, but his larger fingers were no match for her slender ones. Not to mention the fact that he had no fingernails at all. In minutes, she had the animal freed. The frightened raccoon scooted away, jumping over the edge of the porch and heading for the cover of a thick bush.

"Not even a thank-you," Merissa said, standing up and watching as he disappeared.

"But he did us a favor." Merissa turned as Cagan pointed to the box he had tripped over. Reaching down, he pulled out the five-gallon bottle of Kentwood water that had almost sent him tumbling. "Drinking water. Bottled and capped."

"Wet and clean," she added, licking her lips and twirling like a schoolgirl. She completed a pirouette and then bent low to hug the bottle. "Tonight we drink."

"And after that, you can drool over me the way you're doing that bottle."

"I plan to do a lot more than drool over the water," she teased.

"And I plan to satisfy a lot more than your thirst."

Cagan watched Merissa's face turn from bronze to pink. For all her sensual beauty, it was her innocence that touched him the most. So totally feminine, she made him feel that much more a man. Picking up the bottle, he started through the door before he forgot just how thirsty she must be. Before he started something he couldn't stop.

"Wait, look at this," she said, picking up the net that had snared the raccoon. Holding it as high as her hands would reach, she let the snarled webbing unfurl. "There's a crawfish caught in the net. That's what attracted the raccoon."

"Fish bait," Cagan said. "Only this time it almost caught a raccoon."

"Fish bait? You wound my Louisiana spirit. This mudbug, my friend, is some of the best eating you will ever experience."

"That dried-up specimen? You go ahead. I'll pass."

"Not this one. Crawfish have to be alive when you drop them into boiling water. This one's dead, but he hasn't been dead for more than a few days, if that long."

"So we just missed rescue."

"That's the bad news."

"Dare I ask what the good news is?"

"If someone caught crawfish here in the past few days, there must be more nearby. Grab that net and follow me."

Cagan watched Merissa take off down the back steps and into a cluster of trees. "I really like energy bars myself. Besides, don't you think we've had enough exercise for one day?" he yelled after her. She ignored him. No surprise.

By the time Cagan caught up with her, she was standing near a tree, her foot resting on a pirogue that had been turned over and pushed beneath the edge of a sheltering bush.

"How in the devil did you find that?"

"Pure talent, just like you used to track me. I thought there might be a boat around since the cabin is still used by fishermen. It's not unusual for people who live or play around here to have several pirogues. Water's the only mode of transportation in these parts."

"Unless you do it our way. By foot."

"Not anymore," she said, turning the boat over and running her hand along the splintered edge. "We're back in business."

"So now all we need is a bayou. I guess you can provide that, too."

"If you'll be a little quieter," she warned, putting a finger to his lips. "Listen."

He did. An owl hooted from the top of a tree. The grass rustled. Tree frogs continued their chorus. "I don't hear anything unusual."

"You will. Not unusual, but well, just wait, you'll see."

She stood statue still, her head held high, her features angelic in the misty gray of twilight. Cagan stared at the curve of her neck, the soft lines of her shoulders, the swell of her breasts. His body hardened.

"Did you the hear that splash?"

He shook his head, not trusting his voice to hide the desire that had suddenly overtaken his body.

"Then you'll never be a bayou hunter."

A bayou hunter. The terms and all its connotations ran roughshod across his brain as he followed Merissa toward the sound of the splash and the bayou. He'd come into the bayou country a little over twenty-four hours ago to hunt for a woman with a fifteen-thousand-dollar bounty on her head. Now he had her, and his problems were just beginning.

"Okay, partner," she called. "Take your end of the net. We're going to sweep it through the water and catch our dinner."

"I can hardly wait," he lied.

They fished for the odd-looking creatures, dipping the net into the water again and again. After each catch, Merissa dropped the crawfish onto a giant lily pad she'd pulled from the edge of the bayou.

Cagan began to relax, soothed by the exotic beauty surrounding him, intrigued by Merissa's laughter. If anyone had ever told him he could be lost in a dangerous swamp and having fun, he would have sworn they were crazy.

He would have been wrong.

They dipped the net again, and Merissa lifted her end of the net high in the air, marveling at the ring of crawfish wiggling in the middle of it. Her sensual body was silhouetted against the gathering dusk and the steamy fog that circled up from the water. Cagan stared without speaking, desire rising inside him like a suffocating heat, forcing his mind to accept what his heart had known for days.

He wanted Merissa as he'd never wanted any other woman. Maybe even loved her. But in the end, it wouldn't matter. He'd do what he had to do. No matter what it cost him.

No matter what it cost *her.*

"One more sweep, Cagan. Then we should have enough for dinner. Heave-ho," she called, her laughter riding the humid air.

They swept the water again, pulling in at least a dozen wiggling crawfish, a few minnows and a bouncing crappie. Merissa reached into the net and retrieved the crawfish, then tossed the net so that the rest of the catch could fall to freedom. He went over to help her gather the rest of the crawfish into the net for carrying.

"Food, water, a dry place to sleep. And you. I wish I could stay for here forever, Cagan."

"You'd get tired of it. You'd miss your work."

"What work? I no longer have a job."

She shuddered, and he took her in his arms. He couldn't bear to see her confused and afraid, not after knowing what she was like laughing and free.

"What's next, Cagan? After we eat."

"When it's completely dark, when there's no risk of being seen by the helicopter hunters, we'll set out again. We'll take the boat and follow the bayou, hopefully back to the Atchafalaya River and our cars."

"Traveling at night is dangerous, Cagan. There are snakes and alligators, and I don't know these waters. We might wind up deeper in the swamp."

"It's a chance we'll have to take."

"And if we fail, if the helicopter hunters find us first?"

"They won't." Cagan used one hand to pick up the net filled with crawfish. He used the other to wrap around Merissa's waist. "Now about that mudbug dinner."

"You're going to love them," she said, but the lilt had gone out of her voice.

CAGAN SAT ON THE back porch of the cabin, watching darkness descend. A red-eared turtle crossed the area of stunted grass in front of him, taking his time and minding his own business. A staccato cry sounded from overhead as one of the many nocturnal birds began its night of prowling, and a small swamp rabbit scurried by the turtle and disappeared into a hole at the base of a willow tree.

But the uniqueness of the swamp was lost on Cagan. The unraveling mystery at his fingertips was too consuming. He'd been working on this case ever since he'd arrived in Baton Rouge over four months ago now, and the only fact he was sure of was that Bracer was in the laundry business. Two days ago, Cagan had been sure Gaffner was in on the operation with him. Now it was hard to be certain of anything.

But illegal campaign funds, payoffs from gambling establishments, whatever you wanted to call Bracer's huge supply of ready cash, it was being washed and returned to his pockets as clean profits.

At least some of it was. The rest was being spread around banks in the Cayman Islands to sit there until he needed it. Bracer operated in manure and came up smelling like a rose.

Too bad Jeff hadn't stayed out of it. It would have saved him his life. Now Cagan had to find out what was in the locker that was worth killing for. And he had to get his hands on it before Bracer did.

The aroma of spices and fish drifted to his nose, and Cagan shifted so that his back rested against the shaky railing. From this position, he could look through the dingy screen and into the kitchen. Merissa was standing over the butane burner, stirring a steamy pot of boiling crawfish, her blond hair finger combed now, but still falling semiwild around her shoulders. As always, his heart constricted at the sight of her.

Making love to her this afternoon had not begun to satisfy the hunger that raged inside him. She was not a murderer. He'd stake his life on that. In fact, he had. The only thing he wasn't sure of was her involvement, if any, in the money laundering.

Being with her like this, it was easy to convince himself she was totally innocent. But the people he had to answer to would only rely on facts. That's why he had to have them, the sooner the better, while he could still help her. Before her stalkers silenced her forever.

A ball of lead the size of Texas settled in his gut. He wouldn't let that happen, not while there was breath left in his body. He took his gun out of his pack and he cradled the hard steel in his palm, his expression hardening. He hoped he didn't have to use it, but he would if he had to. He'd done it too many times before to become squeamish now.

Chapter Eleven

Merissa watched Cagan pick up a boiled crawfish and dangle it headfirst toward the table.

"What am I supposed to do with this thing?"

"Pinch the tails and suck the heads. Like this." She pinched off a curved tail and slipped her thumbs beneath the shell, peeling it off in one piece. With a slow, deliberate motion, she dropped the tail into her mouth, chewing and savoring the flavor. "Absolutely divine."

"I'm glad it's the tails you expect me to eat. I was afraid it was that head you were going to down, feelers and all."

"No, you only suck the juices out of the head." Holding the crawfish head between her thumb and forefinger, she placed the neck end into her mouth and sucked the spicy juices. A drop gathered on her lips and she used her tongue to catch it.

"I could have done that for you," Cagan teased. His message was light, but his voice was husky and warm.

"I bet you could. But then we might forget to eat, and I'm famished."

"Me, too, but I'm still not convinced this fish bait is edible."

"You will be in a minute." Merissa quickly peeled the tail from another crawfish. "Open up," she instructed, leaning over and placing it in his mouth. His lips wrapped around the tail and part of her fingers. A warm tingle slithered through her, and even as hungry as she was, it was difficult to pull her fingers away.

"Hey, not bad," Cagan said, licking his lips. "Spicy as hell, but not bad." He reached for his glass of water.

"The crawfish by themselves are rather bland. It's the salt and spices that bring out the flavor."

Cagan grabbed another crawfish, this time awkwardly peeling it himself. "You mean you used that package of weird-looking stuff that was in the mesh bag?" he asked, swallowing the tail and reaching for the head.

"Right." Merissa's stomach growled, noisily demanding more now that she had offered the first bite of temptation. She peeled and ate another half-dozen crawfish before she stopped long enough to continue the conversation. "Too bad we don't have the extras. At home I would have added new potatoes, corn on the cob, onions, garlic cloves and some smoked sausage to the pot."

Cagan picked up speed, his fingers quickly learning the art of separating the crustaceans from the shell. "You can invite me over for dinner anytime. Not that I'm as excited as you are about these mini lobsters yet, but they're starting to grow on me. And I have to admit, they're better than the stale energy bars."

"Your compliments overwhelm me." At least they gave her food for thought. Cooking dinner for Cagan Hall, not out of necessity like tonight, but for pure pleasure. The idea was full of intriguing possibilities. But it wasn't likely to happen. Not with her life going steadily downhill.

Talk settled into silence as manners gave way to hunger. Merissa's fingers flew as she stripped the shells from the tails and ate so fast she barely tasted them. And new as Cagan was at the pinch, peel and suck routine, his pile of heads and shells grew almost as fast as hers.

When she was sure she couldn't manage another bite, she poured a tall glass of water and drank it slowly, like fine wine. Never again would she take the satisfying taste of water for granted. Never again would she take the term "dying of thirst" lightly.

"Don't stop eating now," Cagan urged. "There's plenty more."

"I'm so full I could burst. And it feels wonderful," she added, stretching her legs in front of her and pouring yet another glass of water.

"Laissez les bons temps rouler."

"So, you have picked up a little Cajun since you've been in Louisiana. Although being stranded in a swamp isn't everybody's idea of letting the good times roll."

"That's because they haven't been here with you."

Desire gleamed in Cagan's eyes and dripped from his words, suffusing Merissa with an inner warmth. This afternoon, she'd reveled in the full power of his passion. The experience had touched her in ways she would never forget, but it hadn't really changed anything.

It couldn't, until this whole mess was cleared up and the real killers were behind bars. Only then would she and Cagan be free to explore fully the emotions that crackled like lightning every time they were together. Only then could they discover if the fire that melded them together was more powerful than the issues that tore them apart.

Her grandfather would have approved of Cagan, would have admired his make-my-own-rules attitude. Like bayou justice, he would have said. Take care of your own business without interference from outsiders. But in Merissa's eyes, the end did not necessarily justify the means.

"How many people have you killed, Cagan?" She asked the question and then cringed inside, not wanting to hear the answer.

"A few."

"That must have been difficult, taking a life."

"I did what I had to."

Ice water flowed through her veins, and she pulled her hand away from his. "I suspect you know a lot more about the recent murders than you admit, Cagan."

He didn't answer, and she looked into his eyes. They were bottomless depths, dark and mysterious. But she wasn't afraid of him. She couldn't fear a man who burned with passion the way he had today and yet touched her so tenderly she ached for the moment of climax never to end.

"Tell me what I'm up against, Cagan. I can take it."

"I know." He stroked her neck with his thumbs, running them up and down her flesh. "You've got far more courage than most men twice your size."

"Only because I've had to. But I'm tired of fighting for something I can't understand. What was Jeff mixed up with that cost him his life?"

Cagan hesitated, letting silence wedge between them. When he finally answered, his voice was hard and distant. "He was blackmailing launderers. He had cut in on a million-dollar deal. And he was apparently in pretty deep."

A look of incredulity crossed Merissa's face. "Who has that kind of money?"

"James Bracer."

"Senator Bracer?" Merissa repeated in astonishment. "This is too ludicrous, Cagan. Bracer's been involved in Louisiana politics for years," she added, sure Cagan was wrong. "He's one of the most influential men in the state senate."

"Need I say more?"

"Yes. A lot more. But stick to the facts, Cagan, if you have any."

"How much do you know about Gaffner's involvement in Mardi Gras Lights?" he asked, knowing that he was about to break one of the few rules he lived by.

"I know that when gambling was approved in Louisiana, Gaffner put up the lion's share of the money to buy the riverboat casino," she answered. "I don't think it was doing as well as he expected, though. Rumor had it he might lose his investment."

"Rumor had it at least half-right. He borrowed the money using LPI as collateral. At one point, he had been on the verge of losing both businesses to the lending institution that had backed him. The main stockholder for the loan company is none other than his good friend, Senator Bracer. That's why Gaffner didn't hesitate to become a partner in Bracer's scheme."

Merissa pushed away from the table and walked to the back door, staring out into the darkness. "How would you know this, Cagan? You're just a security guard, a cop who lost his job in New York and moved to Baton Rouge on a whim. Do you really expect me to believe Bracer and Gaffner took you into their confidence?"

"No, they didn't tell me anything, at least nothing truthful. But I am asking you to believe me." He walked up behind her and circled her with his arms, locking his hands beneath the swell of her breasts. "I'm asking you to do the same thing you asked of me. Believe me without proof. And trust me." He cuddled her back against his chest. "I can't tell you more, not yet, but I can tell you that Bracer has enough at stake to make murder a real possibility. Especially if blackmail was involved. I'm hoping your bus-depot locker holds some important clues."

"Why would Bracer need LPI for his operation?"

"That's one of the things I plan to find out."

Merissa shook her head slowly. "Murder, corruption, blackmail. All from men who already had more than most. It doesn't add up."

"It never does." Cagan touched her earlobe with his lips. "Let it go for now, Merissa. In a couple of hours, we'll have to start out again. In the meantime, we need rest." He let go of her waist and took her hand. "Lie down beside me," he said, leading her to the ramshackle bed, "and let me hold you close. For a few minutes, we can forget the craziness, at least put it on hold."

He dropped to the lumpy mattress, pulling her down beside him. She leaned into him and touched her lips to his. But the comfort he'd promised didn't come.

MOONLIGHT DAPPLED the water, riding the ripples like fireflies as Cagan and Merissa climbed into the small pirogue. Merissa settled in the front of the boat as Cagan used one of the oars they'd found under the bed to push the boat away from the muddy bank.

"We're off," he said, "homeward bound."

"We hope. Like I told you before, this bayou may be a quick trip to nowhere."

"Quick I like. But not to nowhere. According to my compass, we're going west-northwest," he said, taking a seat behind Merissa.

"That's the general direction we need to follow. Hopefully, this bayou will feed into the Atchafalaya River or into another bayou that does." Merissa broke the water's surface with her oar, fitting her hand into the groove that had been worn into the wood by the real owner.

"We're lucky the moon's so bright. It would be pitch-black out here without it." His words hung in the silence that followed. Lost in her thoughts, Merissa rowed steadily, praying for the best.

A loud splash sounded to their left, and Merissa and Cagan turned in unison. An adult alligator, seven feet or more in length, had crawled from the bank and slid into the water. His rough snout floated just about the water's surface as he swam along beside them.

"I hope he's coming along for the company and not for dinner," Cagan commented.

"Relax. I'm sure you've faced a lot more dangerous enemies on the streets of New York."

"Hoods don't frighten me. Large, sharp teeth and strong jaws do."

"How do you feel about poisonous fangs?" she asked, using her oar as a pointer to show him a snake swimming in front of them. The water moccasin was as big around as her leg and every bit as long.

"Cripes!" He shuddered. "And to think you had me wading and dipping my hands into that water to net those crawfish. I must have been crazy."

They kept on rowing, passing from a relatively clear area to a spot where huge moss-draped cypress trees made a spooky ceiling over the water. Leaves rustled above them, and birds called to each other warning of humans invading their world.

"It's strange that you would choose to come here when you were afraid," Cagan finally said. "I mean, if you were looking for safety and solace, it seems other places would have been more inviting."

A breeze stirred, whispering through Merissa's hair, feathering her skin with a surprising coolness. She breathed deeply and caught the fragrance of rich earth and sweet blossoms. Memories of summers past washed over her in tantalizing keenness.

"Some of my happiest memories were made here," she said, trying to put her feelings into words. "It's where I learned about life, important things like who and what I am."

"Untamed beauty. Now that I think about it, the bayou country suits you well."

"You mean it marks me as an oddity. It always has. When I went back to the city every fall, I never quite fitted in with the rest of my school friends."

"I'd never think of you as an oddity." His gaze traveled the length of her body. "Exotic, sensual, intelligent. All of those, but never an oddity."

Merissa felt the color rising to her cheeks. A word, a touch, that's all it took from Cagan to awaken longings she'd thought she didn't possess.

"Is the bayou country the reason you moved back to Baton Rouge?" he questioned, his oar smoothly moving through the still water.

"No. That's a long story."

"We have all night."

He was right, but that part of the past seemed so distant, she had to search her mind to remember the details. Even then, she wasn't sure she wanted to talk about it. But Cagan waited silently for her response. "I was engaged," she began, searching her heart as well as her mind for what actually prompted the broken engagement. "It didn't work out. So when I ran into Jeff at a convention in Dallas and he raved about LPI, I decided to take his advice and fly in for an interview."

"You must have left a heartbroken man behind."

"He got over me quickly enough. He's married to someone else now."

"And how about you? Are you over him?" Cagan's tone told her this was not a casual question.

"A week ago, I would have told you I didn't know. Now I realize there was never anything to get over. We were comfortable together, but there was never any magic. Not like..." Her voice trailed off.

"Not like there is between us?" he finished. His words sparked the electricity that always crackled in the air between them, their unspoken desires never dissipating. "You may as well admit it," he said when she didn't respond to his question. "I can't keep my eyes or hands off you. And you can't deny having the same problem. This afternoon was no accident." His observations were sensually teasing, but true.

"You're awfully sure of yourself."

"I just know when I'm right."

Conversation stopped abruptly and so did the boat.

"Now what? Just when things were starting to move along nicely."

"We're stuck," she said, peering over the side of the boat into the watery darkness.

Cagan leaned over the edge, working his oar under the boat, probing until he hit something solid. "We're jammed between something. Feels like a couple of cypress knees." Balancing precariously, he shoved and prodded until the boat nudged free.

"Good work. You might learn to maneuver this bayou after all."

"Not unless I learn it tonight. Once I get out of this swamp, I'm not planning to give it another crack at me."

They were moving upstream again, but their relief was short-lived. The bayou narrowed, and the vegetation grew thicker. Isolated clumps of blooming water hyacinths increased in number and size until the bayou became choked with them. They dug their oars deeper into the water, but the knot of plants caught and entangled the boat.

"Looks like we're back to walking," Cagan said, aggravation straining his composure. "And there go our chances of getting out of here by sunup."

"Not necessarily. We can carry the boat and walk along the bayou's edge. With luck, the water will clear upstream, and we can launch the boat again."

"Then let's go for it."

Burying their oars in the muddy bottom of the shallow bayou, they forced the pirogue to the bank. Cagan stepped over the side of the boat and sank ankle deep in the slimy bog.

"Give me your hand, Merissa, and take it easy. It's going to be a long, wet night."

THE SUN PEEKED OVER the horizon, casting its first glow of gold over the cloudless sky. Shadows that had seemed threatening during the night gave way to scenic beauty that in other circumstances would have left Merissa gasping in awe.

She stretched and bit back a groan as pain shot through her back and neck. Last night's adventure had left her with aches in places she didn't even know she had. But she wasn't complaining. Not when they were back in the Atchafalaya River, with nothing worse than a few scratches and sore muscles. Thankfully her arm wound had not become infected.

"Civilization," Cagan said, pointing to a pile of trash left along the bank. A paper bag poked out of a web of exposed cypress roots and a couple of foam cups bobbed in the water.

"The marina isn't much farther," she said, reaching for the plastic bottle they had refilled with fresh water. She unscrewed the top and took a long sip. "Do you think our cars will still be where we left them?"

"Not likely, at least not mine. But a welcoming party might be."

Never think for a moment the worst is over. New surprises were always around the next bend. "Do you think the police have set up camp to wait for my return?"

"It's not the police I'm worried about, although I'd just as soon avoid them, too. But you can bet Bracer's hired goons are looking for you, ready to finish what the hit man in the power boat failed to do."

Apprehension struggled with the waves of nausea that flooded her stomach. "So how are we going to get out of here?"

Cagan reached into his pocket and pulled out a small bird-dog device. "I didn't bother retrieving the mate to this thing from your car the other night. If your marina friend moved your car far enough out of sight, it might still be there. If we're lucky, we can drive it away without a soul seeing us."

"And what if they do see us?"

Cagan grimaced and flexed his fingers. "Then it might get a little ugly."

"Ugly. Cop-style, I guess. Guns, threats, whatever it takes?"

"Good work, Merissa. Now you're starting to think like a lawman."

"Heaven help me."

The beeping was soft, but Merissa turned as if she'd been shot.

"Looks like we have transportation nearby," Cagan said. "Now the fun starts." They rowed the next half hour in near silence. Finally, Cagan pointed to a spot on the bank where a swamp willow hung low over the water. "That looks like as good a docking spot as any."

Minutes later, the boat was out of sight, tucked away under a cluster of thick bushes. Merissa retrieved the bottle of water and stuffed it into Cagan's bag. The sun and the temperature were climbing steadily, and she had learned first-hand about the discomforts of real thirst.

Cagan took off through the bog. The beeper was in his pocket now, almost silenced through the fabric of his jeans, but obviously still loud enough to guide his footsteps. Merissa followed a few steps behind. Something irritated her right foot, and she turned her heel, limping slightly to ease the pain.

Then it might get a little ugly. Cagan's words echoed through her mind. If Bracer's men had found the car and were there waiting for them... She pushed the thought away.

She tramped on, first to the left, then to the right, two steps forward and one step back, following Cagan through thick underbrush. And the pain in her foot had switched from annoying to downright brutal. Either something was in her sock, or the damp boots had rubbed a blister on the sole of her foot. She stopped and leaned against a tree.

Cagan walked on a few steps and she let him go. She'd catch up. Stopping abruptly, he turned and stared at her. Strength and determination drew his muscles into definitive lines and hardened the jut of his chin. Suddenly, she felt a lot safer. Even Bracer's hired guns would be no match for him.

Only his clothes indicated the ordeal they had just gone through. A jagged rip extended from his left shoulder down to the hem of his T-shirt, and mud streaked his clothes.

"Are you okay?" he asked.

"There's something in my shoe," she said, bending to untie the leather boot. "You go ahead. I'll shake it out and catch up."

"No, we need to stay close together in case there's a sudden change in plans." He came back for her. Stooping, he eased the shoe from her foot and slipped his hand inside it.

"Nothing here," he said. He dropped the shoe to the ground and tugged off her sock. "Here's the villain." He rolled a tiny fragment of shell between his fingertips and held it up for her inspection. "Little, but sharp as glass."

"Thanks." Quickly, she pulled on her sock and boot.

Cagan settled her foot on his leg and tied the laces into a tight bow. "Just hang in there for a little longer. It's almost over." He took her hand and led her along, keeping her on a short rein. He took the beeper from his pocket, then flicked a switch and muted the sound. "It's close, Merissa. I want you to wait here, behind this tree. Don't make a sound, and don't try to follow me, no matter what you hear. If it's safe, I'll come back for you."

Merissa waited, but not silently. Her heart pounded against her chest, noisier than a beating drum. The seconds dragged into minutes, and her imagination wrested itself from her control. She could see Cagan lying in a pool of his own blood, the same way she'd found Jeff. The same way she'd found Gaffner.

Shudders shook her body, and she wrapped her arms around the tree for support. Not Cagan, please don't let it happen to Cagan. The prayer careened about her mind and flooded her senses.

Tears burned in the corners of her eyes, and she squeezed them back. She had to stay in control. And she had to believe Cagan was safe.

Footsteps rustled in the grass, and her breath caught in her lungs and pushed against her chest. But it was Cagan who stepped from behind the cluster of trees and made his way through the undergrowth.

"All's clear," he whispered, reaching out and wrapping a strong arm around her trembling body. "Let's get out of here."

MERISSA SIPPED FROM the cup of hot coffee Cagan had placed in her hand and waited while he finished showering. They had picked up breakfast at a drive-through and then he'd insisted she come with him to his apartment. It would be safer there, he'd explained, while he made arrangements for the trip to New Orleans and to the downtown bus depot.

He'd spent the first few minutes after they'd arrived speaking in hushed tones on the phone in his bedroom. Just checking on their status, he'd told her. The police wanted her for questioning, but a warrant had not been issued for her arrest as yet. They expected to issue one at any time, though. That meant Cagan and Merissa would have to work quickly.

Her arrest. The words should be sending her into orbit, but a dull dread numbed her senses. Deadly problems had become too commonplace to register. Holding her hands out in front of her, she focused on the mundane. Besides her bullet wound, her hands and arms were scratched, her fingernails cracked and broken. Two days in the Atchafalaya Basin and she looked like she'd been trekking in the Amazon.

The bedroom door opened and Cagan stepped out. The shirt he wore was cotton, a muted design in shades of green, open at the neck. It topped a pair of clean but faded jeans that hugged his buttocks and skimmed brown loafers. From bedraggled to devastating, the change was impressive.

He stepped toward her, and the clean smell of soap and shampoo made her suddenly aware of her own condition. "I need a shower, Cagan. And something to wear."

"I left one of my robes on the bed, and there are clean towels and washcloths on the rack behind the bathroom door. The shampoo is on the shower rack."

"I can't run around in your robe forever, Cagan. Sooner or later, I have to go home and get clothes. I prefer sooner."

"No." His tone was emphatic. "You can't go back to your house, and you can't go anywhere without me. I have to leave for a few minutes to take care of some business. I'll pick up some clothes while I'm out." He wrapped his arms around her. "Don't answer the phone while I'm gone, Merissa, and don't open the door under any circumstances. Do you understand?"

"Of course I understand, but—"

"No buts." He reached into his pocket and took out a folded piece of paper. If you need me, call this number. It's to my cellular phone. I'll answer immediately."

She took the paper from his hand and unfolded it, pressing out the crease with her finger.

"Remember, don't answer the phone, don't open the door, and if you need me for anything—"

"I'll call you at this number."

He took her in his arms again, holding her close, his mouth resting at the tip of her ear. "I'll be back before you even have time to miss me, sooner if you call."

He kissed her lightly on the lips and then headed out the front door at a near run. Merissa double-checked the locks, then stepped out of her clothes as she headed for the bathroom.

She climbed into the shower and turned the water on full blast and as hot as she could stand it. Cupping her hand, she filled it with liquid soap and rubbed it onto her skin, coating her arms, legs and stomach with thick layers of frothy foam.

Throwing back her head, she let the tingling spray rush through her hair, saturating it completely before she lavished it with shampoo. She stood under the shower, rinsing and reveling in the feel of cleanness until the hot water began to cool. Then, grabbing a towel, she stepped onto the tiles and padded into the bedroom.

More relaxed than she'd been in days, Merissa toweled her long strands of hair until the dampness had almost disappeared. The towel tied around her body loosened with her activity and slipped to the floor. Stepping from it, she pulled on the fluffy robe Cagan had left for her. The smell of him was in it, masculine and fresh, and for a moment she almost forgot the nightmare she was living in.

The moment was short-lived. The piercing ring of the doorbell hit like a dagger to the heart. She waited silently. It didn't ring again. She peeked out of the bedroom, letting her gaze linger on the front door. It was then she heard the sound of a key turn in the lock and saw the knob turn and the door ease open.

The head that poked through belonged to James Bracer.

Chapter Twelve

Face-to-face, Merissa stared at the man she'd only seen before on television and in newspaper photos. Clutching the front of her robe, she pulled it tighter, fighting the dread that rocked her insides. "Are you looking for Cagan?" she asked, her voice strained and shaky.

"No, I'm looking for you." He stepped inside, closing the door behind him.

"How did you know I was here?" She swallowed the lump that caught in her throat, but another took its place.

"Because I get what I pay for."

"You haven't paid for me."

His gaze walked across her from top to bottom. She shuddered as if he'd touched her with filthy hands.

"No? Then why do you think our honorable ex-cop followed you through the swamp? Surely not for justice." Bracer chuckled at his own joke, a shallow, heartless laugh. "I offered him fifteen thousand for your return. He delivered just like he said he would. I'm beginning to like the man."

Fear of betrayal clutched Merissa's heart. "You're lying," she said. He had to be. She'd known all along Cagan wasn't telling the full truth, but not this. "Cagan will be back any minute," she threatened, "and when he gets here, he'll make you eat your words." Her voice broke, and her challenge turned futile.

"Don't worry about Hall," he said, walking over to stand beside her. "It's yourself you need to worry about now."

"Why, because you plan to kill me like you did Jeff Madison and Marshall Gaffner?"

"Of course not. I'm a lot of things, but I'm not a killer. I don't have to be. There are people like Cagan who will do that for me for pocket change."

Pocket change. Fifteen thousand to find her and deliver her to Bracer. Another few thousand to put Jeff's fillet knife through his heart, and still more to take care of Gaffner. Chills shook her body. She willed them to stop. It couldn't be true. Cagan had been so loving, so thoughtful...so *thorough.* He'd found her and delivered her to Bracer.

"Where's the money, Merissa?" Bracer's voice was cold, his eyes calculating.

"I have no idea what you're talking about."

He grabbed her forearm, squeezing so tightly she bit back a cry of pain. "You and Jeff were in on the deal together. Everyone knows that. If the truth were told, it was probably you who caused his death, you and your Goody Two-shoes philosophy. Too bad. He would have done well if he'd just kept dancing with the one who brought him to the party. But no, he had to stick his nose where it didn't belong. Even after he got yanked out of marketing."

Confusion played havoc with Merissa's mind. Nothing Bracer was saying made sense unless... Could the money Bracer was looking for be hidden away in a storage locker in New Orleans? She'd have to play along with him, keep him talking, if she was to find any answers. Or even maybe to get out of this alive.

"Is that why you sent the hit men after me, Bracer? To coax me into telling you where the money is? Or were they an extra precaution just in case Cagan failed?"

"So you do know something." One hand still gripped her arm; with the other he caressed her neck. His fingers threatened, moving in tiny circles around her jugular vein. "Start talking," he ordered, "while you still can. Where is the money?"

She met his gaze, her head high and steady, the fire inside her directed at him. Her life depended on her ability to play the role fate had assigned her. "You won't kill me, because if you do, you'll never get the money you were trying to launder. So, Senator, it looks like you'll have to deal with me on my terms."

"I make deals, not take them." He dropped his hand from her neck, letting his fingers slide down her arm. His touch was loathsome, clawing and foul. She held her breath, fighting back the nausea that churned in her stomach.

"Then I guess you'll have to kill me. I'm not turning over anything to you until we deal." She was bluffing, playing out of her league. Her terms. She didn't have any terms, didn't even know for certain she had access to the money he was talking about.

She had a key. Nothing more. But handing the key over to Bracer now would be the same as signing her own death warrant.

"Let's hear your deal." He stepped closer.

"I give you what Jeff stole from you. You call off the police."

"I have no control over the police."

"Don't hand me that, Senator. You have a hand in everything that goes on in the southern part of the state. Besides, we both know I wasn't responsible for the murders. You set me up, and you can clear me." She was acting out a role as if her life depended on it. Which it did. She only hoped she could carry it off.

Bracer prowled the room, stepping over the shirt she'd let drop to the floor and kicking her jeans out of the way. His gaze stopped on the silk panties that fell from inside the jeans as they took flight, and her stomach turned.

"Is that all you want?" he asked, stopping and turning to face her.

"No, I want a hundred thousand dollars. You're paying fifteen thousand to have me delivered into your hands. You should be willing to pay a hundred thousand to learn where the money is and to get me out of your hair at the same time. After all, you can't keep killing everyone who stands in your way. Even in Louisiana, someone might eventually get upset and question your role in all of this."

"And what guarantee do I have that I'll be rid of you?"

"You have my word. A hundred thousand and I'll leave town, resettle somewhere far away from here."

He walked over to stand beside her, his eyes dark and glinting, more threatening than a knife. "Why should I trust you?"

"Because I'm not crazy. Two people who double-crossed you are dead. I have no desire to be the third. All I want is the police off my back and enough money to put LPI and all of this mess behind me."

"You are wise as well as beautiful." His hand brushed her skin, and her flesh crawled. "I'm sure finding you in the bayou must have been pure pleasure for Cagan," he said. "Maybe for you, too. Is that pleasure how he convinced you to come to his apartment and wait for me here?"

The suggestive gleam in Bracer's eyes made her stiffen with outrage, and she struggled not to beat her fists against his chest. She was angry not because he was wrong, but because he was right. She'd fallen so easily into Cagan's trap, believed what he said, trusted his touch.

And even now she couldn't quite convince herself that Bracer was telling the truth. She'd been so sure Cagan cared for her. She couldn't bear to think he'd tracked her through the swamp for a bounty. Tracked her down and left her here for the murderous Bracer to claim.

Special delivery. Straight into Bracer's hands. Cagan had told her not to let anyone in. She hadn't had to. He'd given Bracer the key to his apartment.

"That's it, isn't it?" Bracer said, amusement and lust curling his fat lips into a grin. "You fell for the rogue cop."

"Like you said before," she said, fighting feelings she couldn't bear to deal with, "we don't have to worry about Cagan. This is between you and me now."

"Then hand over the million dollars, Merissa, and you have yourself a deal."

"It's not quite that easy. The money's in New Orleans."

"Where in New Orleans?"

"We've already established I'm not stupid, Bracer. So you surely don't expect me to tell you where the money is. I'll deliver it to you. But not when you're alone. I want a public place, a crowd of people, where there's no chance for you to forget your end of the bargain. Nothing to keep me from walking away safely."

"We'll do it your way, but I want it tonight. I'll be in New Orleans. At seven o'clock I'm addressing the Citizens for Better Government. After that, I'm attending a private party for the mayor at the Rasperson home on St. Charles Avenue. Show up there eleven o'clock sharp. I'll tell the hostess you're coming." Reaching over, he tore off the corner of a piece of newspaper and used the pen from his pocket to scribble an address. He pressed it into her hand. "Eleven o'clock sharp."

"I'll be there," she said, her mind boggled by the situation she had engineered. She'd prolonged her life for a few hours by dealing with the devil. She didn't dare think about what would happen when the deal fell through.

Bracer's lips parted, revealing a row of perfect white teeth. A politician's smile, full of empty promises. She listened to his parting words, warning her what would happen if she tried to trick him. Her only response was a nod of her head. Her mouth had suddenly grown too dry to speak.

He pulled the door shut behind him, and the room closed in around her. Bitter reminders of Cagan were everywhere. The scattered newspaper, his boots at the door, a paperback mystery with dog-eared pages lying open to the passage he'd read last. Even the air smelled of him—clean, fresh, and totally masculine.

Her heart constricted painfully, and she stood silently, absorbing the hurt. She needed to feel every piercing pain. That way, she would never be taken in by someone like Cagan again.

If only she'd listened to her mind from the first instead of to the deceptive passion that had ruled her heart and body. He had told her from the beginning he wasn't one of the good guys. At least that time he had told her the truth.

Panic surged again and with it a new dose of motivating adrenaline. She had to get out of here now, before Cagan came back. She couldn't deal with him, couldn't bear to see him, couldn't stomach another of his lies.

Fear slithered along her spine, icy and ominous. She had to forget Cagan and concentrate on saving her life. Only then could she worry about justice.

Bracer hadn't tried to hide the greed that drove him or the limits he'd go to get what he wanted. And she was sure he hadn't lied when he said he didn't take deals. He'd wait for her to deliver the money, but there was no way he would allow her to leave town alive. He would take care of her the same way he'd dealt with Jeff and Gaffner. Having her killed was the only sure way to keep her from squealing.

Hands shaking, she jerked open Cagan's dresser drawers, rummaging through them one by one until she found a pair of gray running shorts and a T-shirt. They were miles too big, but they'd have to do until she could find something better. She couldn't go outside in Cagan's robe.

She wiggled her feet into a pair of Cagan's socks, then pulled on her shoes and grabbed her jeans from the floor. The letter and the key were still stuffed in her front pocket where she had put them. Right there for Bracer to take had he only known.

She was running now, out the door and down the steps, her breath ragged and painful, her pulse racing with her feet. She wouldn't run away again, but she couldn't stay in Cagan's apartment. Somehow, she'd get to New Orleans and retrieve the money or whatever Jeff had left for her when he'd drawn her into this madness.

If it was in fact a million dollars, then she'd have to go to the police. It was the only option open. She'd demand to see the chief himself and pray he'd believe her. Believe her over Senator Bracer, the man of the hour. It was her only chance.

She had just rounded the first corner when she caught a glimpse of Cagan. He had already spotted her. Like a dragon, he raced in her direction, fire flying from his eyes and nostrils. She stopped and waited, knowing she was no match for his brute strength.

"I told you to stay put," he said, wrapping his arm about her waist and pulling her against his chest.

"Get your hands off of me."

Cagan covered her mouth with his hand and tightened his grip. Placing his mouth next to her ear, he whispered his demands. "I don't know what's come over you, Merissa, but we're going back inside. Through the front door, quietly, walking side by side like two normal people.''

She struggled, but he tightened his grip, his fingers digging into her flesh. ''You don't have to keep me here any longer,'' she grated through clenched teeth. ''Bracer was already here. You can collect your fifteen thousand.''

A string of curses flew from Cagan's lips. ''If he laid a hand on you—''

''Cut the act, Cagan. I know everything.''

His hand ground into her back as he pushed her up the steps. ''No, Merissa, you don't know everything. But it's past time you did. And what's one more broken rule on top of everything else?''

A door opened a few yards from them, to their left and down the walkway that fronted the second level. Merissa's muscles tightened as a man stepped outside.

Instinctively, Cagan yanked her around, pulling the gun from his waist in a single motion. ''Walk,'' he said, keeping her at an angle where the gun wouldn't be seen. ''And a smile wouldn't hurt, either.'' When they topped the last step, Cagan twisted the knob and kicked the door open, pushing her inside. ''Sit down,'' he ordered, the slight catch in his voice the only clue this wasn't as easy for him as it seemed.

''Or you'll shoot?'' she challenged, her heartbreak overriding her fear.

Frustration brought new lines to his face and he shook his head and raked quick fingers through his hair. ''Damn it, you know I'm not going to shoot you. But I won't let you go off half-cocked and let someone else get the chance to kill you. Now tell me what happened.''

''Let your boss tell you. The one who's paying the bounty.''

''Where's Bracer, Merissa?''

"He's on his way to New Orleans. To wait for me. You turned me in. I have no other choice than to return the money you both think I stole. You should be happy, Cagan. You get your money—Bracer gets his."

He shrugged. "This isn't what you think, Merissa. I want you to sit down and listen carefully to what I have to tell you."

"I'll stand, thank you. And keep it short. I've already heard way too much."

He continued to stand, as well, the muscles in his arm tightened into corded lines. "You could have been killed." His voice cracked on the words and he looked away. "I told you not to let anyone in."

"I didn't have to. He has his own key. But then, you would know that already, wouldn't you?"

"No, I didn't know it. But I'm not surprised. One way or another, Bracer seems to get everything he wants. I'm sure my landlady listened to some story he concocted and jumped at the chance to befriend our next governor."

"Do you deny that he offered you fifteen thousand dollars for my return?"

"Oh, he offered all right. I told you he stops at nothing. He'd offer a bribe to the Pope himself if he thought it would get him somewhere. But right now, I don't give a damn about Bracer." He took her hands in his and looked into her eyes. "I care about you."

Something in his tone grabbed her, and for a minute she almost forgot the anger that flared inside her. For a minute, the arrogant ex-cop disappeared, and the man she'd made love to in the bayou country was here beside her. She cursed her weakness and forced a hardness into her heart.

Cagan made her face him. "I'm not who I've pretended to be. I'm not Cagan Hall. In fact, there is no Cagan Hall."

Merissa sucked in a ragged breath, confusion returning with suffocating force. "You promised the truth," she demanded, determined not to be taken in by his games again. "Your lies won't work anymore. There is a Cagan Hall. And he's right here beside me."

"It was an act."

"No. The act is now. Jeff said Gaffner checked everything out before LPI hired you. You were suspended from the police force in New York for repeated offenses, for bending the rules to suit your own agenda. They even sent your picture."

"The New York story was manufactured. For me. For this operation. My real name is Cagan Lawrence Samuels."

"It's too late for your lies." She whirled and started to walk away.

He wrapped his hand around her waist and stopped her. "You're right. That's why you're getting the truth." He waited until she met his gaze. "I'm an undercover agent for the FBI."

She rocked back on her heels, for a second almost buying his story, almost giving in to the weakness inside her that longed to believe him. Gathering her courage and good sense, she jerked from his grasp. "And I'm one of Santa's elves. Give it up, Cagan. The game is over."

Cagan turned and strode to the bedroom. "My identification is in here. I didn't carry it on me in bayou country for obvious reasons."

He disappeared behind the open door. It was the perfect time to run, only Merissa couldn't. Her feet might as well have been nailed to the floor for all the good they did her. True or not, she had to hear Cagan out.

In minutes he returned, holding a folded leather wallet in his hand. "See for yourself." He thrust it toward her.

Fingers shaking, she opened the wallet. Appearances had fooled her. It was not a billfold at all, but an embossed badge. And a photograph of Cagan. "Fake IDs. You can get them everywhere," she challenged, slamming it back into his hand.

"Right. I have several myself, all provided by the FBI. The Cagan Hall character was created by the Bureau— driver's license, credit cards, social security number, the works. When our homework was done, we'd produced the kind of guy that Jeff would hire to work in the security department at LPI. All I had to do was arrange to meet him."

Merissa dropped to the couch, the scenario Cagan was describing bouncing wildly through her mind. It was crazy. "You expect me to believe this was all an act and that your performance worked so well Gaffner stepped in and made you head of security."

"I'm a good actor."

"Or maybe just a good liar."

"Both. But I'm telling you the truth this time."

"Why? Why, after making everything between us a mockery, would you tell the truth now?"

Cagan sat down beside her, his gaze locking with hers. "Because it's too dangerous not to." He took her hand and wrapped it in his.

Gooseflesh climbed her arms, and her heart constricted painfully. God, how she wanted to believe him, more than she'd ever wanted anything in her life. She struggled to force her rational mind to rule. The odds were not in his favor.

"It's been dangerous ever since Jeff was murdered," she reminded him, "yet if I choose to accept your story now, that means you continued to lie to me about everything. Even when—" Her voice broke, and she stopped in mid-sentence, not wanting to remember the way things had been between them, the passion that had seared clear through to her soul.

"Even when we made love." He said the words for her. "I was a fool. I wanted to tell you the truth. I tried to convince myself I could trust you then."

"But you didn't." Raw hurt clouded her senses. "So if I buy the FBI story, the truth is I don't know you at all. The only person I know is Cagan Hall, a man who doesn't exist."

And she'd never really known him.

"You know me, Merissa. Maybe better than anyone ever has. The real me is the man who followed you into the bayou because I was desperate with the need to protect you."

"To protect me, or to make sure I didn't escape? Or maybe to collect a little extra bounty?" She strained to hold off the traitorous tears that burned the back of her eyelids.

Cagan stared at her, his eyes dark and haunting, his face rugged and hard. "You have the wrong man again. I'm Cagan Samuels, and I have *never* been bought."

"But you have been wrong."

"More than once." His voice dropped to a husky whisper. "All I ask is that you take my word, Merissa. Not because I deserve it, but because it's the only way I can keep you safe. Bracer is dangerous. Far more dangerous than we expected when we followed up on Jeff's claims that he was involved in money laundering."

"You came here because of Jeff?" The roller coaster in her mind began again. "Are you telling me Jeff knew who you were all along?"

"No. No one knew. It was safer for Jeff not to know who I was, safer for all of you. Besides, the truth was that you were all under investigation. Bracer was not working alone. We wanted to find out exactly who was involved and how. And we needed hard evidence if there was any hope of getting a conviction with a man as politically connected as Bracer.''

Merissa cradled her head in her hand. Too much, too fast. Comprehension flickered but didn't hold. Did she dare believe Cagan's story?

"We suspected Bracer was into laundering money. Now it looks like he's capable of murdering to cover up his crime. For some reason, you have something he wants. It might be money. My guess is it's something more.''

"Like what?''

Cagan eased an arm around her shaking shoulders. "Like proof that would help us put him away. You'll have to work with me on this, Merissa.''

"And why should I trust you any more than you trusted me?''

"I don't know. I only hope you do. But whether you do or not, I won't let anything happen to you. Not if I have to handcuff you to me day and night." Cagan pulled her close. With one hand, he turned her face toward his and tipped her chin to meet his steamy gaze. "All you have to do is give me the key. I'll take care of everything else."

She stared into the depths of his eyes and saw the strength, the power, the smoky desire that had drawn her to him the first week at the lake. She had never been able to resist him. She took a deep breath and straightened her back. This time she would.

"The key was given to me. I plan to go to the bus station myself and collect whatever Jeff put there.''

"You're gambling with your life.''

"It's an everyday occurrence." Her voice broke and a tremble shook her body.

Cagan wrapped her in his arms and rocked her to him. "Then we'll do it together," he said, holding her so tight she thought he'd never let her go. But this time, even his arms weren't enough to still the fear or stop the trembling.

PRISCILLA GAFFNER SAT in the darkened living room of her home and stared at the picture of her and Marshall that hung above the mantel. It had been painted twenty years ago. Her face had been soft then and laughter crinkled the skin at the corners of her eyes.

Marshall had been so handsome. His hair was dark and wavy and covered his whole head instead of just the sides and back edges as it did now. No. There was no now for Marshall. It had ended for him when Merissa Thomas had walked through his office door and shot a bullet into his heart.

It was ludicrous that the police hadn't arrested her. Witnesses at the casino had seen her walk into his office. They'd also seen her leave. Pale and shaking, that's how one person had described her appearance when she'd made her exit. Minutes later, Marshall's body had been discovered.

Sen. James Bracer and Merissa Thomas. She didn't know exactly how they were connected, but she was certain that they were, no matter what Bracer had said about justice. Bracer had robbed Marshall of his money. Merissa had stolen his life. She hated them both with a passion she didn't know she possessed after so many years without experiencing it.

She didn't hate them because she'd lost her husband. She'd lost him years ago, or maybe they'd lost each other. He lived his own life, played big shot at LPI and Mardi Gras Lights and slept with a string of bimbos, although the playing around had slowed down in recent years. Whether from lack of energy or fear of disease, she wasn't sure. The reasons hadn't really mattered.

She'd lived her own life, as well. Shopping, traveling, attending boring luncheons. Her nights had been spent alone. Men could have their indiscretions. Women in her social circle didn't. Circle. Such a fitting name. Moving in circles got you absolutely nowhere.

Nowhere and alone. Now poverty would be added to the list. And life without money was the worst cut of all. With money, she could have ended the nowhere and the alone. Rich widows were welcome in any circle. Especially a rich widow who still harbored a passion for love and for life and whose body still fitted into a size eight dress.

Priscilla left her chair and walked over to the corner table. She tapped her long, fake nails on the polished wood, her mind still toying with ideas her conscience wouldn't entertain. Slipping her fingers around the bronze handle, she slid the door open and took out the silver pistol Marshall had given her years ago. For protection, he'd said, during the many nights she spent alone.

She carried the gun back to her chair, running her fingers up and down the short barrel, massaging the cylinder the way she might have done a lover. Not for protection. It was the need for revenge that tormented her now.

Revenge against Bracer and against Merissa Thomas. Her life was over. Theirs should be, too. Taking the gun with her, she walked back to her bedroom. There was a party in New Orleans tonight, a celebration and fund-raiser for Bracer's campaign.

She hadn't been invited. A woman in mourning didn't go to parties. Tonight would be different. They would all be surprised to see her, especially Bracer. And, with a little bit of luck, Merissa might show up, too.

She had no proof of that. Just another of her hunches. Merissa had murdered her husband, so she had to be in league with Bracer, one of the partners in the plan to foreclose on all that should have been hers. The two of them would live the good life and she'd have nothing.

Her pulse quickened, and she slipped the pistol into her handbag. Double revenge would be sinfully sweet.

Chapter Thirteen

Merissa sat beside Cagan in the front seat of the new Lexus he'd been driving when he returned to his apartment. Provided by the FBI, he'd explained. It would be much safer driving to New Orleans in the Lexus than in Merissa's car. If Bracer had actually bought her story, he would have called off his dogs for the day, but the police were still looking for her.

Cagan gripped the wheel with his left hand and fingered the radio with his right. He passed a rock song and a couple of commercials before stopping on an instrumental, haunting and familiar, a theme from a movie whose title she couldn't quite remember.

"Something soothing," he said, reaching over to lay his hand on hers. "You've had a rough few days."

"Life on the edge. The scary thing is that I'm starting to get used to it." She turned to face Cagan. Intensity deepened the lines in his brow and pulled his mouth into tight lines. It did nothing to lessen the rugged masculinity that still drew her to him like a magnet.

He squeezed her hand. Disillusionment stirred uneasily inside her. She'd met and fallen hard for Cagan Hall, a no-rules cop who mystified and mesmerized her. A man who drove her wild with longings, but a man whom she could never really trust. Now she wondered how different that man really was from Cagan Samuels.

"How long have you been associated with the FBI?" she asked, still trying to accept and understand the new identity of the man who rode beside her.

"Ten years, but not continuous. I took a couple of years off."

"What did you do during that time?"

"Nothing much."

"Then why did you leave?"

"Personal issues." He gripped the wheel more tightly. "Looks like traffic's building up," he said, his eyes glued to the road in front of him. "We might be a little later getting to the bus station than I thought."

Obviously, she'd hit a nerve. He wasn't interested in talking about his two-year vacation. And there was no reason for her to push the subject. Cagan Samuels was an FBI agent on assignment, a man who would be out of her life as quickly as he had entered it. His secrets weren't her business.

She stared out the window. Interstate 10 stretched out in front of them, a ribbon of highway lined with two lanes of traffic speeding into New Orleans. Cagan drove in silence, leaving Merissa to her thoughts. And to her memories of the past few days. Memories. Soon, that's all her time with Cagan would be.

The hourly news came on the radio at three o'clock. Cagan reached down and switched it off before the broadcast could begin. She knew he was saving her from more details about the murders and continued speculation about her disappearance. His unexpected smile warmed her.

"Tell me, Merissa, how did you come to be interested in prosthetics design?"

She knew he was trying to keep her relaxed, and she also knew it wouldn't work. "My grandfather lost part of his leg in a hunting accident. I was only eight at the time, but I remember it well."

"He must have been devastated."

"Nothing devastated my grandfather. He'd show me his replacement limb and say, 'See, little one, this goshdurn contraption's better than the real thing. Not a bit of rheumatism in it.'"

"So you decided to go into the business of making those *goshdurn* contraptions."

"That and the fact that my dad always said, 'The best way to be happy is to keep busy doing something that helps others.'"

"Too bad they can't see you today. They'd be proud of you." Cagan reached over and gave her hand a squeeze.

She leaned back in the seat, realizing that Cagan's attempts were working. Just thinking about her family had brought some calm to her pounding heart. "How much farther?" she asked, eager now to get everything over with.

"We're coming into Metairie. That should put us downtown in about twenty minutes, barring a major traffic jam. Let's go through the plans again. We can't afford any slip-ups."

"There's no way to slip up, Cagan. We've gone over this a half-dozen times at least. We go in, retrieve the contents of the locker and take a cab to the downtown Hilton. Two other agents will meet us there."

"That's not the part I'm worried about your forgetting."

"I know. Don't arouse suspicion. Act as if we know where we're going. And if trouble starts, let you handle it."

"That's the part. Getting involved in operations like this is what I get paid for, but it's no place for civilians. It's not too late for you to back out. You can leave everything to me and the other agents, and we'll make sure you're protected.''

''No, Jeff sent the key to me. I've gone this far. I want to finish it. Besides, what could possibly go wrong?''

''Everything. Bracer's already killed twice for something Jeff took, or at least had someone do the killing for him. Unless I'm way off base, that something will be in our hands in about twenty minutes.''

''A million dollars. That's what Bracer said I'm supposed to have.''

''A million dollars. A lot of people would kill for that, but I'm not sure Bracer would. Remember, he has a lot at stake here. As a crooked governor of Louisiana, he stands to make even more money in paybacks than he's made in the senate, and he's already a wealthy man.''

''Then you think Jeff took something besides money?''

''I think it's possible. Evidence of some kind, I'm hoping.''

''Isn't the money enough to convict him?''

''Not in the real world. In case you haven't noticed, that's where we live. You could testify you handed over a million bucks to him. It's your word against his. He's a hero around here. You're a murder suspect.''

''But I could testify about what he told me this morning.''

''Still his word against yours. No case.''

Anger knotted in Merissa's chest. ''You mean that unless you come up with absolute proof, Bracer is going to get away not only with money laundering but with murder? And then possibly be elected as the next governor?''

''That's exactly what I mean. He won't be the first to dupe the electorate. Unfortunately, smart men do it far too often.'' Cagan gunned the engine, shooting around a car that crawled in front of them. "But I'll be damned if it happens this time." The lines in Cagan's face were taut, and the muscles in his arms stretched the fabric of his shirt almost to tearing. "He's dodged and sidestepped every trick we've tried, but he's not walking free. I'll get him if I have to do it on my own, doing whatever it takes. The same way he operates."

Cold shudders shook Merissa, and she wrapped her arms around herself. Once again, it was Cagan Hall beside her, making his own rules, playing to win on his own terms. Or was this more of his act?

"What makes this case so different, Cagan?"

"You." His voice grew husky. "If I don't get him, Merissa, he'll get you. He won't rest until he does."

The feeling was there again, all-encompassing, filling the air between them like thick smoke. A oneness, an affinity she couldn't describe or understand. Cagan Hall, Cagan Samuels, the name and the background had changed but not the person. And not the emotions inside her.

Talk ceased between them, and Merissa leaned back, lost in her own thoughts while Cagan fought the increasing traffic. It had clogged to a crawl by the time Cagan pulled off the exit in downtown New Orleans. They rounded a corner and pulled into a parking lot that was only half-full. Cagan slowed and parked between a beat-up van and a late-model Ford.

"This is the Amtrak terminal, Cagan. Are you sure this is the right place?"

"Yeah. I checked everything out. Amtrak and Greyhound both pull out of here."

He slid out from behind the wheel and slammed the door behind him. By the time he reached her side of the car, she was out and walking away.

Cagan grabbed her arm and stopped her. "Don't worry about a thing, Merissa. Just walk beside me. Briskly." Once inside, Cagan dropped four quarters into a slot and pulled out a rickety wheeled cart. "I'm not sure how heavy the package will be, but I want my hands free. Just in case."

Free to go for his gun. He left the words unsaid, but Merissa knew what he meant. She did as he said, walking beside him through the main lobby and down a corridor that smelled of perspiration and stale cigarette smoke.

A young woman passed them, her jeans faded and tight, her hair cropped above her ears. A large brown duffel swung from a shoulder strap, and her hand rested on the zipper closing tab. She eyed Cagan from top to bottom, and Merissa's nerves skittered crazily. But the woman merely smiled and kept walking.

So far, so good, Merissa decided as they reached a wall of locked compartments. She stuck her hand deep into the pocket of the slacks Cagan had bought for her to wear. The key was there, safe and secure.

Cagan scanned the numbers on the compartments. Number fifty-seven. She saw it at the same time he did. Third from the bottom. Cagan stood back and let her move in closer.

"Open it," he said. "Then move behind me. I'll pull the package out."

The key jiggled against the lock, her fingers too shaky to push it in place. Sucking in a deep breath, she tried again. This time, the key slipped into the lock and turned easily. The door swung open and she stepped out of the way as Cagan reached inside the locker.

Heavy footsteps sounded behind Merissa. She spun on her heels as two teenagers rounded the corner and headed in their direction. In an instant, Cagan pushed the locker door shut, then turned and lounged against it. The boys ignored them, walking by and stopping a few feet farther down the corridor.

"Let's just get the package and get out of here," she whispered.

Cagan smiled but didn't budge, not until the two youths had dropped off their canvas duffels and walked away. Then, whistling an old rock song as if he didn't have a care in the world, he reached into the compartment and pulled out a cardboard box.

"Bingo!" Cagan whisked one box into the cart and reached in for a second one.

"They're just packing boxes, Cagan. Sealed and addressed to Sancleotus Medical Supplies in Mexico. They could be anything."

"People don't usually kill for just anything, not people like Bracer anyway." His gaze scanned the near-empty hall, settling on a tall man who was standing a few feet away and staring at them. Cagan nodded at the man and flashed a broad grin. "Looks like we picked a hot time to visit New Orleans."

"You said it. We came in on Amtrak a few days ago. My wife's complained constantly about the heat, but it hasn't slowed down her spending any." The man stepped closer, and his hand slipped into his jacket pocket.

Cagan stepped in front of Merissa, holding his own hand up near his waist. He looked so calm, so relaxed. But she knew better. She'd already seen the speed with which Cagan could pull out his gun and take aim.

"She's out there now buying one last souvenir," the man continued. "You know, a package of that square doughnut mix. Beignets. Something like that."

Cagan curled the fingers of his left hand around the cart and gave it a gentle shove, obviously deciding the man wasn't after their loot. "Hope you have a nice trip back," he said.

"Yeah, you folks, too."

Merissa took control of the buggy, pushing it down the narrow corridor, Cagan at her side. Her heart pounded in her chest, and she fought the urge to break into a run. Minutes later, they were in the car and headed toward the hotel. Only then did she draw a steady breath.

MERISSA STOOD INSIDE Room 544 of the downtown Hilton and watched Cagan slide the sharp blade of his pocketknife through the mailing tape and slice it open with a quick stroke. Two male FBI agents stood by his side. One of them, the one called Tommy, had been the man in contact with Jeff before his death. The other, a tall, redheaded guy with a quick smile was called Luke. He had apparently flown in to join the team after Gaffner's murder.

Tommy lifted the lid, and Luke started to dig into the box with both hands. Cagan slid the box from his reach. "If there's anything here, Merissa deserves first crack at finding it. She's paid her dues." He scooted over and made a place for her in front of the box.

Merissa took her place at the table and dipped her hands inside the cardboard container, then pushed aside handfuls of packing peanuts, letting them spill onto the table, some sliding silently to the carpeted floor.

Hands shaking, she pulled out a foam packing cradle and eased off the top section. Apprehension knotted her stomach as a familiar prosthetic device came into view. She eased the plastic device out and cupped it in shaking hands.

She rolled the piece over her palm. There had to be some mistake. Jeff wouldn't send her a key to a box of connectors for artificial limbs. Devices she had designed herself and had access to every day of the week.

Cagan was the first to give vent to his frustration, spitting out a loud curse as Merissa opened another packing cradle with the same result. And then he moved with lightning speed, yanking everything from the carton, mumbling and groaning, rage tearing away at his self-control.

"Somebody made fools out of all of us," Luke grunted, tearing into the second box. "There's nothing here but a stinking bunch of plastic." He banged a fist on the edge of the table and bit back a curse.

"And Bracer's going to walk. Two murders at his hand, and a bank account worth millions, most of it acquired illegally, and he's going to walk," Tommy barked, his voice hoarse with unchecked anger.

Cagan had regained his composure, his mind working overtime. "He's not going to walk." He took out a sheet of paper and started scribbling. "I want a cool million bucks, Luke, in recoverable funds. I don't care what you have to do to get it, but make it fast. If Bracer finds out Jeff didn't have a scrap of evidence against him, the case is back to square one."

"There's no such thing as a fast million with the FBI and you know it. Besides, what good would it do you? You can't plant evidence."

"I won't have to, not if you get the money. Merissa made an appointment to meet Bracer tonight at a party in the Garden District. I'm going to keep that appointment for her."

"Wait a minute. First you tell us the man's out to kill her. Now you tell us she's partying with him. What is it, Cagan? You're not changing the rules as you go again, are you? You know what Hampton said."

"Who's Hampton?" Merissa asked.

"The big boss," Tommy answered. "And he's warned Cagan already. The media's down Hampton's throat right now over the last case Cagan headed."

"We got our man."

"Don't push it, Cagan. Hampton warned you. One more broken rule, and he'll chew you up and spit you out. We have to follow the established procedures in this case to the letter."

"Just get the money. I'll worry about Hampton. And you know what I need to carry this off. My favorite mike and recorder. I'd feel a lot safer with the reel-to-reel, but we'd never be able to set that up without detection in a private home."

"Need another gun?"

"No. The one I have will do fine. But pick up the old standby. Just in case."

Merissa listened to the exchange, a language too foreign to register. Disappointment clutched her heart. They'd expected so much from the key, from the boxes. Half listening to Cagan and the other agents, half wallowing in should-have-beens, she walked back to the empty boxes and stared at the pile of plastic disklike devices.

"The equipment we can get. No sweat." Tommy's voice carried across the room. "The immediate million is a no go, and you know it."

"Get what you can. We'll have to make do."

"Okay, Mr. Miracle Man, we'll do our part and you get Bracer to confess that the missing money's his and that it was on its way to be laundered. Then have him confess to the two murders, and we can wrap up this case and get out of here."

"I'll drink to that," Tommy said, adding his approval to Luke's proposal. "The sooner the better. I'm sick of this Louisiana heat and humidity. By the time I get home at night, every stitch of clothes I have on is dripping. I haven't been this wet since I was potty trained.''

"So get to work," Cagan said, ushering them out the door.

"You got it, boss man." Luke nodded his head, a look of determination firing his eyes. "Tommy and I will be back in a couple of hours with everything you need, short of your million, of course." His lips widened into a broad smile. "Let's get the bastard."

Merissa watched them leave and then picked up one of the prosthetic devices, thoughtfully turning it over in her hand. It had worked well—one of her first and best designs since coming to LPI last year. It had been in big demand. Still, it was hard to believe a supply house in Mexico had ordered this many at once.

Rolling it between her fingers, she slid her thumb over the smooth edge. Only it wasn't smooth. A rough spot caught on her fingernail.

"Come here a minute, Cagan, and bring your knife."

"What is it?"

"Slide your blade between this seam. Something's not quite right."

With deft fingers, Cagan pierced the seam with his knife, breaking it open. The top half fell off and bounced across the floor unnoticed. Cagan reached inside the circular piece of plastic and pulled out a tightly folded bill.

"The money!" Merissa's pulse quickened as Cagan smoothed the bill and then used his knife to dig out eleven more. A dozen hundred-dollar bills in just one plastic disk.

Cagan paused just long enough to kiss her hard on the mouth and let out a couple of victorious shouts in between rescuing the remaining bills from their plastic cages. Minutes later, they were standing in a pile of discarded plastic, a mountain of hundred-dollar bills on the table in front of them. Cagan took a handful and tossed them into the air, letting them fall like confetti on their heads.

"Looks like I'll be going to the mayor's party tonight," Cagan said, wrapping an arm about her. "With *Bracer's* million dollars and evidence that it was cleverly hidden and on its way to the cleaners. Hidden away in prosthetic devices. All addressed to Sancleotus Medical Supplies."

"That's why there were so many being sent. That's why Jeff was going through the files, checking out all the shipping records. He must have figured out that Sancleotus is a bogus operation."

"And then switched the boxes." Cagan finished the thought for her. "Bracer wouldn't have known the boxes had been switched until the carton of unaltered prosthetics reached its destination. And that's when someone decided Jeff made the switch and came to the lake to get him and the money."

Merissa dropped to the side of the bed, weaving her fingers behind her head and stretching her neck. It was still a puzzle, though, with jagged pieces that didn't quite fit. "But who killed Jeff at the lake, and how did they find out Jeff had taken the money-stuffed prosthetics?"

"I don't know, but I'd wager that Bracer does. If he didn't do the deed himself, he ordered it done. He had to know that if these boxes fell into the wrong hands, it would trigger an investigation that would reach all the way back to him."

"Only the investigation had already been triggered. Jeff had done that when he reported what he suspected to the FBI and they sent you to Baton Rouge."

Cagan sat down beside her. All traces of the jubilance he had experienced on finding the money had vanished. He raked his fingers through his hair, but it rebelled against his touch, slipping back over his forehead in a dark wave. He placed a reassuring hand on Merissa's thigh, and she felt the heat of his touch through the crisp linen of her slacks.

"Jeff went to the FBI, but when the evidence came through, he wavered. That last night at the lake, he said the big guys always took what they wanted and no one cared. Now it was time for one of the little guys to get their share."

"But he wouldn't have gone through with it, Cagan. I know he wouldn't. He was unhappy, but he wasn't a crook."

"I think you're probably right. When we argued, he told me I should leave LPI, that all hell was about to break loose. But he wouldn't tell me what evidence he'd found."

"Are you saying he never mentioned the boxes to you at all?"

"No. He only said he had some goods on Gaffner. And he mentioned you. He said you held the key to everything."

"And from that chance remark, you decided I was in on the money laundering." Her lungs constricted, squeezing out her breath, and she felt as if her heart would break. "One comment from a confused man held more weight than all you knew to be true about me."

She got up from the bed and paced the room, finally stopping to stand in front of Cagan.

"That's the real reason you followed me into the bayou, wasn't it, Cagan? Now everything makes sense. You were doing your job. What was it you said? Using whatever means it took. Pretending to care about the suspect from the very first. Even making love to the suspect."

Merissa's voice was trembling. She didn't care. Her gaze had locked with Cagan's, but she could read nothing in the dark brooding that met her stare.

"No, Merissa. None of that happened by plan." He touched her hands, and she felt his sensual power flow through her. She tried to back away, but he pulled her closer.

"The last thing I wanted was to feel the way I did about you." He stood up, taking her chin in his hand and tilting her face toward his. "The last thing I wanted to do was love you." His lips moved closer, so close his heated breath feathered her skin. He ran his fingers through her hair, stopping at the back of her neck and cradling her head in his hands. "Loving you broke the one rule I'd vowed never to break again. But *not* loving you was impossible."

His lips brushed hers and then opened, pressing against hers, hard and demanding. Her breath caught in her throat, the longing inside her so powerful she ached from it. Still, she pulled away. There was so much about him she didn't know and couldn't understand.

"Why, Cagan?" she asked, putting words to her fears. "Why is falling in love with me so wrong?" He stared at her in silence, and Merissa felt the ache inside her intensify until she thought she'd die from it. She shuddered, the question she knew she had to ask tearing her apart. Trembling, she managed a ragged breath. "Is there someone else? A lover? A wife?"

"Not anymore." He wrapped her in his arms, hugging her to him. "At one time, I thought I was in love, but I was dead wrong. *Dead* wrong." His words were dry, caked with bitterness.

"What happened, Cagan?"

"It's not important now."

"Maybe not, but honesty is. There have been too many secrets between us already."

Cagan dropped his arms from around her. "Then sit down, Merissa. The story's not long, but it's ugly." He shook his head, regret dulling his usually fiery eyes and pulling his face into rock hardness. "Worst of all, the ending's always tragic. And all my fault."

Chapter Fourteen

"Five years ago, I was working on a case in Kansas City."

Merissa cringed. Cagan's voice was strained and distant, as if it belonged to another person, another time. But the pain burning in his eyes and twisting his lips was brutal assurance that his story was all too real.

"The case involved blackmail and a series of murders that were spread over three states. The gruesome details aren't important now, only my own weakness, my own mistakes."

Cagan paced the small hotel room, a tiger, hunted and condemned.

"The prime suspect was a young woman," he continued in the same hollow monotone. "She was beautiful, almost ethereal, with black hair that hung to her waist. She had a way of moving, of walking into a room, that went right through you, if you were a man." He shook his head, and his fingers knotted and then flexed in rapid succession. "And she aimed all her ammunition straight at me."

Merissa's heart constricted, and the heaviness of the moment settled like bitter gall in her stomach. She'd been wrong. She didn't want to hear this. "You don't have to go on, Cagan. That's all past."

"No. I thought it was. But when I met you, it all came back in vivid color."

She nodded, not trusting herself to speak again.

"Every scrap of evidence pointed at her, but I was too infatuated to believe her capable of such brutalities. She feigned innocence, and I fell into her trap." Cagan stopped pacing and planted his feet in front of the window, staring off into the gathering twilight.

Merissa walked over to stand beside him. "You made a mistake, Cagan. Everyone does sooner or later."

"Everyone's doesn't cost like mine did," he said. "I was in love with her, or at least in love with the woman I thought she was. I took her into my confidence and told her everything, even the name of our informant. I convinced myself I was doing the right thing, breaking rules to protect an innocent."

Cagan shook his head, but the muscles in his face stayed drawn and tense.

"I met her that night at a rendezvous spot she'd chosen, a shabby motel on the edge of town. While I was making love to her, her accomplices kidnapped and murdered my informant. But silencing the witness wasn't satisfying enough for them." His voice grew rock hard. "They also killed my partner, Beth. I was the one who found her body, stripped and—" His voice broke.

Icy dread hammered Merissa's heart, and she struggled for a calming breath. Telling this was hard enough on Cagan. Her revulsion would only add to his pain and self-recriminations.

"It was her first assignment and the night of her twenty-third birthday. Her cake was still on the table."

Merissa closed her eyes against burning tears, but still they escaped, the hot drops sliding down her cheeks. Cagan silently wiped them away and put an arm around her.

She rested her head against his broad shoulders, sure he needed the comfort as much as she did.

"If anyone had to die for my mistakes, it should have been me. And all I could do was wish it had been. I left the FBI. It was two years before I got my life back together enough to try again."

A shudder shook her body, and Cagan held her closer, rocking her gently in his arms. "If I'd known..."

He touched a finger to her lips. "It was nothing you did, not consciously anyway. I was attracted to you from the first moment we met. The feeling frightened me then, but it wasn't until you became a suspect in Jeff's death that I knew I had to back off."

"But you didn't."

"I tried. It didn't work. You were like a drug, potent and dangerous. I couldn't stop thinking about you, couldn't stop wanting to touch you, to hold you, to protect you, even though I realized I could never trust you completely until I knew the whole truth."

"So instead of telling me the truth about the FBI's suspicions, you let me run for my life?"

"That's why I came after you. I had to make sure you were safe."

"But I wasn't safe. If the man who shot me in the swamp hadn't missed his mark, I'd be dead."

"I know." His voice dropped to a hoarse whisper. "And once again I would have been to blame." He closed his eyes and took a deep breath, then stared directly at her. "And this time, I could never have lived with myself."

Her insides quaked as feelings she'd tried to drive into oblivion forced their way through every nerve. She pulled away from Cagan.

"I know it's not a pretty story, but it's who and what I am. All part of the package. How do you feel now that you

know the real me, Merissa? I'm Cagan Samuels, a man
who's made deadly mistakes. A man who's so afraid of
trust, he strangles his own emotions."

Merissa could hardly find the words to speak. "I'm—I'm
glad you told me. It makes everything easier to understand."

Cagan reached out and circled her waist with his arm,
pulling her to him. "You didn't answer my question. How
do you feel about me?"

Her mind searched for the truth. "I'm not sure," she
murmured, her breathing jagged and shallow. "So much
has changed. Even who and what you are."

"My feelings for you haven't." Cagan touched his lips to
hers, a whisper, a promise. His hands knotted in her hair,
and his lips found hers again. This time, he didn't stop until she struggled for air. "I care for you, Merissa. More than
I ever dreamed possible. And you care for me," he murmured, his breath torrid on her skin.

He slid his mouth down her chin and neck, then nuzzled
the soft flesh that edged the swell of her breasts. Desire
coursed through her. She'd never known hunger like this,
never tasted such sweet desire. He skimmed her body with
his hands, and her pulse skyrocketed. She was his, and he
had to know it. Maybe she'd always been his, since that first
moment their eyes had met.

Or maybe it had happened in the swamp, when he came
looking for her, following the trail through deep bogs and
ragged underbrush that teemed with snakes and rustled with
the movements of alligators. Maybe it had happened when
he'd touched the soothing water to her dry lips.

Cagan deepened his kiss, his tongue inside her deliciously probing and thrusting. Merissa let her hands rove his
back, massaging and kneading his flesh, pulling him so close
she could feel his heart against her chest. Passion stronger

than she'd ever imagined swelled inside her, straining for release.

Cagan relinquished her mouth, touching the tip of her nose with his lips and looking into her eyes. His finger traced a tender line from her brow, down her cheek to the corners of her mouth. "I love the feel of you," he whispered, his mouth at her ear. He nibbled her earlobe, his tongue flicking on her burning skin. "And the taste of you."

He swung her up in his arms and carried her to the bed, laying her across the soft coverlet. Merissa cuddled against him, aching to let go of all her inhibitions, to trust Cagan completely. He wanted her, and she wanted him. For now, that had to be enough.

His fingers snaked from her lips to the base of her neck and then lower, dipping beneath the fabric of her blouse and slipping the buttons between the narrow holes. In seconds, he had loosened the front, pushed the fabric aside and slipped his fingers under the clasp of her bra.

"Let me undress you," he said. "Slowly, so I can see each beautiful part of you. The first time I made love to you was frenzied and wild. This time, I want to savor each moment, discover what excites you, bring you as high as you bring me."

She lay back, reveling in the look of love in his eyes as he slowly stripped the clothing from her body and then quickly tore away his own. His mouth traveled her body, leaving a trail of fire, finding each crevice and sending her emotions spiraling.

Finally, when the pain of arousal became so intense she thought she might die, he pulled her on top of him, sliding inside her and driving his passion home. She gasped for breath and cried out in pleasure as desire shot through her in crashing waves.

A half hour passed before she was able to lift herself from the bed where they had shared such ecstasy. She was certain a lifetime would pass before she would forget it.

"YOU DIDN'T EAT MUCH," Cagan said as he watched Merissa push away the shrimp salad she'd barely touched. "It's not half bad for room service."

"I'm not hungry." She leaned back in the chair and stared out the hotel window.

"I don't see how you can keep from eating every bite after our period of swamp fasting."

"I keep thinking about tonight."

Cagan finished the last of his salad and swigged down the rest of his iced tea. "What about tonight?"

"What makes you think Bracer will deal with you?"

"I have what he wants. A cool million bucks that he planned to have laundered in Mexico." Cagan gave Merissa a rueful smile.

It pained him that the afterglow of their love had to be replaced so soon with the problems at hand.

"Exactly how does the money laundering work?" she asked, twirling the ice in her tea. "If the money just leaves the country and comes back, how is it changed?"

"It comes back accounted for. Bracer is wallowing in cash, a lot more than he's earning. We think most of it comes from illegal contributions, from people who expect favors in return for their substantial cash donations. They don't want any records kept and neither does Bracer, so the money changes hands under the table."

"And you think he sends it to Mexico and someone there sends it back under the pretext that it's payment for prosthetic devices?"

"Something like that, only LPI is not officially in his name. It will be soon, since he's foreclosing, but it hasn't been until now. We think that's why Gaffner's in debt up to his ears, at least on paper. Bracer pretended to lend him huge sums of money to invest in the casino and in LPI. Actually, he probably only loaned him a fraction of that amount.''

Merissa drummed her fingers on the windowsill. "Let me see if I understand. You're saying the company in Mexico writes checks to Gaffner, supposedly for prosthetics, and Gaffner pays the money to Bracer for loans he doesn't really owe.''

"That's about the size of it. Only Gaffner did owe some money. From what we've been able to uncover, that's how he got involved with Bracer to start with. When he couldn't repay, Bracer likely offered him a deal he couldn't refuse. He'd forgive the loans if Gaffner would help him out. Gaffner paid fake loans with money that was already Bracer's. Gaffner didn't lose his investments, and Bracer had a neat laundry situation that wouldn't be easily detected. In fact, it's turned out to be the devil to prove.''

"So LPI doubled as a legitimate business and a front for a money-laundering operation. The prosthetics could be returned and used over and over for the shipping operation.''

"You got it. And the prosthetic business was a perfect cover. It's humanitarian, catering to medical supply houses, hospitals and doctors around the world. Even if the shipment was opened by customs, who'd believe it was anything but needed medical supplies?''

"But somehow Jeff found out." Merissa stared at the opened boxes. "But I'm still puzzled. How did Jeff know what he had? The boxes were still sealed.''

"There's only one answer for that.''

"You think he saw them being packed?''

"That's exactly what I think. He switched the boxes, probably planning to turn the ones we found over to the FBI. But once he had the money in his hands, he had second thoughts about letting it go. I think he wanted the week at the lake to think things over."

"But someone knew or at least suspected it was Jeff who made the switch. It cost him his life." Sadness edged her voice.

Cagan reached out and took her hand in his. "It will all be over soon, Merissa. It won't bring Jeff back, but Bracer will pay. His games are about to come to an end."

"I hope so. What are the chances you can get the evidence you need on Bracer tonight."

"They're fair."

"Fair isn't good enough."

Merissa's brow furrowed, and she chewed nervously on her bottom lip. Cagan could all but see the wheels turning in her brain. His nerves hovered on the brink. He didn't want her involved any more than she already was.

"He's not going to level with you, Cagan." Her smoky gray eyes met his, dark and gleaming with determination. "He doesn't trust you."

"He offered me a bounty. He thinks I'm a dirty ex-cop."

"He offered you money to find the woman accused of murdering his friend. But he's not going to spill his guts to you. A man like him never fully trusts a cop, ex or otherwise. You said it yourself. He has too much to lose."

"Maybe. That's a chance we have to take."

Merissa pulled her hand from his and stood up, a look of concentration hardening her features.

"Don't get any funny ideas, Merissa," he warned, afraid even to guess what she might be thinking.

"I'm the one who was invited to the party tonight. I'm the one who should go." She looked him squarely in the eye and delivered her statement like an ultimatum. "The straighter we play this, the less likely we are to arouse Bracer's suspicions."

Cagan leaned back in his chair. "I know you want to help, Merissa, but this is way too dangerous for a civilian."

"It's not as if I'm not already involved up to my eyeballs. Besides, I'm not afraid, Cagan. You'll be there to protect me. Tommy and Luke, too. And if I'm successful, we'll have an airtight case against Bracer."

Cagan felt the pressure building at his temples. He rubbed the painful areas with the tips of his fingers. "Forget it. Under no circumstances are you going to the party tonight." His voice rose a few decibels. He didn't care.

A sharp knock at the door cut short his next protests. He checked the peephole and then jerked the door open. Tommy and Luke walked in slowly, eyeing the two of them suspiciously.

"What's the yelling about?" Tommy asked, glaring at Cagan. "You two sound like an old married couple."

"No," Merissa said, walking over to stand beside Tommy. "Cagan is just excited that I've agreed to go to the party tonight and worm the confession out of Bracer."

Tommy's jaw dropped and Luke shot Cagan a doubtful look. "Is that right, Cagan?" Luke asked, closing the door and snapping on the dead bolt.

"Yeah, and we're expecting a frost tonight." Cagan didn't hide his sarcasm. The situation was getting out of hand, and he planned to put a stop to it before it went any further.

"It makes sense," Merissa insisted, aiming her arguments at Tommy and Luke. "I deliver the money like I promised. Bracer gives me my cut. I bring up the fact that he was sending it away to be laundered. He admits it.

There's no reason for him to lie tonight. He already admitted it to me this morning. And you get everything on tape."

"She's got a point, Cagan."

"Not on your life." He bit back the curse that tumbled around his tongue. "You're all nuts. Merissa is not setting one foot out of this hotel room until the party is over."

"Why? She's willing. And you know good and well she has a much better chance of getting a confession than you do. It's just too bad we didn't have a mike on her this morning."

"We can make up for it tonight," Merissa said.

Cagan continued to growl his disapproval. Bracer had confessed to Merissa all right. Cagan knew exactly what that meant. The senator would make sure she wound up a corpse. The reprieve was only in effect until he could get his hands on the incriminating million.

The argument went back and forth, and Cagan was losing. No wonder. It sounded simple enough. What could go wrong with three FBI agents all nearby and primed to protect?

Only things did go wrong. No one was saying it, but they all knew it was a distinct possibility. Merissa put up her hand to halt the argument. "I'm going to the party. Now all I need is something to wear." She walked to the dresser and ran a comb through her hair. "I can buy a dress in the Riverwalk. The shopping center's attached to the Hilton. I won't even have to leave the building." She walked toward the door. "Anyone want to come along?"

Her mind was made up and she'd be hell to stop. Especially since she was the best person for the job. Cagan had to admit that fact to himself even though his insides quaked at the idea. Apprehension churned in his gut as he followed Merissa out the door.

CAGAN'S HEART TWISTED inside him as Merissa applied the second coat of bright red lipstick. Her lips matched her dress in color and vibrancy. He walked up behind her and rested his hands on her bare shoulders.

As he stared into the mirror in front of her, his gaze traveled to the low-cut neckline that revealed a tempting touch of cleavage. From there, the dress shimmered and hugged her tiny waist, sweeping out below the hips to swirl above her knees and make a delectable topping for her shapely legs.

"You'll have the men falling at your feet." He massaged her shoulders as he spoke. She looked cool and in control, but the tightness in her neck and shoulders told him he was not the only anxious participant in this charade.

"I don't want anyone to fall at my feet." Her voice was low but steady. "I only want James Bracer to talk." She reached a hand behind her neck and checked the clasp on her necklace.

Cagan covered her hand with his. "The necklace is secure, Merissa." He ran his other hand along her neck and slipped his fingers under the silver heart that dangled from the chain, assuring himself that the mike was in place.

It had taken Tommy a full hour to secure the mike to the heart in such a way it wouldn't be noticed, but he had done a perfect job. He was the best technical man in the business.

"I know Tommy and Luke will be outside the gate, but where will you be, Cagan?"

"In the kitchen, making a delivery. We'll hear when you start talking to Bracer. At that point, I'll drive up in a catering van with boxes of French pastries. It's all arranged."

"I feel like a character in a James Bond movie."

"And you look the part." He touched his lips to her earlobe. "Just be careful, Merissa. Do exactly as we said. Don't leave the house with Bracer under any circumstances. Scream, yell, whatever, but stay in the populated areas. If you do leave the premises with him, protection will be a lot more difficult.''

''I won't leave with him. In a house that size, there must be a room where we can have privacy.'' She leaned against Cagan, and he wrapped her in his arms, his mouth nuzzled in her golden hair.

''It's not too late to change your mind.''

''It's two murders too late. And I'm next on the list.'' Resolute, she stiffened her shoulders as she turned to stare at the clock.

Reluctantly, Cagan dropped his arms from around her. It was ten-thirty. The plan was in place. He had to let her go.

''Tommy and Luke will be following your cab. They'll be in a green Ford, a sedan. They'll be able to hear everything you say from the time you enter the Rasperson home. As soon as you connect with Bracer, he and Luke will move in closer.'' Merissa moved away from him. Cagan grabbed her hand and pulled her back for one last kiss. ''Go get him,'' he whispered as she took a deep breath and slipped out the door.

MERISSA STEPPED INSIDE the Rasperson home and into a world of wealth and dazzling glitter. Loud voices, tinkling glasses and music from a mini orchestra mingled in the smoky air, creating a symphony all their own. She stood quietly, soaking in the atmosphere and sizing up the situation.

''My, my, and to think I'd already pegged this as another of mother's dull parties.''

The voice came closer, and Merissa paired it with a man who looked to be in his early thirties. He was handsome enough, with a flirtatious smile, a slim build and a confident air that screamed money. Holding out a hand in her direction, he stopped in front of her. She switched the oversize valise to her left hand and extended her right to him.

"Raymond Rasperson." He introduced himself, grasped her hand warmly and held it longer than necessary. His gaze wandered from the top of her head to her toes, pausing at every nook and cranny in between before he let it return to her face.

At another time, Merissa would have shot him a frigid look that would have frosted his conceit. Tonight she merely smiled.

"Mother never told me she had a friend who looked like you," he said, still standing too close and smiling like a Cheshire cat. "If she had, I would have been camped on her doorstep."

"My name's Merissa Thomas. And to tell the truth, I've never met your mother. I'm a friend of Senator Bracer's."

"In that case, I forgive Mother." A waiter walked by with a tray of filled champagne glasses. Raymond grabbed one and handed it to her. "I'm a Scotch-on-the-rocks guy myself, but you look like champagne, all shimmering and seductive."

"Looks can be deceiving."

"And you're clever, too."

She searched the room for a familiar face. None appeared, so she smiled at Raymond. She'd have to cut away from him soon, but he might suffice as a capable guide through the crowd while she looked for Bracer. Besides, Tommy and Luke were undoubtedly finding his schoolboy antics entertaining.

"Now why are you carrying a briefcase to a party, especially one that size. Surely you don't plan to work."

"I'm afraid so. I've brought some papers for the senator."

"Here, give that disgusting case to me. I'll put it somewhere out of sight for you."

"No. I'll carry it." She tightened her grip and started to walk away. Raymond stuck an arm under her elbow and tugged her in the opposite direction. Another waiter stopped in front of them, this one carrying a tray of hors d'oeuvres that rivaled most works of art. Raymond pointed out a couple that he said couldn't be passed up. He took one and held it to her lips. She nibbled and then chewed appreciatively. The man was right. The pastry shell was so light and fluffy it could have floated, and the succulent filling of crabmeat and oyster danced on her tongue. "Your mother knows how to throw a party."

"She should. She's spent her adult life perfecting the art. Besides, she likes jumping on the bandwagon of candidates who are sure to win."

Merissa let Raymond's comment ride while she scanned the crowd. "Have you seen Senator Bracer?" she asked. "I really should let him know I'm here."

"Don't worry. I'm sure we'll run into him sooner or later. He's a politician. He doesn't let anyone get out without a handshake." Raymond led her through a pair of French doors and onto a terrace that sparkled like diamonds.

Stars over New Orleans were usually invisible, lost in the lights and haze of the city, but here in Raspersonland, the night twinkled with man-made stars that hung from the lower limbs of giant oaks. The small orchestra was set up in the far corner of the brick terrace, and dancers snuggled and twirled in the dreamlike setting.

"May I have this dance?" Raymond asked, taking the crystal champagne flute from her hand and handing it to a passing waiter. "I can't wait to hold you in my arms. Of course, you'll have to shed the briefcase."

"I'm afraid I can't do that. It's work first. Then play."

He faced her, resting one hand on each side of her waist. "You are a serious one." The music started up, and he began to sway, his hands coaxing her to move with him. He took the briefcase from her hand and placed it on the floor at their feet. "Relax," he said. "We won't let it out of our sight."

Merissa rested her foot beside it, making sure she could feel it pressing against her shoe. She had to admit it was a relief to set the heavy bag down for a minute. Not even a minute. Thirty seconds was her limit. Then she'd pick it up again.

Keeping the case in her peripheral vision, she studied the dancers and clusters of people who dotted the edges of the terrace. A lone woman dressed in black caught her attention. She was backed up against a brick wall, a drink in her hand. Shadows played across her face, but even in the half darkness, she looked familiar.

Raymond swayed closer, and Merissa strained her neck for a better look. The woman turned toward them. No wonder she looked familiar. It was Priscilla Gaffner.

An unexpected tremor snaked up Merissa's spine. Priscilla was here at a party for a man who was responsible for her husband's death. Merissa knew that but wasn't sure if Priscilla did. But even if Priscilla didn't know that Bracer had had Gaffner killed, she knew he had foreclosed on LPI and Mardi Gras Lights. In one fell swoop, she had lost both husband and income. She couldn't possibly think of Bracer as a friend.

"I'm being ignored," Raymond said. "You shouldn't torment a guy like that."

"I'm sorry. I was looking at the woman in black. Isn't that Priscilla Gaffner?" Her words were more for Tommy than for Raymond, but he twirled around to look in the direction she had been facing.

"The woman in black? No. I met her when she came in. I don't remember what she said her name was, but it wasn't Gaffner."

Merissa was sure Raymond was wrong. She didn't get a chance to tell him so. Someone stood in front of her, and she looked into the piercing eyes of Rick Porter. "Rick, what are you doing here?"

"Didn't you know? I'm one of Bracer's most loyal supporters."

A twisted grin played on his lips, telling Merissa more than his words had. So Rick was tied up in this, too. She should be surprised. She wasn't. Nothing surprised her anymore. She bent down and reached for the briefcase. Rick beat her to it.

"I hate to break this up," Rick said, facing Raymond, "but Senator Bracer wants to talk to Merissa. I'll return her to you as soon as their business is over. That is, if she wants to be returned."

"I'll hold you to that." Raymond lifted Merissa's hand to his mouth and placed a lingering kiss on her fingers. "And do make it quickly. Miss Thomas and I are just beginning to get to know each other."

Rick held the leather case in one hand and circled Merissa's waist with the other. "I trust you brought what Bracer wanted," he whispered, his mouth so close she felt his breath on her skin. The cloying sweetness of his after-shave was stifling and strangely familiar. She shuddered as if someone had walked on her grave. A stupid reaction when she needed to stay cool.

She went along with him, walking quickly away from the crowds and moving toward the edge of the terrace. Then he hurried her onto a carpet of grass.

"This way, Merissa."

"Where are you taking me?" Her breath came raggedly, her heart thundering against her chest.

"To meet Bracer. He's expecting you, and he doesn't like to be kept waiting." He increased his speed, dragging her behind him an arm's length away. He ducked from the path and into the trees. A shroud of darkness covered them, and the lights and music grew distant.

Digging in her heels, Merissa skidded to a sudden stop. "The house is the other way, Rick."

"So it is." He grabbed her arm and jerked her forward.

"I'm not going with you. If you try to make me, I'll scream. We're not so far away that people won't hear us." She issued her warning through clenched teeth despite the fear that churned inside her.

"I don't think so, Merissa."

Before she could follow through with her threat, he covered her mouth and nose with a damp cloth. The smell of ether—or was it chloroform?—filled her nostrils, burning into her brain. Struggling for air, she pushed at Rick as hard as she could.

He grabbed her around the neck, and she heard the terrifying click as the clasp of the necklace popped loose, sending the silver heart flying through the air.

"Cagan!" She cried out his name, but the sound never even reached her own ears before the world began its crazy spinning and she was swept into darkness.

Chapter Fifteen

The next thing Merissa knew, a pair of large hands had attached themselves to her backside and were shoving her into the back seat of a car. Her hands were tied behind her back, the rope digging into her flesh. An acrid smell filled her nostrils, and she struggled to swallow. It was all but impossible. The cloth Rick had stuffed in her mouth had swelled to suffocating fullness.

"Good job, Rick. Now we have to get out of here fast."

The female voice purred. Merissa recognized it at once. Lana Glass. So much for her pretense of being a friend.

"Did anyone see you walk away with Merissa?" Lana asked, slamming the back door and rounding the car.

"Yeah. Mrs. Rasperson's son, but he thinks she was going to see Bracer. This will work out perfectly." Rick opened the back door on the other side and tossed in the large briefcase. He held the door open while Lana slid in beside Merissa.

"I'll sit back here to keep you company," Lana said, smiling at Merissa as if this were a pleasure trip. "And to make sure you don't try anything."

The engine roared into life and Merissa was thrown against the back of the seat as the car jerked into motion. Lana pulled the large case from the floor and balanced it on her lap. "A million dollars," she drooled, "and it's all mine."

"Not quite, sweetheart."

"Mine and yours, Rick. You know that's what I meant. After all, you're the one who figured out it was Jeff who'd switched the boxes."

"That was easy enough. He was the only one still on the floor that night."

Lana fingered the catch on the case. "What's wrong with this thing?" she asked. "It won't open."

"It has a combination lock."

"You mean you didn't check inside when you grabbed it. How can we be sure it's the money Jeff took?" Her voice grew to a shaky high.

"We can't. Not yet, but we will soon. We'll shoot it open if we have to. Then we'll take care of Merissa the same way. Too bad we didn't get to do it the other day from the helicopter. Or the night we had her in the swamp. Especially after the episode with the damn snake."

"Forget the snake. You panicked for nothing. It wasn't even poisonous. Besides, it will be much better this way. Everything done at once. Clean and final. The way I like it."

"Lana, my girl, I like the way you think. Do you still have the gun?"

"Of course."

"Then take it out and keep it ready, just in case our friend back there gets any ideas about escaping."

Realization settled rock hard in Merissa's chest as Lana took a snub-nosed revolver from her pocket and tapped Merissa's ribs. It had been Rick who had attacked her in the Atchafalaya Basin, who'd shot her and left her to wander wounded and on foot through the stifling swamp. No wonder the smell of his after-shave had nauseated her moments ago.

And the other figure in the swamp had been Lana.

The car swerved to the right, hurling Lana into Merissa's side. The gun punched her hard in the ribs, and Merissa winced in pain. Righting herself, she gave a silent prayer of thanks that the gun hadn't gone off.

She forced herself to think. It was useless to try to guess Rick's and Lana's motives. She needed her reasoning power to figure a way out of this mess. And soon, before they reached their destination. Her last destination if the two of them got their way.

Merissa tried twisting her hands, but the rope only dug deeper into her wrists. A trickle of blood ran down her fingers, hot and sticky, and the knots in her stomach grew as painful as the ones on her wrists.

"Pull the gag out of her mouth," Rick barked as they rounded a corner. "At least until we get out of town. We don't want someone looking over at a red light and alerting a cop about a woman with a rag in her mouth. Besides, the gun will be enough to keep her quiet."

Lana jerked the cloth from Merissa's mouth. She swallowed, and her throat burned, the bitter aftertaste clinging to her tongue. Coughing, she turned and stared out the window. They were driving along St. Charles Avenue, heading toward downtown.

A police car pulled alongside them. Merissa's pulse quickened. She had to do something to alert him to her predicament. A signal, a movement, the fear in her eyes. He speeded up and drove on without a glance her way. She blinked back a wasted tear.

Don't leave the house. Cagan's warning echoed in her mind. He'd said that her leaving the premises would make protection a lot more difficult. Her mistake had been going along with Rick and following him into the darkness. He'd silenced her then with a chemical poured on a rag. So simple. And so effective. And now there wasn't even a mike to guide Cagan to her.

Rick left St. Charles, turning toward the on-ramp for the bridge crossing the Mississippi River. Her hopes plummeted, the same way her chances for rescue would once they crossed the bridge.

Cagan Samuels. Appeared from nowhere at the first sign of trouble. She'd complained of that once. Now she prayed for the sight of him. His image coalesced in her fevered mind and she shivered uncontrollably. She closed her eyes and pretended his arms were around her again.

There were so many things she wanted to share with him, but they'd never gotten the chance. She'd never even told him that she loved him.

CAGAN DROVE LIKE A MADMAN, pushing the catering van to its limits. The portable emergency lights he'd pulled from beneath his seat and stuck on the roof spun dizzily, painting the night in pulsating blue, echoing the frenzy that coursed through his veins. This was all his fault. He should never have let Merissa go to that party.

He swerved into the passing lane, flying across the bridge as if it was his own personal speedway. Fortunately, it was almost empty this time of the night, and the few cars traveling it with him gave him a wide berth.

Once on the west bank, he took the Highway 90 expressway. Tommy and Luke were behind him somewhere, moving more slowly since they were without the flashing lights that cleared his path. But they wouldn't lose him. And he wouldn't lose Merissa.

Determination and rocketing fear pushed his adrenaline levels to overdrive. Rick and Lana. He'd known Lana was involved in the LPI operation. He just hadn't known to what extent. From fingerprints he'd lifted off her coffee cup last week, he'd learned she had a record. Petty stuff in Houston. Bad checks and even a little hooking in her younger days.

Now she had graduated to murder one. A bitter curse sailed from Cagan's lips. He knew she had at least one more murder planned. And time to stop her was running out.

He took the Lafayette Street exit. That's where the tan Chevy Rick was driving had last been seen. Ten minutes ago.

A tan Chevy, two doors, with a dent in the left front fender. A perfect description, the one that allowed him to track them this closely. He even had the license number.

He whispered a prayer of thanks. Help came from the most unusual places. This time, it had been Priscilla Gaffner who'd come through. Delivered a miracle just when he needed it most.

He drove his foot into the accelerator again as he crossed Lapalco Boulevard and took the road to Belle Chasse. He had to find Merissa fast. There were a million hiding places in Plaquemines Parish, with its dark wooded roads where a car could disappear completely.

Cagan drove through the tunnel, past businesses closed for the night and a beer joint crowded with pickup trucks. A car turned in front of him, to the left. The sign said to Algiers, but the road curved into the darkness. A hunch, a wild hunch. Cagan swerved behind the car. He lived and died by hunches.

"END OF THE ROAD." Rick made the announcement as calmly as if he were giving a report on the weather.

Merissa shuddered, her hands clammy and knotted together, still tied behind her back. Rick brought the crawling car to a full stop and stepped out, swinging her door open.

"Get out," he barked. "It's show time. Get her the briefcase, Lana."

Lana walked over and set the briefcase on the hood of the car. Merissa didn't move. The reprieve was short lived. Rick grabbed her roughly by the arm and dragged her from the back seat. Her insides shook, but she held her back straight and her head high.

A scream lodged in her throat. She bit it back. They were on a dirt road somewhere, nowhere. Not a house, car, or even a trash pile had appeared for the past two miles.

"What's the combination, Merissa?" Lana asked the question, her voice low and harsh, without a hint of her usual purr.

"You don't need me. Let your boyfriend shoot it open like he said he would."

Rick threw the case at her feet. With a quick motion, he grabbed a pistol from the front seat of the car and aimed it at Merissa's head. "Open it. Now!"

"Zero, four, nine, six," Merissa whispered. They'd shoot her soon enough, but she wasn't about to rush it.

Rick lowered the pistol, and Lana grabbed the briefcase and heaved it back onto the hood of the car. In seconds, she'd twisted the numbered panel until the top of the case flew open.

Shaking, Lana picked up a stack of bound bills and flipped through it with her thumb. A sigh escaped her lips and she leaned against the car for support. "It's here. Real money. Enough that we can fly out of the country before daybreak and never come back again."

Rick wrapped his arms around Lana, but his eyes never left Merissa. One wrong move and the pistol would point at her. And he wouldn't hesitate to pull the trigger. The thought kept her nailed to the spot.

"Tomorrow night we'll be in South America, lying on the beach," Lana said, nuzzling against him.

"You'll still be murderers." The words flew from Merissa's mouth. There was no reason to stay silent any longer. "Will a million dollars let you forget that, let you live with yourselves?"

"Sure. Why not? Bracer lives with himself." Rick spit the words contemptuously. "The privileges of the rich. He'll climb to the top, stepping over everybody beneath him and grinding them under his heel. The mighty senator himself is the one who planned this whole thing, except for tonight's action. Lana gets the credit for that."

"And it's all Bracer's fault it's ending like this," Lana said.

Merissa stepped back, watching how Lana's face hardened. "How can this be Bracer's fault?" she asked, buying time any way she could.

"He starts all the fires and then gets nervous when he gets too close to the heat. This million was to be his last laundering. After that, he was going to go straight. So straight, he's even going to try fidelity." A bitter laugh escaped her lips.

Rick stared at Lana, his face twisting into angry contortions. "What's that supposed to mean?"

"Now I get it," Merissa taunted. "A woman scorned. Bracer decided to go straight along with putting in his bid for governor. That meant he was getting rid of all his excess baggage. You included."

"I wasn't baggage. I was the best thing that ever happened to him. We'll see how happy he is now, flitting around political circles with that boring wife of his."

Rick grabbed Lana's arm and pulled her closer. "You told me you weren't seeing Bracer anymore. That it was over between the two of you months ago. What else have you lied about?''

Rick's grip on Lana's arm tightened, the flesh of her arm bulging over his fingers. She beat her fist into his hand, and he slapped her hard across the face. The sound reverberated through the woods.

Merissa sucked in a ragged breath. No one was paying the slightest attention to her. It was now or never. Silently, she turned and started running, ducking under and around protruding tree limbs, not daring to look back.

CAGAN PASSED A CLUSTER of houses and then hit desolation. No streetlights, no car lights, not even a neon sign to brighten the night. A mile of nothing, and he squirmed in his seat, cursing the crazy hunch that had brought him here.

He'd radioed Tommy and Luke when he'd made the last turn. They were staying on Belle Chasse Highway, but if they found any sign of Merissa, they were to signal at once. Cagan slammed his fist into the steering wheel and cursed the damning silence.

Another mile, and he'd turn around, retrace his path and get back on the road to Belle Chasse. The road curved hard to the right, and he slowed to keep the van on the asphalt. Something caught his eye a few yards ahead.

He flicked his lights to bright and followed the beams. There was a road of some kind. It cut to the right, through an opening in the scrappy trees that bordered the road.

Cagan slowed and made the turn, switching off his headlights. Easing to a stop, he climbed from the car and directed his flashlight toward the ground. The roadbed was red clay, dry and hard. No way to tell if a car had passed.

There was nothing but darkness in front of him, a road to nowhere. There was no reason to go on. None except the clawing in his gut, demanding he drive a little farther.

A dark road for a dark deed. He drove, windows down, listening and scanning the blackness for any sign of life. A mile passed and still there was nothing. Panic clutched at him now, giant hands wringing his heart.

A ray of light flashed through the trees. Cagan slowed to a stop and radioed his location to Tommy. Seconds later, the light flickered again, appearing and disappearing like a phantom. Someone was in the woods. He left the car and started walking.

Weapon in hand, he followed the light. And then the quiet was broken. The sound of gunfire blasted through the night air, and Cagan took off like a shot.

"Merissa."

Merissa stood silently, the beating of her own heart hammering in her ears. Lana was following her through the woods, calling for her.

"Came back, Merissa. I won't hurt you. I've never hurt anyone. You're safe. We both are. Rick can't hurt us now. I killed him, just like he killed Jeff and Gaffner. Just like he planned to kill you."

Merissa wasn't fooled. Lana wanted her to come back so she could shoot her the way she'd just shot Rick. Stealthily, she moved to the next tree. A twig snapped behind her, and she whirled around.

"Don't scream! It's me."

"Cagan!"

"I'm right here." He stepped from behind a tree and extended his arms. She fell against him, shaking so hard she could barely stand, and he held her all the tighter.

"Merissa!"

The call came again, wafting on the night air, soft yet bone chilling.

"It's Lana," Merissa whispered, lifting her chin from Cagan's chest. "She and Rick kidnapped me. I think she's shot Rick." Her words spilled out.

Cagan dragged Merissa behind an ancient oak. "Answer her, Merissa. Bring her into the open. Let her know you're here, waiting for her."

"She has a gun."

"Then we're even."

"I'm over here, Lana," Merissa called softly, but she couldn't disguise the tremble in her voice.

"I'm coming to get you, Merissa, but there's nothing to be afraid of. I just want you to go into town with me."

"Keep her talking, but don't move." Cagan stepped away from Merissa, slipping out of sight in the bushes. Fear knotted her stomach, but she kept on talking.

Lana was closer now, only a few yards away. She stepped into the opening. One hand was in front of her. The other was at her side. "You can't trust anyone but me, Merissa. Not even Cagan. He's like everybody else. He wants the million for himself."

"You're right." Cagan spit the words and then stepped from behind a scrubby pine.

Chapter Sixteen

Cagan locked his arms around Lana, pinning hers to her side. With one forceful swing of his arm, the gun went flying from her hand.

"I want the million," he said, slipping a pair of handcuffs around Lana's wrists. "Every dollar of it. It's just the evidence I need to put slime like you and Bracer away."

"Don't be ridiculous, Cagan." Lana's voice grew soft, pleading. "You can't give up a million dollars. Especially this kind of money."

"What makes this million so different."

"It should be mine. Bracer owes me. Besides, he has more than he needs. He'll never miss it. You and I could take it. We can leave the country tonight on a private jet to South America. It's already arranged."

"And you arranged it, didn't you, Lana? Only the booking is for one."

"It doesn't matter. The pilot will do whatever I say."

"Like Rick did. Poor, trusting Rick. But you planned to kill him all along, right after you had him do the rest of your dirty work. You needed him to help you get the money and kill Merissa. After that, his services would be terminated, fatally."

"So what if I did? It doesn't matter now, and you can't prove anything."

"He won't have to."

The voice came from the darkness, low and shaky. Merissa spun on her heels toward the sound, just in time to see Rick stagger from the bushes, Lana's gun clutched in his unsteady hand.

"I'll testify to everything," Rick whispered, then took one more step before his legs collapsed under him and he dropped at Merissa's feet.

A round of applause burst from the trees. Merissa turned as Tommy and Luke broke through the brush and into the clearing. Tommy sank to the ground beside Rick and checked his pulse. "So you're going to testify. In that case, old buddy, I'll make sure you live."

Luke grabbed Lana's arm. "And I'll do my best to make sure you live, too. In a cozy cell where you'll have lots of time to dream about what you would have done if Cagan here had taken you up on your offer."

"Wait a minute. How long were you two out there listening in?" Cagan asked, moving to Merissa's side.

"Long enough. But we weren't worried, boss man. There wasn't a chance you would break the rules and go off into the sunset with Lana." A broad smile spread over Tommy's face. "We knew you were already taken. So why don't you take your lady home, and we'll take care of these two."

"You've got yourself a deal." Cagan pulled Merissa close, nestling his chin in her hair. "May I take you home?" he asked. He tilted up her face. "With me?"

"I thought you'd never ask."

"ARE YOU GOING to sleep forever?"

Merissa opened her eyes as Cagan's lips touched hers.

"I brought you coffee. The rest of breakfast is on its way." He bent over and set a steaming mug on the bedside table.

"What time is it?"

"Ten after ten."

"It's after ten! I have to get up." She threw her legs over the side of the bed.

"Don't you dare." Cagan reached down and grabbed her feet, lifting them back to the top of the covers. "I've been slaving in the kitchen for half an hour so I can bring you breakfast in bed. You deserve some serious pampering. I could tell as much last night when you passed out the second your head hit the pillow."

"I guess I was a little tired."

"You were exhausted. A week of running scared will do that to you. Especially when the action comes to an end." He kissed her again, warm and sweet, like café au lait.

The glow spread over the rest of her body as she watched him disappear through the door. Looking down, she ran her hand across the front of a T-shirt twice her size. She had a vague memory of changing clothes last night. Slipping into Cagan's shirt and climbing into bed. Alone. That was the last thing she remembered.

Quietly, she slipped out of bed and padded into the bathroom. She looked into the mirror and made a face. Her hair tumbled wildly around her shoulders, and her eyes were still groggy with sleep. Filling her hands with cold water, she splashed her face and then patted it dry.

A toothbrush was too much to ask for, but she rummaged in the medicine cabinet for toothpaste. Using her finger as a brush, she rubbed her teeth and gums vigorously and then rinsed with a bottle of green mouthwash.

Cagan was waiting when she got back into the bedroom, a tempting smile curling his lips. She sighed and walked closer. Even in the morning, he was devastating. He placed a loaded breakfast tray in the middle of the bed.

"Bacon, eggs, croissants, juice and fresh raspberries. From the kitchen of Cagan Samuels."

"I'm impressed."

"You should be." He fluffed two pillows, piling them up against the headboard. "I only do this on special occasions. And for very special people."

She crawled back into bed, sliding snugly between the sheets. "Will you join me?"

"I'd love to." He sat on the opposite side of the bed. Choosing a raspberry from the bowl, he slipped it between her lips. Desire tingled inside her. It would be so nice to cuddle beside Cagan, to lose herself in the morning's pleasures. But first she had to have a few answers.

"Have you heard about Rick?" she asked after she'd swallowed a bite. She hated to break the mood, but she had to know. "Is he going to make it?"

"According to the doctors, he'll live to testify and serve time. He's already confessed to his part in the murders and the money laundering. His testimony, Lana's midnight confession and the million dollars wrapped in prosthetics should be enough to seal the case against Bracer, Lana and Rick."

"So it was Rick who killed Jeff and Gaffner."

"No, he killed Jeff. Lana took care of Gaffner. All of it on Bracer's orders. When the wrong package turned up in Mexico, Rick suspected Jeff was the one who had taken the original shipment. He came to the lake that night and was hanging around outside the camp. While I was in your tent, he took the knife and followed Jeff down the path to the water."

"And Jeff was unsuspecting and at least thirty pounds lighter. He couldn't have been much of a match for Rick."

"No. In fact, Rick said Jeff admitted to him he'd taken the money. When Rick demanded he tell him where it was hidden, Jeff tried to run. Rick caught up with him in the woods where you found him. Jeff started to call for help, and Rick killed him."

"But Rick's fingerprints weren't on the knife. Only mine."

"Rick wore gloves, proof that he'd planned to kill Jeff all along. The knife was handy, out in plain sight, as he tells it, and much quieter than the gun he had brought with him."

"It sounds like everything was pretty much the way you had it figured."

"Yes. Only now we have the evidence to back up my theories."

"But why kill Gaffner? Wasn't he in on everything?"

"According to Rick, Gaffner was running scared after Jeff's murder. He was worried about what Jeff might have told you and where the missing money was. Bracer was afraid he would panic and squeal."

"So how did they convince him to have me called into his office the morning he was killed?"

"It was part of the plan. Lana kept me in the coffee shop and out of the way while she set you up for Gaffner's murder. She called Gaffner from the coffee shop and told him you knew where the money was. She told him to stay at the office because you were on your way there. Then she had your lawyer call you in, saying he would be there, too. That way she knew you would show."

"And Lopen went along with it?"

"Another one of Bracer's boys, bought and paid for. He did as he was told. Of course, he's claiming now he had no idea what was really going on."

"But Lana beat me to Gaffner's casino office."

"Right, using a key to his private office, one she'd gotten from Bracer. No one even suspected her, not after they'd all seen you go in and then rush out. The only thing we're not sure of is why Gaffner printed my name. My guess is he was passing out and hoped the first person who found him would call for me. At that point, I was probably the only person he trusted. But by the time someone found him, it was already too late."

"And while I was being framed for murder, Rick was in my house searching for anything that might lead him to the money. He must have been the one there the night before, too."

"He was. He said he hadn't planned to attack you. You came out while he was going through the boxes that had Jeff's name on them. That's when he hit you over the head and took off."

"Those dreadful boxes. I never wanted Jeff to leave them at my place, but he was insistent. He wanted to go through them in private, and he had no place to keep them in his tiny apartment."

"Somehow he had gotten hold of those files and sneaked them out of LPI. He'd lost access to shipping and sales records when he was bumped from his job as head of marketing."

"That's why Gaffner put Rick in Jeff's place." Merissa leaned back against the pillows. The clues had all been there. She just hadn't known how to read them.

"Rick was eager to play the game," Cagan agreed. "Especially with Lana as his loving accomplice. And she was on the inside from day one. She'd worked with Bracer on his last campaign."

"And all the while, she was playing up to Gaffner, too." Merissa nibbled at her scrambled eggs. "There's still one thing I don't understand, Cagan. How did you follow me across the river last night after I'd lost the mike?"

"That was the surprise of the evening. Priscilla Gaffner was at the party. No one has any idea why, but she was watching when Rick dragged you into the bushes. She followed him to the car. When I showed up, she gave me a detailed description. It was poetic justice at its best. Bracer had her husband killed, and she was one of the main players in getting the goods on Bracer."

Merissa shook her head. "It's almost too much to think about. I'm just glad it's over."

"Not everything is over, Merissa. At least I hope it isn't." He moved the tray from between them and leaned closer, propping himself up on his right elbow. He captured her with his gaze, and she felt the power that drove him, the passion that pulled her to him and never let go.

The piercing ring of the telephone stopped them short. Cagan muttered a few choice words under his breath as he grabbed the receiver. The conversation was brief, but the look on his face told her breakfast was over.

"It's the police. They want to meet with me. This will be a joint effort between the local police and the FBI. I'm afraid I'll have to go."

"I understand. You have a job to do."

He kissed her again. Hard but quick. "I hate to leave."

She curled under the sheets as he walked away. She still had so many things to tell him, so many things she wanted to hear from him. But there was no hurry now. They'd have forever.

Only one thing couldn't wait.

"Cagan."

He stopped in the doorway and turned to face her.

"I love you, Cagan Hall Samuels. All of you. I just wanted you to know."

He came back to the bed and took her into his arms, lifting her off the mattress and cradling her against him. His lips touched hers, and suddenly she knew he'd known all along. Somewhere deep inside, they both had known.

"And I love you," he said. "I'll prove it every day for the rest of our lives." His kiss deepened, and the heat inside her started to rise.

She trembled deliciously. Every day. Forever. And even that would never be long enough to put out the fire.

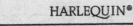

The Spencer Brothers—Cole and Drew...
two tough hombres.

Meet

Cole Spencer

Somehow this cowboy found himself playing bodyguard.
But the stunningly lovely, maddeningly independent
Anne Osborne would just as soon string him up as let
him get near her body.

#387 SPENCER'S SHADOW
September 1996

Drew Spencer

He was a P.I. on a mission. When Joanna Caldwell-
Galbraith sought his help in finding her missing
husband—dead or alive—Drew knew this was his
chance. He'd lost Joanna once to that scoundrel...he
wouldn't lose her again.

#396 SPENCER'S BRIDE
November 1996

The Spencer Brothers—they're just what you need to
warm you up on a crisp fall night!

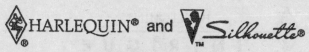

HARLEQUIN® and **Silhouette®**

are proud to present...

HERE COME THE GROOMS™

Four marriage-minded stories written by top Harlequin and Silhouette authors!

Next month, you'll find:

The Bridal Price	by Barbara Boswell
Annie in the Morning	by Curtiss Ann Matlock
September Morning	by Diana Palmer
Outback Nights	by Emilie Richards

ADDED BONUS! In every edition of *Here Come the Grooms* you'll find $5.00 worth of coupons good for Harlequin and Silhouette products.

On sale at your favorite Harlequin and Silhouette retail outlet.

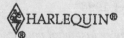 

HARLEQUIN®   **Silhouette®**

HCTG1096

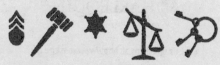

Merry Christmas, Baby!

A romantic collection filled with the magic
of Christmas and the joy of children.

SUSAN WIGGS, Karen Young and
Bobby Hutchinson bring you Christmas wishes,
weddings and romance, in a charming
trio of stories that will warm up your
holiday season.

MERRY CHRISTMAS, BABY! also contains
Harlequin's special gift to you—a set of
FREE GIFT TAGS included in every book.

Brighten up your holiday season with
MERRY CHRISTMAS, BABY!

Available in November at
your favorite retail store.

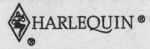

HARLEQUIN ®

Look us up on-line at: http://www.romance.net   MCB

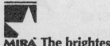